A DEATH
IN THE SMALL HOURS

Also by Charles Finch

A Beautiful Blue Death

The September Society

The Fleet Street Murders

A Stranger in Mayfair

A Burial at Sea

A DEATH
IN THE SMALL HOURS

Charles Finch

Minotaur Books ✹ New York

A DEATH IN THE SMALL HOURS. Copyright © 2012 by Charles Finch. All rights reserved. Printed in the United States of America. For information, address St. Martin's Press, 175 Fifth Avenue, New York, N.Y. 10010.

www.minotaurbooks.com

The Library of Congress has cataloged the hardcover edition as follows:

Finch, Charles (Charles B.)
    A death in the small hours / Charles Finch.—1st St. Martin's Minotaur ed.
        p. cm.
    ISBN 978-1-250-01160-2 (hardcover)
    ISBN 978-1-250-01816-8 (e-book)
    1. Lenox, Charles (Fictitious character)—Fiction.   2. Politicians—England—London—Fiction.   3. Private investigators—England—London—Fiction.   4. Murder—Investigation—England—Somerset—Fiction.   5. London (England)—Fiction.   6. Somerset (England)—Fiction.   I. Title.
    PS3606.I526D43 2012
    813'.6—dc22

                                                          2012033901

ISBN 978-1-250-03149-5 (trade paperback)

Minotaur books may be purchased for educational, business, or promotional use. For information on bulk purchases, please contact Macmillan Corporate and Premium Sales Department at 1-800-221-7945 extension 5442 or write specialmarkets@macmillan.com.

D   10   9   8   7   6

This book is dedicated with great love to three people:

Charles Baker Finch, 1920–1996
Angela Havens Finch, 1920–2001
William Payson Finch, 1956–1999

*until we die we will remember every
single thing, recall every word, love every*

*loss: then we will, as we must, leave it to
others to love, love that can grow brighter*

*and deeper till the very end, gaining strength
and getting more precious all the way*

Acknowledgments

I owe a particular debt, as this book comes to press, to my editor Charles Spicer, whose constancy and acuity exceed what any author has a right to expect. Surrounding him at St. Martin's are a group of exceptional people, to whom I am also very grateful: the formidable Andrew Martin, Hector DeJean, Matthew Shear, Laura Clark, Allison Strobel, David Rotstein, and, especially, April Osborn.

Enormous credit must also go to the three people at ICM—Kate Lee, Jennifer Joel, and Kari Stuart—who have worked so energetically and creatively on my behalf. Kate, thank you so much for your friendship, both in the years that have passed and in the years to come.

My wonderful wife, Emily Popp, is supportive and loving—what a stroke of luck that she's an eagle-eyed editor, too. I am also thankful, as usual, to my mother, Mary Truitt, who gave the book her customarily invaluable attention and improved it a great deal.

For giving me a quiet place to write a particularly difficult passage, love and thanks go to Tim and Jenny Popp.

Finally, it's been too long since I mentioned four very dear friends, Rachel Blitzer, Matt McCarthy, John Phillips, and Ben Reiter. Their e-mails get me through the dry spells. Thanks, guys.

A DEATH
IN THE SMALL HOURS

CHAPTER ONE

Charles Lenox sat in the study of his town house in Hampden Lane—that small, shop-lined street just off Grosvenor Place where he had passed most of his adult life—and sifted through the papers that had accumulated upon his desk, as they would, inevitably, when one became a member of Parliament. In fact now they were like a kind of second soul that inhabited the room with him, always longing for attention. There were outraged letters about the beer tax from his constituents in Durham; confidential notes from members of the other party, inviting his support of their bills; reports on India, anarchism, and the poor laws; and oh, any number of things beside. It hadn't been an easy year so far, 1874. As his stature within the House increased, as he progressed from the backbenches to the front—aided, in part, by the knowledge of international affairs he had gained on a trip to Egypt that spring— the amount of work increased commensurately.

While he organized his correspondence, Lenox's mind worked over each problem the papers presented in turn, going a little ways on one, then turning back to the start, then going slightly farther, like a farmer plowing a furrow, setting out to break still newer ground. If he could get Cholesey and Gover, of the Tories, to agree to vote for the Ireland bill, then he might just permit Gover and Mawer to let it be known that he would stand behind the military bill, in which case Mawer might—so his thoughts ran on and on, ceaselessly formulating and analyzing.

Eventually he sighed, sat back, and turned his gaze to the thin rain that fell upon the window. Whether he knew it or not he had changed in the past few years, perhaps since his election, and would have looked to someone who hadn't seen him since then indefinably different. His hazel eyes were the same, kind but sharp, and he was still thin, if not positively ascetic, in build. His short brown beard had been clipped only the evening before to its customary length. Perhaps what was different was that he had developed the air of someone with responsibility—of multiple responsibilities, even. Thinking of one of them now, however, his face changed from discontent to joy, and though his eyes stayed on the street a great beam of a smile appeared on his face.

He stood. "Jane!"

There was no reply, so he went to the door of the study and opened it. This room of his was a long, book-filled rectangle a few feet above street level, with a desk near the windows and at the other end of it, around the hearth, a group of comfortable maroon couches and chairs.

"Jane!"

"Keep quiet!" a voice cried back in an urgent whisper from upstairs.

"Is she asleep?"

"She won't be for long, if you hullabaloo about the house like an auctioneer."

He came out to the long hallway that stretched from the front door to the back of the house, rooms on either side and a stairwell near the end of it. His wife came down this now, her face full of exasperation and affection at once.

"May I go up and see her?"

Lady Jane reached the bottom of the stairs. She was a pretty woman, in rather a plain way, dark-haired and at the moment pale, wearing a gray dress with a pink ribbon at the waist. Above all the impression she left on people was of goodness—or perhaps that was the impression she left primarily on Lenox, because he knew her so well, and therefore knew that quality in her. For many long years they had been dear friends, living side by side on Hampden Lane; now, still to his great surprise, they were man and wife. They had married four years before.

Better still, to add to his great happiness and evergreen surprise, at long last they had received a blessing that made him stop and smile to himself at random moments throughout every day, as he just had in his study, a blessing that never failed to lift his spirits above the intransigent tedium of politics: a daughter, Sophie.

She had been theirs for three months, and every day her personality developed in new, startling, wonderful directions. Almost every hour he snuck away from his work to glimpse her, sleeping or better yet awake. Granted, she didn't do much—she was no great hand at arithmetic, as Lady Jane would joke, seldom said anything witty, would prove useless aboard a horse—but he found even her minutest motions enchanting. Babies had always seemed much of a muchness to him, but how wrong he had been! When she wriggled an inch to the left he found himself holding his breath with excitement.

"Hadn't we better let her sleep?"

"Just a glance."

"Go on, then—but quietly, please. Oh, but wait a moment—a letter came for you in the post, from Everley. I thought you would want it straight away." Lady Jane patted the pockets of her dress. "I had it a moment ago. Yes, here it is." She passed him the small envelope. "Can you have lunch?"

"I had better work through it."

"Shall I have Kirk bring you something, then?"

"Yes, if you would."

"What would you like?"

"Surprise me."

She laughed her cheery, quiet laugh. "I doubt Ellie will surprise you very far." This was their cook, who was excellent but not much given to innovation.

He smiled. "Sandwiches will be fine."

"I'll go out for luncheon, then, if you don't mind. Duch invited me to come around. We're planning the Christmas ball." Lady Jane, rather more than Lenox, was one of the arbiters of Mayfair society, much sought after.

"I shan't see you for supper, either."

"Dallington?"

"Yes. But we'll put Sophie into bed together?"

She smiled, then stood on her toes to kiss his cheek. "Of course. Good-bye, my dear."

He stopped her with a hand on the arm, and leaned down to give her a kiss in return. "Until this evening," he said, his heart full of happiness, as so often it was these days.

After she had gone downstairs to arrange his lunch with the butler and the cook, Lenox remained in the hall, where he opened his letter. It was from his uncle Frederick, a relation of Lenox's late mother.

Dear Charles,

Please consider this a formal invitation to come down for a week or two, with Jane of course and the new Lenox; I very much want to meet her. The garden is in fine shape, and then, Fripp is very anxious to have you for the cricket, which takes place Saturday week. I haven't seen you in more than a year, you know.

Yours with affection &c,
Frederick Ponsonby

Postscript: To sweeten the pot, shall I mention that in town, recently, there have been a series of strange vandalisms? The police cannot make head or tail of them and so everyone is in great stir. Perhaps you might lend a hand.

Lenox smiled. He was fond of his uncle, an eccentric man, retiring and very devoted to his small, ancient country house, which lay just by a village. Since the age of four or five Lenox had gone there once a year, usually for a fortnight, though it was true that the stretches between visits had gotten longer more recently, as life had grown busier. Still, there was no way he could leave London just at this moment, with so many political matters hanging in the balance. He tucked the note into his jacket pocket and turned back to his study.

Ah, but he had forgotten: Sophie! With soft steps he bounded up the stairs, past a maid carrying a coal scuttle, and toward the nursery.

The child's nursemaid, Miss Taylor, sat in a chair in the hall outside it, reading. She was a brilliant young woman, accomplished in drawing and French—both useless to the infant at the moment, but fine endowments nevertheless—who had a reputation as the most capable nursemaid in London. She cared for a new child every year or so, always infants. Jane had acquired this marvel for them, at great expense, to Lenox's derision—yet he had to admit that she was wonderful with Sophie, with a gentle comprehension and tolerance for even the child's worst moods. Despite her relative callowness—she was perhaps two and thirty, though her complexion retained to an unusual degree the bloom of youth—Miss Taylor was an imperious figure; they both lived in frank terror of offending her. Still, she was used to Lenox's frequent interruptions and indulged them with less severity now than she had at first.

"Only for a moment, please," she whispered.

"Of course," he said.

He went into the room and crossed the soft carpet as quietly as he could. He leaned over the child's crib and with a great upsurge of love and joy looked down upon her. Such a miracle! Her serenely sleeping face, rather pink and sweaty at the moment, her haphazard blond curls, her little balled-up fists, her skin as smooth and pure as still water when you touched it, as he did now, with the back of his fingers.

It was joy beyond anything he had ever known.

CHAPTER TWO

The light rain of the afternoon had thickened into a torrent by the evening. It emptied the streets of London, and even up close the streetlamps, paced fifty feet apart along the pavement, were no more than shrouded yellow smudges against the darkness, while the buildings of Pall Mall loomed above like great, lightless cliffs. As for the driver of Lenox's carriage, he and his horses alike were soaked to the bone—though upon closer inspection one could in the dimness around the driver's face perceive a small dot of orange, growing faint and then brightening every so often: his inextinguishable cigar.

He didn't remove it to call down. "Here we are, sir."

"Thank you kindly," Lenox answered and climbed out of the carriage.

It was a short, wet walk into his destination, Brooks's, one of the gentlemen's clubs along Pall Mall. Lenox was not a member here, preferring the less erratic and more civilized air of the Athenaeum or the Reform nearby. Certainly the average member of Brooks's was quite highly born—royalty were upon its rolls—but they were also almost uniformly wild men, who gambled at cards for days and nights on ends, jousted with cues across the snooker table, and placed with each other the oddest sorts of bets in the infamous club book. This lay open on a marble plinth in the warm, comfortably carpeted entry hall where Lenox stood now; the entry that caught his eye read:

Mr. Berkeley pays five guineas to Lord Erskine, to receive five hundred should he successfully entice an unclothed woman of good birth into a hot air balloon, which must then attain no less a height than one thousand feet.

"Oh, dear," said Lenox to himself.

"There you are!"

Lenox turned and saw his companion for the evening, Lord John Dallington, coming down the club's grand staircase. He was a handsome, compact man of perhaps twenty-seven or twenty-eight, wearing a black velvet blazer with a carnation affixed to its buttonhole.

"Hello, John," Lenox said.

"Have you been peeking into the club book?"

"No—or rather—"

"Good. There's a bet I have with Ollie Pendleton which I don't think you ought to know about—all on the up and up, I swear. It's to do with stealing a certain horse from a certain stable. Damned impudence to call a lock unbreakable—sheer hubris—but never mind, it's neither here nor there. Come along, let's go up, I've reserved us the small room by the library. The wine is open."

Lenox smiled. "Cork it again, then—I have too much work to feel mutton-headed in the morning, these days. Not to mention a daughter."

"How is she, then? Happy, healthy? And Lady Jane?"

"They're flourishing, thank you."

"I'm glad you've been able to get away, nevertheless. I've got a tricky one this week."

Lenox felt a quickening of anticipation. "Oh?"

"It's a poisoning in Belsize Park."

"Have I read about it?"

Dallington, climbing a step ahead of him, shook his head. "It hasn't made the papers yet, because the chap who was poisoned is hanging on to life like a limpet. He's comatose, unfortunately, which means he's roughly as communicative as one too, ha, ha."

Lenox and Dallington sat down to supper once a week when both were in town, always at Brooks's. It was a strange and unexpected relationship. For many years Lenox had heard of the younger man only distantly, the disappointing youngest son of one of Lady Jane's closest friends. Dallington had been sent down from Cambridge under a cloud of angry rumor, and after that had proceeded to investigate every alehouse, gambling pit, and gin parlor in London, usually with a string of unnameable women and several debased aristocratic companions. By the time Lenox first really got to know him, Dallington's reputation had been hopelessly blackened.

Yet now Dallington was probably the premier private investigator in London. Lenox himself had occupied that position for many years, before the whole business of Parliament took his attention away from crime, and during the time when it was still his primary pursuit Dallington had come and asked to be his protégé. Lenox had been deeply suspicious at first, but within a matter of months the young man—neither as pure at heart as Lenox would have wished, nor the wastrel his reputation would have had one believe—had saved his mentor's life and helped to solve the detective's thorniest case in years.

These days they were firm allies, and while Dallington still came to Brooks's, he was a tamer creature, given over more and more to detection. Like Lenox he felt a passion for it; in fact Lenox envied him. While he saw Parliament as a duty—or in fact more than that, a complex of duties, ambitions, and vanities—detection had always been his truest vocation. Now these suppers, at which they discussed Dallington's cases, held for him his favorite relaxation of the week.

They came into a small room, papered dark blue, full of portraits of old members—many now snoozing in the House of Lords, solid ancient Tories, no longer the fire-breathing rascals of their youth—and sat at table, which was laid out for supper.

Dallington rang a small bell. "Are you sure you won't have a glass of wine?"

"One, perhaps."

"That's more like it—just one, there, no, not to the top, apologies. Ah, and here's the waiter. What would you like to eat, Lenox, guinea fowl or beef?"

"Guinea fowl."

"For two, then, and bring all those things you bring, too, please, potatoes and carrots and mustard, if you don't mind." The waiter, who was terrible at his job but too stupid to blackmail any of the men he served, and received therefore a princely remuneration, smiled, nodded, and left.

"A poisoning?" said Lenox, too curious for preliminary chatter.

Dallington retrieved a small notebook from his jacket. "I'm glad you're here, in truth, because I have my suspicions but I can't confirm them."

"Tell me the details."

"The victim is a solicitor in Belsize Park, Arthur Waugh. He—"

"How did you come by this case?"

Dallington smiled. "Inspector Jenkins didn't like the look of it."

"Ah—the old story." Lenox had received cases in the same way, once upon a time. Scotland Yard's men couldn't always devote the time or resources to an investigation that an amateur could. It gave him a pang that they went to Dallington now, though he tried not to show it. "Go on, then."

"This Waugh was apparently a rotten apple. His first wife died five years ago, and it seems almost certain that he killed her, but all of the servants swore up and down that she had fallen down the stairs. It couldn't be disproved."

"He married again, I take it?"

"Yes, and it's she that I suspect, Florence Waugh. Four evenings ago, after supper, Arthur Waugh fell ill. Before supper he had had a toothache, for which he took a dose of laudanum, but he often did that."

"It was his usual prescription?"

"Yes."

"Go on."

"About an hour after he went upstairs to bed his servants heard him crying out for help, and called for the doctor. By the time the doctor arrived Waugh was comatose."

"How much of the laudanum was missing?"

"Precisely what I asked. The answer was that much more than usual was gone, certainly much above his usual dose. So his wife and servants all confirmed."

"Separately?"

Dallington laughed. "You taught me one or two things, Charles. Yes, I asked each of them separately. I don't believe it was the laudanum, though—I think his assailant drained half the bottle in the sink to try to make it look that way. Waugh was in rude health and certainly not suicidal—pigheadedly in love with life, from the sound of it, if anything—and he had been taking laudanum for years without incident."

"What did the doctor say?"

Dallington turned a page in his notebook now. "You anticipate me again. I spoke to him this morning and he believes that it was antimony poisoning. That or arsenic, though arsenic is much more difficult to come by, arousing suspicion as it does when one tries to order at the chemist's."

"Does it? How do you know?"

"I tried it on, once, to see what they would say. On a different case."

Lenox was impressed, as he had been repeatedly at these suppers, with the younger man. There was a doggedness there that the outward flair of personality concealed. "I take it there was skin rash?"

"You've seen antimony poisoning before, then?"

"Oh, several times. There was an ironmonger in Fulham who killed his son with it, I'm sorry to say. The woman he wanted to marry refused him because he had a child and she had no great longing to be a mother. An appalling thing. What did this Waugh look like?"

"There was a red rash all over his hands and arms, but Florence, his wife, said that it had been there for days."

"And the servants?"

"They hadn't noticed, but it's not conclusive. His vomiting and headache might have been from an overdose of laudanum."

"Would she have had access to antimony?"

"I canvassed the chemists in the neighborhood but none of them, including the one she frequents, remember her buying anything unusual at all."

"Of course it would have been the easiest thing in the world to disappear onto a crowded omnibus and go to the other side of London."

"Exactly." Dallington sighed. "So you can see—I feel strongly that something nasty is afoot, but it looks so hard to prove."

There was a noise at the door; the waiter had returned with a heavy tray, and set out a variety of dishes and pots in front of them, all appetizingly fragrant and warm on that cool, wet night. He fixed a few more logs onto the fire in the hearth and withdrew. Dallington poured from the bottle of wine without any objection from Lenox.

"Shall we eat, then, and I'll give you the rest of it afterward? In the meantime tell me of Sophie. Does she roll around on the floor yet? Has she got any children her own age she plays with?"

CHAPTER THREE

Wen their cigars were lit and their glasses of port poured, Lenox and Dallington sat back. The older man spoke. "What was her motive, though, this Florence Waugh? Why do you suspect her? You still haven't said."

"It's just a sense."

"Has her behavior been suspicious?"

"On the contrary, she has been just as one would expect—grieved, bewildered."

"I take it, then, that Arthur Waugh was not as cruel to her as he was to his first wife."

Dallington shook his head. "No. She has a great deal more money than he does, all under her own control, and their acquaintances implied to me that it shifted the balance of power toward her."

"I wonder if you're too influenced by the circumstances of his first marriage. After all, she stands to gain little enough from his death monetarily, and she loses a husband whom, however you may view him, she chose to marry. Mightn't you look elsewhere for your killer?"

"Where, though?"

Lenox frowned. "Who are the other inhabitants of the house?"

"There are a butler, a parlor maid, and a cook. All of them have been with Arthur Waugh since he moved into the Priory, which is what he calls the house."

"They predate her, then?"

"Yes."

"And all three swore that the first Mrs. Waugh fell to her death?"

Dallington's eyes were screwed up tight in concentration. "Tell me, what are you getting around to?"

Lenox shrugged. "I'm not certain myself, to be honest."

"What would any of the servants stand to gain from Arthur Waugh's death, if it comes to that?"

"I don't know. I would only say—and from this very comfortable chair, with a glass of port at hand, which is not the same thing as being in the mix of things as you have been—that he seems perhaps to have had a complicated relationship with these three people. The butler, the maid, and the cook."

"Yes."

"Let me ask you a question: Did Florence Waugh fall ill, after supper?"

"In fact she did, though her complaint was very mild. She hadn't eaten much."

A thought formulated in Lenox's head. Slowly, he said, "Perhaps there's another angle to look at it from, in that case—what if she was the target?"

Dallington whistled. "You believe the servants were trying to kill her? And made a hash of it?"

"Perhaps they mixed up the meals, yes. Or perhaps they were trying to kill both Waugh and his wife! Could they have stood to gain from the two deaths in conjunction? Are they remembered in Waugh's will, perhaps, and is he the automatic recipient of anything she leaves behind? He's a solicitor—it should be written up somewhere."

Dallington was writing furiously in his small notebook. "You're a pip," he said. "I hadn't considered any of that."

Lenox shrugged. "It may be a blind alley, of course, but when there is a large sum of money attached to the scene of a crime, it's often as well to look at the money from every angle."

"First thing in the morning I shall go and look at Waugh's will, and Florence Waugh's too."

Lenox smiled. "Not a late night here, then?"

"D'you know, when I'm on a case I find that I never come here other than to dine with you. Funny, that."

The waiter came in then and cleared away the table. The rain still lashed violently at the windows, while inside the two men smoked their small cigars.

"It's nearly ten," said Lenox with a sigh. "I suppose I had best be off home, soon. Have you any other case at present?"

"I don't. Have you heard of anything?"

"Nothing, no. Ah, but I tell a lie—my uncle has written from Somerset, complaining of vandals in his village. You know how it is in places like that. If they find themselves sixpence shy of the usual tally in the church collection they cry out for Scotland Yard as if Jonathan Wild has moved in above the local pub."

Dallington laughed. "Are you going to look into it?"

"No, no. I'm far too busy in Parliament. There will be an up-and-down vote on the naval bill in three weeks' time, among other things. I can't chase about after a gang of bored schoolboys on their hols."

Dallington smiled gently. "And yet you miss it?"

"Can you tell so easily? I don't mind confessing that I rather do. I'd be curious to clap eyes on this Florence Waugh. For one thing, how did she grow so rich? Is there a dead husband in her history?"

"No. I asked, in fact, and verified her story. Her father was a brewer in Birmingham and brought her to London after he retired. Died two or three years ago, and entailed all the money very specifically upon her and her heirs. Unusual, you see."

"Quite so."

As his carriage rolled him over the cobblestones toward home, the rain somewhat abated but still steady, the night fearsomely cold for so early in September, Lenox thought about his old profession. He had had cause to renew his endeavors in detection twice: once for a friend, once on board a ship bound for Egypt, when of course no member of the constabulary was close to hand. Those cases had been a few years apart, years that had seen him married and, now, a father. In truth he was out of the game.

His meetings with Dallington always filled him with a strange blend of regret and pride. Lenox's father and brother had both taken the family seat in the House, and served with great distinction—in fact his brother was one of the Prime Minister's leading confidants at the moment—and he was pleased to join their ranks. Many members of his small social world had looked upon his work as a detective as folly, more embarrassing than admirable, and though he had put a brave face on the embarrassment he was glad to be distanced from it. There again, he knew Jane was happy, too, for his change of career, though she didn't mention it. It meant an end to the knives and beatings and guns he had encountered through the years.

He also loved politics, but for all his pleasure in the long debates and the hushed hallway conversations of his present life, Lenox had never quite felt as viscerally engaged with Parliament as he had with crime.

The house on Hampden Lane was quiet when he returned, dark but for a flicker of light in two upper windows. Lenox entered quietly and found that his political secretary, Graham, was sitting in the hallway, waiting for him. Graham was a small, sandy-haired man, deeply intelligent; he had for many years been Lenox's butler, but after trying and failing to find an enterprising young man to manage his political affairs, Lenox had given him this unorthodox promotion. So far it had worked beautifully.

"Have you been at the House?" said Lenox.

"Hello, sir. I thought I might catch you here. Yes, I was down with Frabbs, going over the bills for the new session."

"I haven't missed a meeting, have I?"

"No, but something has arisen."

"What is it? You look grave."

"You mistake me, sir," said Graham. "I've good news."

"What is it?"

"Mr. Hilary and Mr. Gladstone have invited you to open the speeches this session."

Lenox's eyes widened. "Is this a rumor? Or a confirmed fact?"

"Mr. Hilary's secretary"—James Hilary was the young and ambitious Secretary of State for the Colonies—"has confirmed it for a fact."

Lenox whistled, taken aback by the news.

It was a signal honor, usually assigned to a member of the cabinet. In such a speech Lenox could lay out his own political philosophy, like Burke or Fox or Palmerston before him, and address the great issues of the day. The House would be full. His party would be reliant upon him, and all of the papers would print the speech in its entirety.

It felt like an enormous responsibility, but even as he thought as much he realized that he was ready for it. He had been in Parliament for years now, working his heart out, and there would likely never be a time when he knew more or felt more deeply passionate.

"In the past," said Graham, "men who have given their party's opening speech—"

"I know," said Lenox.

Graham soldiered on. "They've become prime ministers, sir, cabinet members, been elevated to the House of Lords . . ."

Lenox smiled. "Not much to live up to, then. I suppose I had better get to work." He turned toward his study, forgetting, for the moment, that he had intended to look in on his sleeping daughter and wife.

CHAPTER FOUR

The next day, the skies having cleared, brought instead a new kind of downpour: one of visitors. First there was James Hilary, who substantiated the news.

He was a young man, very handsome, with blond hair and a riding stick under his arm, having apparently come by horse through Hyde Park, on his morning exercise. "I gave the speech three years ago, you know—fearful bother, hours upon hours of preparation—and once I stood up and began to declaim the thing it all seemed wrong, but there you are."

"You did a very fine job, as I recall."

"Ah, well, who can say. Do you know what you want to speak about, chiefly?"

"Poverty, I think."

"Oh?"

It was the single issue that most interested Lenox, but he knew that Hilary, ambitious and powerful, would have a list of other subjects he might want raised on behalf of the party, so Lenox added, "And other things, of course, education, the navy, Ireland . . ."

"Ah, the general approach. Very sound. Listen, I'll leave this here." It was a black leather dispatch bag that bore the royal seal. "I want you to sketch yourself in on its contents before you write your speech."

"What are its contents?"

"You'll see soon enough."

Lenox understood that to mean they involved state secrets. He nodded. "Thank you, James."

The next visitor was a Tory member, Bottlesworth. He had a large, conical head, which tapered toward a magnificently hairless crown, and small round spectacles. There were also several chins gathered around his neck. Both sides of the aisle credited him with tremendous perspicacity, though as far as Lenox gathered the man only ever spoke about eating.

"The great matter is *sustenance*," he said when seated, hands carefully steepled before him—when they weren't darting out for one of the cakes the housekeeper had placed on the table in Lenox's study. "I tell you this as a member of the opposition party, quite freely, you see, because I feel that in the end we are all pulling in the same direction. I hope we are, anyhow."

"Hopefully," said Lenox, and smiled.

"What you'll find," Bottlesworth went on, a picture of seriousness, "is that a half pint of porter *is not enough to sustain you*. There, the great secret of oratory, at your feet! You will need *at least* a pint of porter, perhaps even a pint and a half, and I have known great men, very great men indeed, to take *two* pints of porter, ere they speak before the House. Which is to say nothing of sandwiches, of course."

"Of course."

"I needn't mention to a man of your experience and wit the importance of sandwiches."

"No."

"Horseradish and roast beef I find to be too upsetting to the insides. Perhaps you will have a stronger constitution than I do, though I very much doubt it." He laughed at the idea that Lenox's constitution might exceed his own, eyes screwed shut with merriment and spectacles bouncing. When he had recovered, he said, "What I find is that a gentle *ham* sandwich, even a tomato sandwich, answers capitally. You see the picture?"

When Bottlesworth had left, carrying in a handkerchief the scones that the butler had thought to bring in just before the Tory's departure, there was almost immediately a third ring at the door.

It produced another member of Parliament, this time from Lenox's own party. This was Phineas Trott; and where Bottlesworth found assurance and strength from victuals, Trott—a flustered, red-complected gentleman, who was thought to own more horses than any other claimant in Warwickshire—found them in hunting and the Lord. He, too, took a place upon the red couch near the fireplace.

His approach was direct. "What these speeches want in them is more of Jesus."

"D'you think so?" said Lenox.

"I do. Country sports and Jesus—all of our problems could be solved by one of the two, Mr. Lenox."

"Not the Suez question?"

"Jesus."

"Education?"

"Country sports."

"What, you want the coal miners' children to go hunting?"

Trott frowned. "No, that wouldn't do. Perhaps they could go beagling, though." His face brightened. "They'll certainly want Jesus, I can promise you that."

In his mild way, never given over to much show, Lenox was a God-fearing Christian. Nonetheless he felt compelled to say, "I think they want better food, milk without chalk in it, and not to go to the factory at the age of five, that sort of thing."

"Well; I suppose," said Trott, doubtfully. "I wouldn't put that about too much in your speech. This is England, after all, we're not a raft of Hindoos."

"What do you think I should say, then?"

"It starts with Jesus," replied Trott, more firmly now. "Stick to Jesus, and country sports, and you'll get through it very well."

"Thank you ever so much, Mr. Trott."

Trott went; and in his place came the worst of the lot, Lord Brakesfield. This white-haired, tenebrously attired fellow, born to a butcher in Ealing, had succeeded in making himself one of the richest men in London by exporting soap of startlingly poor quality to all of the country's counties. The most recent New Years' Honours had seen him receive a lordship for services to Her Majesty's Government, and he had immediately released a soap called Brakesfield to capitalize on the notoriety of his newly bestowed name.

"Mr. Lenox, I have found in business that honesty is the best course."

"No doubt."

"Here is my proposal, then. I will pay you a hundred pounds if you mention Brakesfield soap in the first three paragraphs of your speech."

Lenox almost laughed out loud. "But I don't want a hundred pounds," he said.

"Nonsense. Everyone wants a hundred pounds."

"Not I."

"You don't?" the lord asked incredulously.

"No."

Lenox's guest considered this turn of affairs. "Perhaps I might raise my offer to a hundred and fifty pounds."

"I don't want a hundred and fifty pounds, either."

"Hm. Your way, then, make it a hundred if you simply mention my name—don't have to say anything about soap—but it has to be in the first two paragraphs." The lord sat back, well-satisfied with this gambit. "Can't say fairer than that, get the Brakesfield name out there. People know about the soap already, after all, but a mention in the opening address to the House of Commons would give it such a touch of dignity."

"I'm afraid I won't be able to accept your offer," said Lenox.

After Brakesfield left—also with a handkerchief full of scones, for he had never turned down the opportunity for something free in his life—there was still another knock at the door. Lenox sighed, and felt that if the days leading to the speech would all be this way, they could have it back.

This knock, however, brought a more welcome guest: his older brother, Edmund.

"Thank God it's you," said Charles.

Edmund chuckled. "Have you been receiving guests?"

"You wouldn't believe it if I told you. And a dozen more have left their cards for me down in Whitehall, Graham says, all to talk about the blasted speech. It will be the death of me."

Edmund and Charles looked rather alike, though the older brother—the ninth baronet in his line, and the heir to Lenox House, where both had grown up—was haler; his cheeks were red and he always looked fresh from the country, which was indeed where he generally would have preferred to be. Despite that preference he had risen to be very powerful in the Commons.

"Is it you I have to thank for this opportunity?" asked the younger brother. "I'm grateful, of course."

"You must stop believing me to have a hand in your success, Charles. You're a rising man."

"Then it wasn't you."

"No. I say, you couldn't get Kirk to fetch me in some tea, could you?"

"Oh, instantly."

They sat companionably while they waited for their refreshment, talking as brothers will about any number of things, each seemingly unconnected to the last from the outside, their line of connection clear to the two speakers. Bessie the cow had given birth; the Marquess of Broadhurst was ill; there was to be a party for Toto McConnell the next Wednesday; and so forth.

When they had their tea the conversation returned to Lenox's speech. "What do you want to say?" asked Edmund.

"I'd like to talk about the poor. So far I haven't had a moment to think, however. Only a series of visitors."

"It will be worse when you go down to the House. Everyone will be in your ear."

"What I need is somewhere quiet."

Edmund shrugged. "That's done easily enough. Go to Lenox House."

"I couldn't leave now, with the speech in three weeks."

"On the contrary, through the years many people I've known have left London to write the opening speech. People will consider you statesmanlike, I imagine, if you disappear to have a deep think through things. It implies an appropriate seriousness. Really, honestly."

"I wonder . . ." said Lenox. With a quick tug of excitement he remembered the letter from his uncle Frederick. "Perhaps you're right, after all," he said.

CHAPTER FIVE

Before supper Lenox and Edmund had a visit with Sophia. Her affectionate uncle dangled his pocket watch over her crib and she happily batted at it, smiling and laughing.

"I wish I had had a daughter," said Edmund, rather wistfully.

"How are the boys?"

"Oh, they're in excellent form. Teddy is still aboard the *Lucy* with Captain Carrow, as you know, and happy as can be. Have I shown you his letters? Remind me to, when you next come to see me and Molly for supper. The ship has acquired a pet monkey, apparently. He sleeps with them in the midshipman's cabin. But a little daughter, to dote over . . . I should have liked it above all things."

"At any rate you may dote over Sophia, provided it doesn't interfere with my schedule of doting."

Edmund laughed. "A generous and fair proposal."

As he was walking his brother downstairs, Charles said, "Uncle Freddie has invited me down to Everley, in fact."

"Has he? It would be an ideal retreat, I should say. The most excitement I ever saw in those parts was the three-legged race at the summer fête. Then again you were always fonder of it there than I was."

They were at the door, Edmund putting on his cloak and his hat. "I liked the country, it's true."

"And you were Freddie's favorite."

"Perhaps."

Edmund smiled and tipped his hat. "Congratulations, Charles. Really, I'm excited to hear what you'll say. It will be brilliant, I know as much as that."

"Good-bye, then. I'll write to tell you what I'm doing."

"Tell Jane I'm sorry I've missed her."

Even as Edmund walked away from the house, someone was approaching it from the other direction. It was J. G. Reese, the member for Dover, who was perpetually convinced that the French were at that very moment bracing themselves to cross the channel and climb his constituency's white cliffs.

"Ah! Lenox! Capital, I was just coming to see you. Want a word about France. I hear dire things about their gunnery, really you won't believe it when I tell you. Beastly frogs, their budget for pig-iron alone would make you shiver."

"I've no doubt at all."

"At a bare minimum we need to double the budget at the Woolwich arsenal, for starters, and shift more men to Dover—hate to think of the poor cliffs—but here, I'll come in, thank you, yes. You haven't got a scone handy, have you? I'm positively famished."

A trip to the country, thought Lenox, as he invited Reese into his study. It was just the thing.

To convince Lady Jane of it would be a different matter. When his final visitor had vacated the study that evening—George Swan, who wanted to outlaw Catholics from sitting down in Hyde

Park—Lenox waited for her to arrive home, wondering how he could convince her to come along for a week in the country.

When she arrived it was with a bustle of boxes and parcels. "Oh, there you are!" she said to her husband, who was waiting in the hall. "How is Sophia?"

"She's asleep. Can I help you?"

"Would you? I bought ever so much at the food hall at Harrod's— I couldn't stop. There are some marvelous ostrich eggs I want to give to your brother, he is fond of them, and then once I got to the chocolate counter I couldn't resist—but listen to me. How is your speech coming along?"

He had told her the night before of his news, and now he told her about his day, about Bottlesworth, Brakesfield, and the rest of them. "The prospect of setting foot in the Commons is terrifying."

"Won't they stop bothering you after a day or so?" she asked.

"Edmund imagines not."

She furrowed her brow and sat down. "Well, we must think of something to thwart them, these hordes."

"I quite agree. Would you suggest tipping hot oil over them?" She removed her gloves, and looking at her thin, lovely fingers he felt a wave of love for her. "How are you feeling, incidentally?"

She looked up at him and smiled. "You're sweet, Charles, but really I haven't felt badly for a month or more, now."

"You look pale."

"Well, it was a long day." He sat next to her and she leaned into his shoulder. "Perhaps I do feel a bit off, if I think of it. It's only that I think I should be able to do what I did before, you see, and when I can't . . ."

It had been a difficult birth for her, and she had been ill, though not gravely, for six weeks afterward. Still she looked too thin to Charles. "I wish you would rest," he said.

She looked up at him, her eyes slightly saddened. "It's London, I suppose. The invitations keep rattling through the door, noon and night, and now we must plan a party for your speech—of course we must, don't shake your head—and, oh, I don't know . . . I wish it could just be the three of us for a little while, don't you?"

"You were cheerful when you came through the door, my dear. I feel guilty."

"When I think of it I suppose I don't feel my best. I try not to think of it."

"Would you like to go to the country?"

He thought he saw hope dart across her face and then vanish. "But you couldn't, of course, you must be here."

"On the contrary, Edmund was advising me we ought to go away before the speech. Thinks it's more statesmanlike," he said with a tiny smile.

She laughed. "Are you to be a statesman, now? As long as you don't get a big head. Oh, but Charles, could you really leave? It sounds heavenly, the country, having walks, skipping breakfast, nobody to see . . ."

"My uncle Frederick offered."

So it was that in due course the Lenox family decided they would depart London for Somerset.

Lenox wrote to Everley immediately to tell them the family was coming, and to expect them as early as the next evening. Kirk, who had been Jane's butler for many years, a fat, severely dignified specimen, was thrown into a panic of packing and sorting out, as was Sophia's nurse, Miss Taylor. For his part Graham was shocked that Lenox would leave town at such a juncture. In the end he conceded Edmund's superior political judgment, but he still refused to look happy about any of it, and kept muttering about the meetings they would have to cancel.

It didn't matter to Charles and Jane, who both expressed, over supper, a feeling of relief, of a burden being lifted.

"In a way," said Lenox, "we've never been alone with Sophia. I've had to work so much, and you were ill."

"You shall still have to work."

"Can't you picture us walking her in the garden, though? And it's still really splendid weather, if we hurry down."

Jane laughed. "I don't think a day will make much of a difference in that regard."

"Come now, I feel happy. That's all I mean to say."

She smiled, indulgent. "So do I, Charles. We can bring the dogs, and not think about London things for a while."

He felt delighted that he had enticed his wife to go to the country. It was only an hour or two after he had congratulated himself on this victory, sitting in his study, that he remembered the conversation over again, and began to wonder whether perhaps it had been the other way around. Had she seen some sign of him wanting to leave town, and let him think he was persuading her to do it? Hadn't she been energetic and happy upon arriving home, and wasn't she busy that very evening, planning a party to follow his speech? It would be consistent with her character, for her to let him think he was tricking her: with her subtlety of mind, her insight into his own clumsily gallantry, her empathy.

One could never quite know the truth of such a dance, even in a marriage as close as theirs. Whatever it was it left him feeling loved.

From all of which it may be inferred that Kirk's momentary unhappiness, and Graham's, and Miss Taylor's, were not in the end of much importance. Anyhow, the sudden change of plans was very exciting for the housemaids, who were to be left behind and hadn't had a holiday for ages besides. They decided they would go to the seaside.

CHAPTER SIX

S ophia passed her first train ride in the kind of stoic silence that Lenox had found all too uncommon among children on public transportation, sleeping most of the while to Somerset. Sharing a compartment were the three of them and Miss Taylor, each with a small valise; Kirk and Jane's lady's maid were traveling behind in a private coach with the great majority of the family's things and the two Lenox dogs, Bear and Rabbit, who loved going out of London above anything. Lenox passed the trip by peering in at Sophia in her bassinet every few minutes, and otherwise gazing through the window at the countryside, imagining with pleasure all the importunate guests who were arriving to find his house and office uninhabited.

"It's surprising to me that she has her own personality, so young," he whispered to Lady Jane. Miss Taylor was reading the *Illustrated London News*.

"What do you mean?"

"I had always thought of babies as being a pretty uniform lot, but

Sophia seems different. Certain things make her happy, certain things make her unhappy—she's almost a small human."

"I should hope so," said Jane and returned to her novel.

In Bath they switched platforms and got onto a tiny single-car train, largely empty, which traveled in no great haste across the western part of Somerset. Through the windows one could see vast unspoiled meadows and orchards—the local cider was famously strong and delicious—and at each small station, the platform often no longer than fifteen or twenty feet, a stationmaster popped his head through the window to make sure nobody had to come off. Then he went to the end of the train and collected an armful of mail from the engineer.

After ten or twelve of these stops Plumbley was close; Lenox knew because he remembered a certain pub by the side of the tracks, and his heart swelled up with happiness at the prospect of returning to a place he had so loved. He felt a fondness all out of proportion for the dusty farmer who had gotten on two stops before, and was now reading the local newspaper in the corner of the car. How different from London it was here!

"We've arrived!" he said, well before the train began to slow, and leaned his head through an open window, breathing in the rush of country air.

At the station there was a cart to meet them, driven by a young man Lenox didn't recognize, but who was expecting them.

"To Everley?" he said.

"Yes, if you please. Our things are following behind."

They went a mile or so along a small cart-path, with ancient stone walls on either side, before they saw the black gates of Everley. Leaning against them, smoking his pipe, was Uncle Frederick.

More properly he should have been denominated Cousin Frederick, for he was the beloved first cousin of Lenox's late mother, but family tradition had claimed him as an uncle and so he remained.

He was a small, friendly-looking, gray-haired man, just nearing sixty now, utterly unassuming—retiring, in fact—with a small belly pushing out at his tweed waistcoat and the healthy air of a country squire. In his lapel was a bright blue ribbon, given to him many years before by the Somerset Garden Society, in honor of his contributions to horticulture. That ribbon about measured the height of his ambitions.

He put up a hopeful hand when he saw them turn the bend. "There you are!" he called out to Charles.

"Hello!" Lenox cried back.

"Come along in, come along in! Hello, Jane! Hello, Sophia, wherever you are in that bundle of blankets! And you, you must be Miss Taylor, Charles said you were going to visit! Very pleased indeed to meet you, madam!"

He hopped nimbly up onto the cart with them, and they drove down the long avenue, past lime trees on either side, which led to the house.

"I couldn't be happier to have you," said the older man. He wasn't smiling—he didn't smile too often—but there was plain and simple affection in his face. "For starters you must play in the cricket match next weekend, Charles, and then you haven't seen my garden—and in truth, you're coming for the best of the season."

This Frederick was the reigning squire of Plumbley, just as his forefathers had been since such a thing called a squire had first come to be in England and begun passing down the family name from father to son, from uncle to nephew, and occasionally from cousin to cousin. There was no unbroken line of male succession, yet each Ponsonby who abided at the great house, as the family called it, had viewed it in much the same light: There had been no profligate along the way who tore down the land's timber to pay gambling debts or sold off the estate's outlying acres for pony-money. Thus the estate—though it was legally unbound and therefore each new heir might have sold it on his first day of taking up the patrimony—had remained intact for many hundreds of years. Only tremendous good luck had held it all together. Or a peculiar, settled sort of inherited trait in all the Ponsonbys. As a group they were similar, all quiet, all bookish, all in love with home. The portraits that lined the front hall showed a long sequence of gentle gentlemen.

Frederick was no different. He was without aspiration to any greatness of personal achievement, was excessively modest, yet was a merry and genial soul, who took great pleasure in company and in other humans. The combination made people love him. Other than a stretch of time at school and then another at Cambridge he had spent all of his years at Everley. He left the estate twice annually and no more, once to visit for a week a small, warmthless, but colorful hovel in Ireland, where he shot birds with three very old friends, and once, for twenty-four hours every April, to the Chelsea Flower Show in London. The exertion of this latter sojourn, it was widely accepted among the people of Plumbley, nearly killed him, and his valiance in nevertheless going inspired in them a broad affection. (In this regard it didn't hurt that he loved the village, shopped with its shopkeepers, gave generously at church, and sent a silver rattle along to every Plumbley child who was born.) Generally he kept to his books, his gardens, his pipe, and his meals.

As for the house, there were greater families than the Ponsonbys in Somerset—many, in fact—yet you could not say there was a finer house than Everley. As they turned the corner of the drive and came to view it, reflected perfectly in the still pond that lay before its front door, all of them but Uncle Frederick fell silent.

For his part, he was saying, "Here we are, then, fetch down, Miss Taylor—but then, she is having a look at the place."

"It's very beautiful," the governess said soberly, gazing upon its littoral calm.

"Well, she's not bad," murmured Frederick, but his tight lips showed that the comment had pleased him.

Indeed Everley was famous in Somerset, famous even in England, among the people who knew of such things, for its serene loveliness. It had none of the grandeur of a palace, or of the great medieval castles—it was only two stories—yet it had a beauty all its own.

In color and build it looked something like an Oxford college, made of the same honey-colored stone, which looked beautiful no matter how the light struck it; it was in the shape of an open-ended square, with a medieval hall at one end, dating from 1220, and opposite that a matching Tudor hall. The front was more recent, dating to the reign of Queen Anne, and had two rows of four great windows and a large archway that led to a grassy inner courtyard. Ringed around it were small gardens with gravel paths, not grand but perfect in their beauty; Frederick tended them very carefully. The whole picture was one less of uniform imagination, like Chastworth or Castle Howard, than of a modest, gradually evolving, lived-in place. Yet the effect, between the pond and the quiet gardens and the house itself, was one of almost supernal beauty.

"It looks as if a nobler race than ours made it," said Miss Taylor.

"You are very kind and I welcome you," said Frederick. "You must admire it later, at length—for now I imagine all of you want tea."

"Oh, badly," said Lenox.

Soon they had been deposited in their rooms, complete with their luggage. He and Jane had a timbered-ceiling sort of hall with at one end a slim window of pink stained glass, which discouraged the light very beautifully against the walls. It was the oldest part of the house.

That evening they all ate supper together, Sophia coming in for a visit just beforehand. Afterward Lenox and Frederick retired to the latter man's small library, a tiny half-moon–shaped room, cluttered with odds and ends, very comfortable for reading. It had just enough space for two chairs and a bottle of port. The rosewood table between the chairs held a chessboard.

"A game?" said Frederick, pouring the port into two glasses.

"With pleasure."

He lit his pipe and opened with his queen's knight. "Well, Charles, I sent you that note without any very great hope that you would come, but here you are."

Lenox smiled. "Thank you for having us all. I've missed it. Hold for a moment—what is this smile you're giving me? You look as if you have a secret."

"No, no. Only I wonder what brought you down here?"

"What can you mean?"

"Was it that postscript of mine? There, yes, put out your pawn, I'll take him soon enough."

"I was intrigued by it, of course, but I came down because—"

"No, I'm only having fun with you. I know you would come oftener if ever you could."

Besides his servants Frederick lived alone; Lenox did wonder whether he grew lonely. "Of course I would." He moved. "In fact I shall come more often. You don't know how it's been, with Jane pregnant, that trip to Egypt—"

"Yes, the reports of it reached me in the *Times*. And your letter, of course, telling me you were safe long after I knew it." The older man chuckled. "Old Rudge, the farmer who lives on the county line, wouldn't believe you were my own cousin."

"We shall have to call on him."

"He's a curmudgeon—would think you a charlatan, I don't doubt. There, I told you I would have your pawn."

"Though it means I take your knight."

"Damn your eyes," he said good-naturedly. "But I may have some plan? No, I look over the board and see that I do not—I thought I had—but no. Still, let's follow the game through. Neither of us is very good, or likely to set the world afire with our brilliance, but it passes the time."

CHAPTER SEVEN

They played on in silence. When Frederick finally spoke again his face had grown more serious. "I'll tell you why I'm glad you've come down, however. I've some news I had rather tell you in person."

"Oh?"

"I'm passing Everley on to Wendell."

Lenox laughed. "Is that so?"

"I'm quite serious, Charles." The older man looked obstinate. "I plan to do it some time in the next eighteen months, in fact."

Wendell was the eldest son of Frederick's first cousin. He was a moon-faced, respectable, surpassingly dull soul, a barrister at Gray's, and Everley had been his due from birth—but not until his cousin died. Lenox felt the disorientation of a sharp shock. It was impossible to imagine Everley otherwise than it had been, and impossible to imagine Wendell appreciating Everley's charms—he was a man full of the same romance and poetry as a fair-sized rock.

"I pray you aren't ill?"

"No, but I am old."

"You're not yet sixty. I don't call someone old until they're eighty-five, these days, and even then I have a look at the withers."

Frederick smiled. "No, I'm not sixty, not for a month, and there's a bit of youth in me yet, but I feel a great strain in taking care of Everley—to be alone here, to be responsible. I am tired, Charles, heartily tired." As he said this, the squire's incipient old age suddenly showed in his eyes. "Wendell has a large family, a good wife. He will be happy here."

"Where will you go?"

"I'll buy a house in the village, I imagine. At first I thought it ill-mannered, to stay so close, but I think Wendell won't mind. He might even let me continue in the gardens—the *Ribes Rubrum* that Rodgers and I planted are very beautiful this year—and I know he will keep on the staff, if I ask him to."

"Freddie, you cannot—"

"Cannot leave? I can, and I shall."

"Is this decision financial?" he asked.

If they weren't relatives it would have been an inappropriate question; it was still very near to being one. "No."

"But Uncle Freddie, how can you leave your library? The card room where the two of us used to play hands of whist with my mother and old Kempe? I cannot understand it."

"Your mother would understand it."

"Would she?" Lenox was beyond forty now himself, a member of Parliament, but he felt the frustrated anger of a thirteen-year-old. "What about your responsibility to the house?"

"If I think that responsibility is best discharged by passing it to a good—to a very reliable—gentleman, then that is what I shall do." Now the squire looked severe. "We might discuss it some other time, but before you say anything else I beg you will consider my position."

Lenox, rebuffed, still bewildered, inclined his head. "Very well. I'm glad my daughter has come to stay here, then, though she will not remember it."

"There's no need to find melodrama in the situation, Charles. Wendell would take any number of your daughters in if you asked him to."

They played their game of chess on in a tense silence. It was Lenox who broke it. "I suppose you have lived here a long time alone."

"Yes, a very long time. I like to believe that I have stood a fine sentry over the house."

"There's no doubt of that."

"The gardens, in particular." Frederick's face looked softer now. "You aren't my age, yet, Charles. When you are, you'll see that it is wiser to make your own decisions than to let time make decisions for you. I hate to think of rotting away here, unable to shift for myself, a burden on everyone."

Lenox pondered this. "My reaction was selfish. I suppose I have the attitude toward Everley that some people do toward church. I don't always go, but it's a relief to know that I always could."

The squire laughed. "Precisely how I felt about leaving. I never thought I would—I love the place too much—but now I find that I would like to do it. Life is strange, I suppose."

"Nobody could contradict that."

"Shall I show you my final project?"

"By all means," said Lenox.

The older man stood, and beckoned his cousin to his small desk. "Here it is. *The Flora of Somerset.*"

"Your book?"

"Yes."

"At long last!"

"Easy for you to say, my boy! It hasn't been quick work."

Lenox leafed through the loose pages, each of which bore a drawing of a different plant. They were artfully done, and at the bottom of each page was a short description. "Will you publish it?"

"The horticultural society in Bath is eager to publish it, but I may take it to a London firm. More professional."

"Is there not a definitive work on the subject?"

Freddie shook his head. "Only a penny-pinching little volume from the year 'twenty-eight, by someone called Horace Hargreaves. I don't think he could have told you a tree from a sheep, to be honest—dozens of mistakes."

"I congratulate you."

Frederick tapped on the window. It was dark outside, but the silhouettes of a line of trees were visible. "Most of these plants I have managed to cultivate out there, too. A living monument. Another glass of port?"

"No, thank you."

Frederick poured his own. "You're tired, I've no doubt—I should let you retire. Yet—"

"What is it?"

"If you are not too upset with me—"

"Never in life," said Lenox.

"Then let us circle back for a moment," Frederick said, sitting. "I do wish you would give me your counsel, your professional counsel, as it were, on the vandalism we've had down in the village. It's giving the constables a fearful time, and to be frank, people are beginning to grow scared. I don't like it at all."

"Is it as bad as all that? I assumed it would be schoolboys."

Frederick shook his head. Outside the wind picked up, rattling the windows. "No," he said. "I fear it is more mysterious than that."

"I would like to hear the facts of the matter."

"Tonight?"

Lenox shrugged. "Why not? Start from the beginning, if you like."

CHAPTER EIGHT

$\mathbf{F}$rederick stood again and began to pace the small room, hands behind his back, brow furrowed. "It began not a few weeks ago, in late August. In a larger town—in Bath, say—I doubt it would have been much remarked at all, or if it were then they wouldn't have taken it very seriously, but of course Plumbley is a very small village."

"Six hundred people as I recall, or thereabouts?"

"When you were a child, yes. Perhaps nearer eight hundred now. The curate could tell you an exact figure. He's been collating the parish registers. At any rate, one sees very few unfamiliar faces in the village. Occasionally a traveling salesman of some sort will pitch up and stay at the Royal Oak for an evening, or a sister from London or Taunton will be resident with one of the townspeople for a month's vacation. Yet I can say with almost perfect certainty that there has been nobody here over the course of the time in which these vandalisms have taken place who is unknown to me."

The chessboard forgotten, Lenox slouched back in his chair, eyes sharp and narrow with attention. "What about over the past year, to take a longer view of things? Has there been anyone new come to town during that time?"

"Captain Josiah Musgrave and his family, yes. He moved into that pretty little house—it has an acre or two attached to it—that Dr. McGrath used to live in, down at the bottom of Church Lane. I'll come to him."

"Pray go on."

"You remember Fripp, the fruit-and-vegetable seller? I mentioned him in my letter?"

"I do. Is his shop still just off the village green?"

"That's the one—little place, not much room to move about inside, but it's by way of being an institution here, not unlike the saddler's or the butcher's. Very little change there."

"He still has the cricket bat nailed over the door?"

"Yes, and he's eager to see your form—but that's for another time. Here, wait there a moment."

"As you like."

Frederick stood and went to his cherry-wood desk now, pipe locked into his teeth, and sorted through the rich profusion of papers, books, and old teacups that concealed the desktop beneath them. At last he found what he had been looking for. "There we are," he said in a quiet voice. "I don't like to look at it, myself."

He passed a piece of paper to Lenox. Upon it, in dark ink, was a stick figure, something akin to a pictograph, of a man hanging by a noose.

It sent a chill up Lenox's spine.

"This was in Fripp's shop?"

"In a manner of speaking. One morning Fripp arrived at his shop—he lives with his mother, who is a very ancient personage, on the Mill Lane—and found all of his front windows broken. There were two or three rocks inside that had evidently done the job. A piece of paper was wrapped around one of them with this image upon it."

"Crudely drawn."

"Yes."

"This is the original?"

"No, that's a sketch, a fairly accurate one, I can confirm, as they sent for me straight away, my being the magistrate."

"Was anything taken from the shop?"

"No—at least, not anything of value. Perhaps they swiped an apple or two as they went, whoever did it."

Lenox studied the simple outline of the hanging man. "Not a happy sight."

"No, and it frightened the poor man half to death."

"I can imagine. He must be close to seventy," said Lenox. "He was in the shop when I was a boy."

"Yes, and his mother well over ninety. They're a hardy lot, the Fripps, but I cannot blame him for reacting unhappily. There was something horrifying about it, Charles, I swear to you—just a mute picture but I shouldn't like to gaze upon it again. It had an ominous feel."

"Who is the police constable in the village?"

"There are two: There is Oates, a good man, who's been in the job twenty years or more, and his new assistant, a boy, not much past eighteen, named Weston."

"They haven't been able to find anything?"

Frederick sat opposite Lenox again, his amiable face now grave. "Patience. We're still near enough the beginning of the thing."

"Go on."

"Fripp was panicked, naturally. He thought it might be a threat of violence—violence at a minimum, in fact, or worse still of murder."

"Had he any cause to believe he had enemies?"

"None. He chaffs the fellows at the King's Arms, the other pub in town, about cricket, but really, I cannot imagine . . . anyhow, after that morning a few of the local men set up a watch around Fripp's house and his shop. That lasted a week. Then the second incident happened, on the other side of town, and rather diverted everyone's attention."

"What was the second incident?"

"It was identical, only it happened to a different man."

"Who, now?"

"Wells, the grain merchant."

"He must be even older than Fripp."

Freddie shook his head. "No, you're thinking of the father, who's been dead for three or four years. His son runs the shop now, Frank Wells, a lad of only thirty or thirty-two. Means business, though. He has much the most prosperous shop in town, and really the only one in Plumbley that attracts people from other villages, in order that they might buy. He's built it up to no end from when his father owned it, and it was a rather sleepy place. I'm afraid it's gone a bit to his head—a gold watch chain, a carriage for his mother. Last year they expanded the building, that high-beamed Tudor place on the corner of St. Stephen's Street. It was a hellish noise, and caused a great fuss because he brought men in from Bath to do it, rather than hiring locally. Ironic, you see."

"And the crime was the same?"

"Yes. All the windows broken, rocks found inside the shop, one of them wrapped in a paper with the same drawing. This time whoever had done it took something of value out of the shop, however."

"What?"

"A brass clock that sat above the doorway. It was there in his father's day, too. Frank Wells minded that far more than the windows."

Lenox's brow was furrowed, the beginnings of half a dozen ideas in his mind. "What did Oates and Weston make of it, your constables?"

"That the criminal was emboldened at going free after the first vandalism."

"What do Fripp and Wells have in common? But no—perhaps you'd better finish by telling me about the crimes. How many of them were there in all? If they can be called crimes?"

"If they can be . . . certainly they are crimes! I would give the man who did it thirty without the option today, if I could. But to answer your question there have been four, the most recent not five days ago."

"Was the third crime another broken window?"

"No. This time—you recall the white doors of the church?"

"Yes."

"Someone had painted on them, in black paint, writ very large, a roman numeral: XXII. Twenty-two, as I scarcely need to inform you."

"How strange."

"Yes."

"The curate had it whitewashed immediately. Then, three nights later, this image appeared on the same door."

Frederick passed across another slip of paper. Like the hanging man it was eerie: a black dog, very simply drawn, and again with an air of definite menace.

"And nothing in the last five days?" Lenox asked.

"No."

For some time Lenox was silent. Finally, he said, "It's bizarre, to be sure, but how can you be sure that it wasn't schoolchildren all along?"

The older man sighed, and swirled the last sip of port in his glass before drinking it down. "We congregated, a few of us men who are concerned with the village's well-being: Mr. Crofts, who has a little land west of here, a very fine gentleman; Dr. Eastwood; Mr. Kempe, who lives now in the old parsonage. There are only thirty-two boys in the village who are of any age to make that sort of mischief. In the end we asked their parents to keep them under lock and key until the problem had been sorted. It seems extreme, I know, but as I said before this is Plumbley, not one of your great cities like Bath, like Taunton. The symbols were very menacing, Charles."

"What happened?"

"The Roman numeral appeared on the door of the church, overnight. We checked in with all of the parents, and none of the boys had been out past dark."

"Boys are very sneaky, you know."

"I had your brother and yourself here once upon a time, did I not? We enquired carefully, however, and though of course it is not a certainty I think it unlikely that any of those thirty-two boys did this. For one thing the images are so strange and unlikely, and for another, I know the boys. None of them are a bad sort. Not that we haven't had those, through the years, but most of them have gone off or grown up."

"I wonder," said Lenox, "whether the second pair of crimes, the defacement of the church doors, is connected with the first pair."

Frederick shook his head firmly. "We might go fifteen years without one incident like any of these," he said. "When there are four in as many weeks they must be connected."

"Yes, very likely."

"The village is trying to pretend that nothing is wrong. Meanwhile all the shops are barring their windows and people are afraid to walk about after dark. It's a terrible state of affairs. I do wish you would put your mind on it."

"I shall be rather busy with my speech," said Lenox, and then, seeing Frederick's disappointment, added quickly, "But I mean to think it over, perhaps even have a word with one or two people. Yes, you may count on that."

Though he fooled himself that he made the promise on Frederick's behalf, in some deeper part of his mind he knew that it was for himself, too; and there swelled up inside him the pleasure of anticipation.

CHAPTER NINE

From a distant part of the house a cry went up.

"Is that the child?" asked Frederick.

"It is, but I must not go to her. Miss Taylor would be fierce with me indeed if I should. Tell me, who do you suspect of these crimes?"

"Still, it's late, now, and you've had a long day's travel. Shall we go on in the morning?"

"If you prefer it."

Frederick's slightly plump, kind face took on again a troubled aspect. "In truth I would like to tell you all now."

"Are you not tired?"

"Me? It's the deuce of a thing, getting older, but I will say in its favor that one sleeps less—and no worse. I spend many hours in this particular nook, in fact, when the rest of the house has gone to bed. And d'you know, I find it rather cozy."

"It's an eligible sort of room," said Lenox.

"I could never use my father's study—the large one. Too much room to think. Here I have my telescope"—he gestured toward the window—"and my books, my papers, and a drop of something to drink. No, I am happy to stay up with you."

"Perhaps you will give me all the facts now, then."

Fate intervened, however. There was a soft knock on the door and without was Kirk, who said, "Begging your pardon, sir, Lady Jane would like a word with you."

"Tell her I'll light along in a moment," said Lenox, and when the butler had gone, said to his uncle, "Here, then, quickly tell me—"

Frederick had risen and was tapping out the ash of his pipe. "No, it's late. Tomorrow I'll give you luncheon, if you like, and we may talk about it then. Good night. It is pleasant to have you here, though—I say, it is."

As he mounted the stairs toward the small set of rooms that his cousin had allotted him and his family, in the old, east wing of the house, Lenox felt rather glad that they would leave some until tomorrow. He was tired. Perhaps the port had gone to his head? Or perhaps it was only the swirl of a long day, a quickly planned journey, the still fresh prospect of the speech . . .

Jane was in a chair by her window, feet tucked under her, a blue shawl of wool wrapped around her shoulders, reading. She smiled when she saw him and put down her book. "There you are."

"Hello, my dear," he said, and bent down to affix a kiss to her cheek. For some reason he didn't feel inclined to tell her that Frederick was giving up the house; tomorrow he would.

She received his kiss very becomingly, and took his hand. "Did I interrupt you?"

"No, or leastwise not in anything significant."

"Your uncle must be happy to have you here."

"And I'm happy to be here. I hope you are, too?"

"Oh, yes. I only called you up because I wanted a sort of family reunion."

"A reunion?"

She pointed. "Look, in the corner."

Sophia was there, in her bassinet. "You overrode Miss Taylor, then?"

"Yes, I said we would take her in here for the evening. I know it's self-indulgent, and Miss Taylor began to be cross with me, but in a new place, I thought—and then, she quieted down right away."

Lenox smiled. "I heard her cry."

Lady Jane stood up. "She's asleep, now."

They spent ten or so minutes, then, in admiring their daughter, the kind of minutes that pass slowly for a stranger introduced to a baby—for even the most precocious infant's conversation cannot be admitted as very sparkling—but which seems to pass in the instant of a breath for two parents. Her skin, which Lenox brushed with the back of his finger, was so warm, and soft! It reminded him of a warm bed on a wet night, of the sun on a mild summer's day, out by a lazy stream—of every comforting thing.

At last they left the child alone. Lenox began to take out his cufflinks and Lady Jane returned to her chair and her book.

Soon she was laughing. "What's that?" asked her husband.

"Only *Through the Looking-Glass*." She had undertaken a project of re-reading her favorite children's books, in order to begin to build a library for little Sophia to hear before bed each evening when she reached a more advanced age. "This part reminds me of us, when Alice and the Queen are running in place."

He went into the small study adjacent to their bedroom and poured a glass of water from the jug left on his desk. "May I hear it?" he asked as he came back through to the bedroom.

So she read out loud:

"Well, in our country," said Alice, still panting a little, "you'd generally get to somewhere else—if you run very fast for a long time, as we've been doing."

"A slow sort of country!" said the Queen. "Now, here, you see, it takes all the running you can do, to keep in the same place. If you want to get somewhere else you must run at least twice as fast as that!"

Lenox laughed but said, "How does it remind you of us?"

"It reminds me of you, you goose. All of your callers yesterday— was that not running in place? Here you may work properly."

"Just so," he said.

"It's not far different for me. Nothing social—nothing more taxing than a walk with Sophia, you know. It's lovely." She put down her book and stifled a yawn. "I think I must go in to sleep, now. Will you be up long?"

"Only a few minutes more."

"Good." She stood up. "It's a funny book, but I think I prefer *Wonderland*. Sophia will like it better, too—I know she will."

"I don't doubt it."

He kissed her and returned to the small study and sat down. Kirk had laid out his papers, his royal dispatch bag, and his blue books—those slim Parliamentary files on the issues of the day, which each member of the House received in avalanches. There was also a fresh notebook in which he might write.

On its first page he found himself sketching out pictures of the hanging man and the black dog.

Soon he was writing in earnest. He made a small map from memory of the locations of the four vandalisms, deciding he would check it tomorrow—it had been many years since he was resident in Plumbley, after all—and at each location wrote a short list of questions to ask. "What sort of paint?" "Who found and reported each one?" "Connections?"

He was by no means convinced that a schoolboy was not in the end behind it all, despite the efforts of Frederick, of Mr. Kempe, of

Dr. Eastwood, and of Mr. Crofts. Yet if an adult had been breaking windows and painting doorways around the town of Plumbley, what could have been his motivation? Did the images convey a message? Or were they only some unhappy soul's bad-natured purgation?

Lenox's own black dog was by his feet, at the moment, Bear, along with his golden companion, Rabbit. They had come down with Kirk in the coach. They were gentle creatures, two retrievers, a present from Lady Jane.

"Why would they've painted a dog like you?" said Lenox in a soft voice.

Of course in folk tradition a black dog meant death. All of the images were therefore deathly, except perhaps the Roman numeral. It made him wonder whether that was the one upon which he should concentrate.

He decided that after he had had the remainder of the story from his uncle, he would go into town and see Fripp, the victim of the first vandalism, and perhaps the grain merchant, Wells. Fripp anyhow was an old friend, and might have some information.

Upon making that decision Lenox set aside his notepad and endeavored to read a blue book upon the subject of rural education in Scotland. He had been much in the committee rooms that produced the report, and felt very strongly on the issue, yet his mind kept circling back to the Roman numeral and the black dog, wondering what they meant, and the broken windows, too.

But of course it was pointless. He had very little information still. With a sigh he snuffed out his candle, patted the dogs on the head, took a final sip of water, and started out for bed, obscurely dissatisfied.

CHAPTER TEN

That mood was gone by the next morning. Lenox rode out early across the fields on a neat little chestnut hack that his uncle kept stabled at Everley, primarily for visitors, occasionally for himself. When the member for Stirrington fetched up to the hall after his ride he was happy, hot, and in a tearing hunger. He fell eagerly to the eggs and bacon laid out upon the sideboard.

"How is Sadie?" asked Frederick when he came into the breakfast room. "Chalmers was delighted to have her taken out. Wishes I did it more myself."

"She was in very fine form, quick as a bee when she jumped the stiles. I must have ridden her eight miles and she was still fresh when we returned."

"I'm glad to hear it. I can never give her enough exercise, though I let one of the lads from the village take her out on Saturdays. Would you like a cup of tea? Or is it coffee?"

"If there's coffee—"

When he had had his two cups of coffee and read the *Times* back to front, and the local paper from Bath more cursorily, Lenox, quite satisfied with his morning, sought out his uncle again. For his part Frederick always took his own breakfast in his study, even when guests were there; he had spread out on a table beside his telescope a single egg in a silver cup, a crust of toast, a blot of marmalade, and a pewter cup full of dark red liquid.

"Oh, Charles," he said, turning at the sound of the door. "Will you join me in a glass of hot negus? It settles the stomach wonderfully, I find."

Lenox sat down. "Thank you, no. I thought we might resume our conversation of yesterday evening, if you remain so inclined?"

"By all means, yes."

"My question was whom you might suspect, or indeed who it is that the town suspects. They must have someone in mind, mustn't they?"

Frederick, who had been standing over his breakfast, occasionally peering into the lens of his telescope, sat down, too. "There we come to Captain Musgrave."

"Who took Dr. McGrath's house."

"The very one, and in fact he has bought the parcel of wooded land that lies behind it from old Turnbridge and is planning to clear it. He's rather rich, I believe."

"He's not from Plumbley?"

"Oh, no, he's from Bath. Tenth Regiment of Foot. I don't think anyone here saw him before six months ago."

"Why does the village suspect him?"

Frederick pursed his mouth thoughtfully, considering how to answer. "I half wonder if it's only because he's new to these parts, yet I confess that I don't like the set of his sails much, myself. He's a very handsome man, light-haired, rather tan, very tall, and even his worst enemy would have to admit that his manners are fair."

"How did he come to Plumbley?"

"He married one of our local girls, Catherine Scales. Do you remember her?"

"I do not."

"No, I wouldn't have thought you would, but she was a very beautiful child around the time you visited Everley most often, working for her mother in the dress shop, always about town, quite beloved—spoiled, you might say, by those who knew her. She has pale skin and black hair."

"A dress shop? I take it their birth is unequal, then?"

"Yes."

"How did that come to pass?"

"Catherine's mother died two years ago. The girl had an aunt in Bath and went to live with her. This aunt had married well herself, to a manufacturer, and just managed to keep a carriage, could nod at some of the finer women in Bath in the streets—was always very hard on her sister when she visited Plumbley, I know, came it very grand. Anyhow she was childless and took an interest in Catherine when the girl's mother died. Catherine met her husband when she spent the season in Bath. Of course, a military man will set his cap at anything, much less a girl of her beauty. I would reckon she won the captain without much difficulty, to be honest, handsome though he may be. Men are fools."

"Nevertheless, I'm surprised that he consented to move here."

"As was I. Stranger still has been their behavior since they arrived."

"How is that?"

"Nobody has seen more than a glimpse of her for these six months, Charles." Frederick looked grave. "If I hadn't nodded hello to her at the church, a few weeks ago, as she was rushing away, I swear I would have feared there had been some foul play."

"How strange."

"Yes, it is. And it has given rise to tremendous gossip, of course."

"What does the aunt say to it?"

"She trusts wholly in Captain Musgrave. I would venture that she stands rather in awe of him."

"Is he much seen, any more than his wife?"

"No. He takes his custom in most things to Bath or to Taunton"—this was a larger town not far away—"and that alone would have made him unpopular, if people hadn't decided that he was mistreating Catherine."

"Yet you said he had good manners."

"Manners; yes. Personally I didn't see the incident."

"Incident?"

Frederick rose and returned to the small table by the telescope, where he took a sip of his negus. "Before Catherine left Plumbley she was, of course, wooed by several gentlemen. One of these was Wells."

"The grain merchant? Whose shop was vandalized?"

"The same."

"And the incident?"

"Captain Musgrave and his wife were walking through town one afternoon and Mr. Wells approached them. Nobody quite heard their conversation—eyes in windowpanes, you see—until Musgrave's voice rose. Said that if Wells was a gentleman he would call him out; that he expected him not to address Catherine Musgrave again; and that he would thank him to continue along his way. Then Musgrave grabbed his wife by the wrist—most cruelly if accounts are to be believed, though it's possible that the myth has grown rather out of proportion to the event itself—and dragged her away. It was after that that we begin to see much less of her about Plumbley. Of course the timing may be coincidental."

"What was Wells's account of the matter?"

"He was very free about it in the Royal Oak—said he had merely been wishing them a good day, and was astonished at Musgrave's reaction. Said a sort of black jealousy came over the man, though he had won his wife fair and square."

Lenox waited, but his uncle didn't say anything else. "And that is all?" the member of Parliament asked.

"Yes."

"Nothing else on earth encourages people to attach Musgrave's name to these acts of vandalism, then? I call it very thin, to think that a captain of the Tenth Regiment of Foot has been setting out about a small Somerset village with rocks and a bucket of paint to frighten the locals, simply because he may be unkind to his wife and has had words with one of her former suitors. Does that seem plausible to you?"

"Not phrased as such."

"And what use could he have with a brass clock that might seem very fine to a grain merchant, but likely not to a gentleman?"

"None. You're right."

"If anything it sounds to me as if he wants privacy. Beyond that we know that he has no fear of speaking directly to Wells, which makes me wonder very sincerely why he would go to the wearisome effort of staying up half the night to break his windows."

The older man frowned, hands clasped behind his back. "Yet there is something in the man's air—well, perhaps you shall see, if you meet him. I fancy myself a judge of character, you know."

"Yes," said Lenox. "And it's all damnably puzzling to be sure." He thought for a moment. "Perhaps I'll have a word of conversation with Oates, the constable, after I drop in on Fripp."

"You'll find that he and Weston are very eager for help."

"Where are they?"

Frederick gave Lenox instructions about where to find the small police station. "Tell them I sent you," he said at last.

"I shall. And is there anything else I ought to know?"

"No. I don't think so, anyhow."

"Nothing about Musgrave?"

"No, I don't— Oh! I quite forgot. I should have added that it is held against Musgrave in Plumbley—held as almost damning, I fear—that he is attended everywhere he goes by a large black dog."

CHAPTER ELEVEN

Lenox sat in the sunroom with Lady Jane and Sophia for a few pleasant moments, during which he told his wife about Frederick's plans to give up the house, and she reacted more calmly than he had—thought it was a sensible idea. Perhaps she was right.

After they had discussed it Lenox said good-bye to his wife and his child, called Bear and Rabbit, put on his black topcoat, and set out for Plumbley.

The clean air had already invigorated him. Few men felt more at home in London than Lenox did, yet even he had to acknowledge the difference it made to his heavy lungs and his stinging eyes to be away from the metropolis. It was a worsening problem; on one day earlier that month the mixture of yellow fog and coal smoke—what residents called the London Particular—had been so bad that the police ordered the streetlamps lit during the daylight hours, not much after noon. Then there were the cattle the year before, brought in from just such a place as this for an exhibition of livestock, who had suffocated to death. It sounded like a joke, but it wasn't. Even every Englishman's favorite accessory, the tightly furled black umbrella, had become that color largely to guard against the discoloration of the polluted air that a white umbrella in London invariably suffered.

The countryside was so beautiful. It was that season when the end of summer and the beginning of autumn get muddled, and one never seemed to know whether to dress for the impending October frost or the lingering September heat. In the small houses he passed on the grassy lane, there was a feel of homeward-turning, of less time outdoors, as if in anticipation of winter, with firewood stacked outside of each chimney again and, visible in the dim windows, congregations by the warmth of the stove, just while the morning chill lasted.

As he walked, he cut a solitary figure, slender, fingers occasionally dragging along the stone wall that guarded the path. The two retrievers gamboled around his feet as he went, one black and one golden. Neither ventured too far from his heel, except once in a while to contemplate for a longer moment some especially arresting scent in a clump of grass along the side of the road, like a scholar who turns a page back to read it again. When whichever dog had been detained by a particular odor was finally satisfied with his interrogation of it, he would sprint forward in bounds to catch up with the pack. As for Lenox he stopped twice during the mile and a half walk, almost as if he had forgotten something at home. Both times his eyes rose to the meadows along the path and his face broke into a radiant smile. He would pause in his steps, then carry on his way, eyes to the ground again, his expression slowly returning from joy to meditation. What had come to his mind, each of these times, was Sophia; what drew his thoughts back away from her were Captain Musgrave, his black dog, and the drawing of the hanging man.

Soon the lane brought him to a small stream, which meant he was close to town. The dogs barked a duck, strolling along its bank, back into the water, and then circled proudly back to their master for praise.

"There're two of you," Lenox said chidingly and nipped Bear on the ear with his fingers.

At the path's final turn, a grove of trees gave way and revealed Plumbley. He stopped, happy to look upon it again.

It was an ancient place of habitation, set at a low point among the few miles of serene countryside that surrounded it, near the strength of the stream. It was entered in the Domesday Book as Plunten, and then round about the year 1160 took the name Plumton; two centuries later it was Plomton; soon enough thereafter it was Plum's Lea; then Plumley, and now, finally, for the past hundred years or so, Plumbley. Whence that superfluous B came no local historian had satisfactorily deciphered, but now, planted where it was, it showed no signs of moving. What was certain was that, as they had nearly a thousand years ago, when they give the village its name, plums still grew on the lea near the great wood. Locals would tell you that they tasted dreadful off the branch but made for a fair jam.

It was an industrious place, full of handsome rows of gray houses. It had two public houses, the Royal Oak (named for the tree in which Charles the Second, pursued by Roundheads, had concealed his august personage) and the King's Arms, which were in a semipermanent state of war, each with fierce partisans; a smithy; a butcher's; a school; and a lovely village green. As Lenox walked down Woodend Lane, toward the fruit and vegetable seller's, he could see twinned above Plumbley its two highest points, the small spire of St. Stephen's church and the cupola of the town hall, freshly painted white, its resting bell, slightly louder than the church's, ready to beat out the time as twelve o'clock in, oh, what now—he looked at his pocket watch—three minutes. Good, the shops wouldn't have shut for lunch yet.

Fripp had replaced his broken window. Stenciled upon it in gold letters was W. F., PURVEYOR, and leaning against the window was a green signboard with white paint that said, in three lines, FRESH FRUIT, FARM VEGETABLES, and OPEN YEAR-ROUND. As Lenox pushed the door open a bell rang. It was a tight space, with crates nailed up tidily along the walls, overflowing with cabbages, potatoes, apples, and much more.

The fruit-and-vegetable seller himself, now five or six years beyond sixty, was at his counter, hunched over a piece of wax paper, intent on some piece of work. He was a wiry, short man, in the pink of health, with fastidious circular spectacles and a carefully maintained black moustache.

He looked up. "Why, Charlie!" he said.

Lenox, who had known Fripp for some thirty-odd years—since Charles was ten—said, "Hello, Mr. Fripp."

Fripp took off his spectacles. "I heard you might be at the great house—but tell me, are you still a batsman?"

Lenox smiled. "If you've a spot for me."

"If we've—we'll only just make the numbers now you're here, you know."

"How are the King's Arms this year?"

"They have a devilish spin bowler, Yates, from after your time. But welcome! And you married, too!" Fripp came around from the counter and shook Lenox's hand.

"And our side? The Royal Oak team?"

Here Fripp began a lengthy, obviously much rehashed description of all the many virtues and vices of the cricket players who frequented each evening the same public house he did. Lenox half listened, as he did so gathering a few choice pieces of fruit to the counter. He would take them back to Jane.

"Is there fig jam left?" he asked in a break during Fripp's voluble recollection of his wicket-keeper's poor eyesight.

"A few jars left, yes. Shall I wrap one in paper?"

"Two if you would." Fripp crouched down beneath the counter, rooting among his preserves. Lenox raised his voice slightly. "By the way," he said, "my uncle told me about your window. Terrible business."

"Yes, it was," said Fripp, rising with the jars in hand. "And then Wells got the same thing."

"I heard. Do you have any idea who might have done it?"

"None, and I still don't feel at ease in my mind about closing up the shop alone. Did your uncle show you the hanging man?"

Lenox's face was severe with sympathy. "Yes. I didn't like the look of it."

"Nor did I."

"You cannot think who might have done it?"

"I would stake my life that nobody in Plumbley wishes me that ill," said Fripp. "Even at the King's Arms, you know, it's only a friendly joke we have with each other."

"What do you and Wells have in common?"

Fripp considered this. "Not very much, I suppose. He rarely takes a pint. His father liked to come into the Oak on occasion, and shopped his fruit and vegetable with me here for many years. The son does, too, but sends his maid around. He's grown very prosperous." He snorted.

"I heard."

"Sells grain and seed to half the farmers in Somerset, it sometimes seems. What similarity could he have to a small shop like this one?"

"And personally? Do you share any family, any friends?"

"Not except insofar as everyone does, in Plumbley."

"What do you make of Captain Musgrave?"

"Mr. Ponsonby mentioned the captain, did he? I can only say that's he's treated very fair with me, buys in his fruit and vegetables weekly, though I know he gives his custom to a butcher in Clamnor, four miles over the country, and not to Richards, here in town."

"Do you think he has been using Catherine Scales unkindly?"

"I think a village knows how to gossip."

"Yet when do villages go very wrong in their judgments?" asked Lenox. "Generally they seem to know their business."

Fripp frowned. "Well, perhaps over time. But the captain hasn't been here longer than six months."

"Do the symbols mean anything to you?"

"Nothing particular-like, if you mean that, though I daresay I can tell as well as the next gent what a picture of a man hanged up by his neck is meant to say. S'nothing good."

They spoke for a few more minutes then, rather unprofitably, about the case. Lenox paid for his fruit and his jam and left, steering the subject before he went to the kinder subject of cricket, and departing with advice about covering shots and leg-breaks in his ears. Then, the dogs at his heels again—they had waited, ears forward and staring in after him, by the door—he set out to meet Plumbley's police force.

CHAPTER TWELVE

Once, as a boy visiting Everley with his mother, Lenox had been scrubbed on his cheeks with soap and water, placed in a stiff collar and a blue coat, and fetched by the purposeful guidance of a junior footman into a wooden seat upon the town green. Alongside the young Lenox then had been his mother and a much younger Frederick. They watched in silence, among a crowd of some hundred or so people, as a man in a tall hat—later revealed to Lenox to be a bishop, that most awesome of creatures after the Queen—took to the church's porch.

"Will Mr. Somers, M. A. Oxon, please rise!"

A tremulous young man, with a long, wet nose and thick eyeglasses, a book under his arm, had stood up from his seat at this request to join the bishop in front of the crowd. The great clergyman—his powerful brow knitted with solemnity, his gray and brown hair stiff against the wind—then led Somers to the door of the church, took him by his two wrists, and placed his hands against the door of the church.

"Now the living is his," Lenox's mother had said to him. She was a religious woman. "He will be a shepherd to these people, Charles. So goes the tradition." Then, after a beat, she added in a whisper, "But did you ever see such a silly thing for grown men to do?" and laughed her light laugh.

As he walked the town green outside of Fripp's, this was the memory that came back to him. He wondered if the man was still there, or if he had moved on to grander things. Funny that he remembered that name, Somers, when so many of the details he had once known about for more important matters had been sifted away from his mind into oblivion.

The office of the police force of Plumbley was in a humble shingled building next to the church on the town green, two stories, with the upper floors occupied by the town clerk, its record-keeper, and its historical documents, and the lower by Oates and Weston, the men Lenox had come to see, and the single jail cell over which they presided.

He knocked at the door. A moment later it opened to reveal a very young, red-cheeked boy, his face still downy. He wore a constable's uniform. As one got older it became harder to guess the ages of young people, Lenox had found, but this boy couldn't be far past eighteen. "Yes?" he said.

"Mr. Weston, I presume?"

"Yes."

"My name is Charles Lenox. I'm staying at Everley."

"Oh?"

"I wonder if I might see Mr. Oates."

"You—"

Weston's opinion of whether Lenox might see Oates was irrelevant, because now a meaty hand had taken him by the shoulder and Oates himself was barging ahead. He was a very large man with a trim, sandy mustache, and a slow, honest, rather stupid face. "Mr. Lenox?" His voice was very deep.

Lenox extended his hand. "How do you do?"

"Honored to meet a member of Parliament, sir. We ain't had one in Plumbley since the last election."

"Is it Mr. Cortwright who sits for you here?"

This was a gentleman who had bought his seat in Parliament much as men might buy trinkets for their watch-chain. He came to sit on the benches, oh, once a year, perhaps. There was of course no mandatory attendance. "The same," said Oates. "Last election he bought every man in town as much beer as they could drink, if they signed down to vote for him."

"Ripping drunk we got, too," said Weston, his face ardent with the memory of that wonderful day.

"Not true," said Oates sternly. Behind the older constable's back, however, Weston winked at Lenox. "Your uncle said as you might come in, Mr. Lenox. Used to be a detective, did you?"

"In a quiet way."

"If you can answer for these broken windows and this church door I'll thank you—but then I reckon you won't be able to, no, not by a long shot. It's the damnedest thing I've seen in a dozen summers on this job. What's the point of it, I ask you?"

"I'm curious to hear the story in your own words."

The quality of the average constable in the bucolic parts of England varied greatly. London itself had only had an official police presence for the last forty-odd years, since Sir Robert Peel had established the Metropolitan Police Force at Scotland Yard. (The members of the new troop had been called "bobbies" in honor of the founder's forename.) It was only in the last ten years that, by law, every town in Great Britain had perforce to hire and pay someone specifically to impose the law.

Oates seemed a fair credit to the profession. There was perhaps no great enterprise in him, but then one could glimpse a certain rural doggedness in his character that might serve just as well for a provincial police constable as cleverness. His relation of the facts of the crimes—the broken windows, the paint on the church door—tallied exactly with Frederick's tale, though he offered precious little in the way of new information. This out of the way, Lenox was free to ask a few questions.

"Tell me, has there been more crime than usual in Plumbley, over the summer?"

Oates shook his head. "No, sir, the normal quantity, or perhaps even rather less. But then, you can ask your uncle about that. He's sitting in two days."

"Is he, though?"

"Yes. Every Monday, in fact, because there's often one or two cases of drunkenness after the weekend."

Frederick, like the long succession of squires of Everley before him, was a magistrate. These men occupied an interesting place in the legal system of England; they were generally local lords or landowners, chosen for their family name rather than training or merit, and they differed vastly in their expertise and judicial temperament. All of the small crimes of Plumbley and its environs came before Frederick. If he felt a case was beyond his purview, for instance if it was unusually violent, he might send it up to the monthly petty session, which consisted of either one or two magistrates in a more formal setting, with more witnesses, or even the quarter session, for which all the justices of the peace in the county met four times a year. The great murders and robberies went to the Courts of Assizes, which ran circuit from London all over the country, and might only come into one's jurisdiction once in a year. Yet it was the judgment of the magistrates that affected the most people. Juries had convicted ten thousand or so men in the past year, magistrates eighty thousand.

"Perhaps I'll sit in with him," said Lenox. "Have any of the crimes in the past months been unusual in their nature?"

"Not in particular," said Oates. "Your garden variety, Mr. Lenox." He gestured at Weston. "We had this one up for fighting over a lass. Fine example."

Weston snorted. "As if I cared a buttercup for her."

"She's married now."

"And very happy I'm sure I hope she'll be." Then the young man added, with a spice of rebelliousness, "Not that it will be easy, with that fool of a—"

"Enough there," said Oates sharply.

"Do you have a list of the crimes other than the vandalisms?"

"We could knock one together if you gave us a day or so."

"Thank you."

"Now, Mr. Fripp and Mr. Wells—can you tell me what you think they have in common?"

The two constables looked at each other. Oates spoke. "They both own shops, less than ten houses apart from each other. We think it might be an attack on the shops of Plumbley."

"But then how to account for the church door?"

"Well, precisely," said Oates. "And the other shops untouched, too."

"Both men have been in town a long time, I suppose."

"Yes."

"Perhaps they're being menaced in the hopes that they will pay off their attackers," said Lenox. "Are they the two richest shops?"

"Wells is doing all right—"

"Better than all right!" said Weston.

"But as for Fripp, I don't think he puts much by. His house is paid for, but his tab is running at the Royal Oak, I know."

"Is it long past due?"

"Not too far, and not for too much. You won't find a motive there," said Oates.

Lenox looked down at a slip of paper he had brought. "The Roman numeral on the church door. Twenty-two."

"Yes?"

"Do you have any thoughts about what it means?"

"We can't make head nor tail of it," said Oates.

"Do any of the street numbers in town go that high? Could it be a date, a time, a numbered gravestone? Who knows Latin, or would be likely to use it? What if it's not a number? Could it be a message, 'two down, two to go,' that sort of thing?"

Weston had taken out a pencil and was writing. "Hadn't thought of those questions," he muttered.

"I'll look at whatever possibilities I can," said Lenox. "Meanwhile, Captain Musgrave. Where does he enter into it?"

Both of the constables' faces darkened. "We're keeping an eye on him," said Oates. "A very close eye."

"Only because he's new in town? And because he has a black dog?"

"If you meet him you'll see why folk're suspicious, Mr. Lenox, sir."

"That woman is in trouble," said Weston sadly.

"Catherine Scales?"

"Yes."

"What makes you say so?"

"Nobody's seen her, have they?"

A troubling thought struck Lenox. "Are you sure she's alive?"

Oates nodded. "Went up to check not ten days ago. She received us, after we fair insisted, but she didn't look well. Weston'll tell you."

Weston had no trouble elaborating on this point—was shocked, most shocked to see the lady so pale—striking beautiful lady, too—damn shame.

"And if you had to assemble a narrative in your minds of what Musgrave is doing, what would it be?" Lenox asked.

"Causing trouble," said Oates.

Weston nodded stoutly. "Causing trouble."

Lenox held back a sigh. "Very well. Perhaps I'll see the captain myself, if I can find the time. In the meanwhile let us hope that nothing further happens."

CHAPTER THIRTEEN

Lenox and the dogs walked home. His mind moved slowly from the mysteries of Plumbley to the mysteries of the nation. When he got back he found the house empty, Jane, Sophia, and the governess on a walk, his uncle working in the muck of the gardens. Lenox went straight to his desk and began to work on his speech.

This age of Queen Victoria, through which he was living, regarded itself as one of great social rigidity, of great propriety—and it was true. The beefeaters stood guard before Buckingham Palace, the banker in his sitting room smoked his pipe and read his evening newspaper, his wife paired people off by rank as they went into dinner, the pound was worth a pound of silver.

Nevertheless, Lenox was persuaded that one day, long after he had slipped out of life and been forgotten, this epoch would be remembered equally for its profound social changes. Look how far they had come! The Reform Act of 1832 had begun the movement toward equality, permitting hundreds of thousands of new people to vote, an expansion that the act of 1867 had widened. The government was growing less brutal, too. In 1849 a husband

and wife, convicted of murder, had been hanged by the neck before thirty thousand people, but five years ago Parliament had finally banned all public executions. Transportation to Australia, whose consequences had been occasionally tantamount to execution, ended ten years before that. Even more astonishing, until 1823 very nearly within his own lifetime, it had been the law—the law!—that a suicide must be buried at a crossroads with a stake through his heart. Those days were gone. Society was growing gentler, more inclusive, perhaps, even, he hoped, less stratified. This was the change he had stood for Parliament in the hopes of achieving.

Finally it was happening. His hardest work as a member had come earlier that year, when he fought for a bill, a special pet of his, called the Agricultural Children Act; it had been a bill he championed in the face of widespread indifference even among his friends, had absolutely forced his brother and the cabinet members he knew intimately to stand behind. The act forbade children under the age of eight—he had been hoping to make it twelve, but was forced to compromise—from working on farms, and, as an extra step won in the compromise, had provided for the education of the same children. Fighting for the bill had been exhilarating, with sleepless night after sleepless night, the thrill of productive work, strong cups of coffee as the House debated into the small hours, the maddening lassitude of the lords. In the end it had passed.

There was still so much to do. That was to be the subject of his speech. Even as he jotted notes now he came across a new fact: apparently a study that year had determined that about a quarter of men and women who registered for marriage signed their name only with the letter X. They were illiterate. He frowned and started a new piece of paper with that at the head.

He knew what the Tories would say—that God would provide for his children—and smiled when he thought of an old quote.

Was there a collected Shakespeare in here? He walked over to the bookcase and saw that there was, the usual ornament of any English bookcase, and found what he had been looking for, by way of preemptive riposte. "Our remedies often in ourselves do lie which we ascribe to heaven."

Occasionally it crossed Lenox's mind that he came to this problem from a perch of exceptional comfort and ease, manufactured for him by hundreds of years of tradition and accumulation. When the thought came he pushed it away, knowing that he lacked the strength to sacrifice any of his personal comfort; ill at ease with himself for it, but also, as a man of his age, forgiving himself, and half persuaded that it was all part of the order of things. Mightn't he do enough good to make it up?

He wrote steadily on for an hour, then two, the thoughts coming to him in phrases, little strings of inquiry. Soon it would all begin to knit together into a speech. He had been writing the same way since his English tutor set him *All's Well That Ends Well* at Harrow, when he was fourteen.

Just when he was thinking that a cup of tea might not go amiss, he heard the door to the east wing open. It was Jane and Sophia returning, the governess with them. He greeted the adults with a smile, then he peered down at the child in her bassinet and chucked her under the chin. She had a curious, mobile face, which broke into a grin now.

"I'll feed her," said Miss Taylor.

"How was it in town?" Jane asked, busying herself with her gloves, her hair, and her shoes before sitting down tiredly in the soft yellow armchair by the window.

"Not bad. I returned with fig jam."

"My conquering hero."

"I thought you would like that. Where did you go?"

"We walked all over creation. Your uncle went along part of the way, but he kept seeing flowerbeds he didn't like the look of, so it seemed cruel to keep him."

"He was in the garden when I returned two hours ago."

Lady Jane laughed. "And still is. We just passed him, down in the dirt, a sight filthier than the gardener who was with him. Oh, did you see you have a letter? I left it on the mantel there, see, yes, that's the one."

"From whom? Edmund?"

"No, Dallington. Just like him to write three sheets, too." The penny post permitted each page to be sent for a penny; any additional pages cost a few shillings, payable by the letter's addressee. In effect Dallington had spent their money with his prolixity.

"I don't know," said Lenox indulgently. He had the letter in hand and was tearing it open. "We've had enough free post from the British government, I suppose."

Because he was a member of Parliament all of his correspondence was franked without charge and sent on. The day he had taken his seat it seemed half his acquaintances had handed him bundles of letters, to be distributed across the aisles. It was common enough practice.

"True," said Jane.

The letter, sent in from the Beargarden Club, read:

Dear Lenox,

How do you do? I trust that the country is still full of all those trees and patches of green that you went to find, a bane to any thinking man, and that you are happy there with Jane and Sophia. Here in the more salubrious climes of London we are well enough. A bit of tedium now that the Waugh matter has been resolved. I'm writing about that, in fact—to tell you about the full confession we've had from Florence Waugh. You'll be surprised to hear it, I know, since you believed the servants to be involved, and yet I fancy in this matter our conjectures redounded to both of our credit, for Florence had the help of one of them. As you guessed, he was named in Arthur Waugh's will, and it was he who poisoned his master's final meal. The constant service of the antique world, I know.

Enclosed you will find Florence Waugh's statement. Apologies about the postage. Inspector Jenkins took her into brig, quite unrepentant. I expect she'll do well in front of a jury. Apparently Arthur Waugh was a brute to her despite her money. The servant fled the day before yesterday, apparently in the direction of Newcastle. Florence Waugh should have been content to let the crime ride on his shoulders, but I found the apothecary where she bought the antimony. It cost me half a sovereign of shoe leather, too, I can promise, traipsing all over London with her photograph. When I finally said "Jensen's Apothecary" to her, just those words, she broke down crying, and from then it was easy.

Letters will find me here. Try not to breathe too deeply down there, the air isn't healthy. Love to all.

Dallington

Lenox spent some time reading over Florence Waugh's confession. He was proud of Dallington—it had taken real effort to find the apothecary who sold the woman the antimony, and the young man had occasionally been more inclined to lazy, penetrating supposition than to tenacious police work in the past—and also, somewhere within, and to his surprise, jealous. The role of mentor had suited him. It had allowed him to keep a hand in the old game, to play the sage, but more and more often now Dallington's judgment surpassed his own. It was rustiness, he supposed.

It made him want to discover who had been threatening Plumbley.

He returned to his desk. He shuffled aside his parliamentary papers, and for the first time in years began to make a complex, encoded chart of the crimes he was tracking, the kind he had made all the time when the cases came in more quickly than he could take them.

CHAPTER FOURTEEN

For much of the next day, however, Lenox was forced to work on his speech. Fresh letters had come in the evening post from his brother and two members of the cabinet, each with detailed thoughts, each franked with Parliament's stamp. It was advice he valued, and he rushed through a very rough outline in time to send it to his brother on Monday morning.

At about ten o'clock, after he had been out riding on Sadie and eaten breakfast, Frederick sent for him.

"Working hard?" he said, when Lenox appeared in the doorway.

"I am. But you're all gussied up, Freddie. Why?"

The older man wore a dark suit and a pair of gold spectacles hung from a gleaming chain around his neck. He gestured toward a robe made of lawn, lying over the arm of his chair. "I've five cases to hear this morning. I thought you might want to observe."

They had spoken about the possibility at supper two evenings before. "Of course," said Lenox. "With great pleasure. I had forgotten."

Like the great majority of justices of the peace, Frederick heard his cases in his own home. The household staff, however, did their best to imbue at least a part of it—the second hall, a large room with very high windows looking out upon the pond, mostly out of use in the daily life of Everley—with the formal mood of a government building.

Frederick sat at the center of a large horseshoe-shaped table, gleamed with beeswax to a brilliant pale brown. Behind him a wood fire was lit. There were a pair of chairs and a small table about ten feet away, with a jug of water and a glass upon it, where the accused would sit. In the corner of the room was a St. George's cross, and upon the table were the seal and rolls of office. Standing at the door, in a suit that had seen better days, was Rodgers, Frederick's gardener, a man whose sensibilities were of profound coarseness in all matters not pertaining to the flora of Somerset. He acted as the bailiff on these occasions. Oates and Weston were in a narrow servants' passage with their five charges, four of whom were well-known enough in Plumbley to have been sent home on the promise that they would appear. The last man, the fifth case for Frederick to hear, had been in the town's lone jail cell.

Lenox took a chair near the window, where he hoped to seem unobtrusive. That was not to Frederick's plan, however. The first cases were two young men of sixteen or seventeen, whom the magistrate had evidently known from infancy. Both were accused of drunkenness and brawling. He lighted into them with identical tirades. "Aren't you ashamed, to be called before me," he said, "and what's worse, what's much worse, on the day when my house is graced by a member of Parliament? A *lawmaker*, no less? I feel ashamed of my village, I promise you I do." And so on, at great length.

Lenox noticed that the appeal to the boys' civic pride was

relatively ineffective; what really struck home was when Freddie began to talk about the shame their mothers would feel, if they heard of their sons in jail. The second boy actually cried.

"Rodgers, what shall I do with him?" asked the magistrate at the end of each testimony. "Jail?"

"Set him to gardening," said Rodgers. This was his invariable advice on the punishment of all criminals, which Frederick liked to hear but had never enacted save once, when the head shrubbery keeper of his rival in this parts, Lord DeMuth—who had a great whacking hall called Saltstow, with miles of gardens—had been scraped up after a fight in the pub; this criminal Freddie had kept for two weeks. Rodgers had been in a state of ecstasy.

"No," said Frederick twice, "I think it had better be a real lesson." Each boy was fined ten pence.

"No worries there, he's a good sort," was all Frederick added, after each had gone. "And neither has a farthing to spare. Rodgers, you know full well they can't take time away from the farms to garden. Of all the advice."

"Humph," said Rodgers, whom long service had entitled to a certain very modest degree of disrespect.

The third case was one of uttering, as it had long been known, or passing bad coin. This one Frederick seemed to take more seriously. The young man in question, a Jack Randall, had paid for a passel of candles with several coins, among them two bad ha'pence. Randall, too, Frederick had known for much of their mutual time upon the earth—he was a man of perhaps thirty-five, ill-favored, with unpleasant hooded eyes—and he questioned him with great ferocity.

This in itself was unusual. In general the criminals who appeared before a justice of the peace were not permitted to speak, but Frederick, once he had heard the testimony of the officer, always gave them a chance.

"You realize that until not long ago you might have been hung for holding a snide, as they call it, a false coin?" Of course he didn't add that the same was true of a host of crimes—opening a tavern on Sunday, doing damage to Westminster Bridge, impersonating an army veteran—that, in practice, had rarely met with capital punishment.

Randall looked unfrightened. "No, sir."

"And if I choose I may still send you to jail, essentially for as long as I please."

This roused Randall out of his insolent silence. "No, sir! Which it was an accident, sir!"

"Your worship, you call him, Jack Randall," chimed in Rodgers. "As you ought to know, being here week in, week out like."

"Your worship, I didn't know! I got them dimmicks off a trader at the fair in Taunton, hand to God!"

Frederick held up the coin in question. "And their extremely battered appearance, their, I would say, unnatural appearance, didn't spark any doubt about their validity in your mind?"

"I trust the Queen," said Randall immediately.

"Hm. Rodgers?"

"Set him to gardening."

Coining was one of the great problems of the age; it had been since the pence, the ha'pence, and the farthing had ceased to be copper and become bronze, some fifteen years before. The Bank of England possessed a machine that could sort good coins from bad, and Lenox knew, from a parliamentary report, that of the nine million coins it sorted each week it threw out two hundred or so. The question was whether the machine was entirely effective.

In the end Frederick let Randall go with a fine, though a rather heavy one, of ten shillings, a half-sovereign. When Weston had escorted him away Frederick said to Lenox, while filling in an official form, "The fine is to keep him out of trouble more than anything.

I doubt he had the sense to know the coins were false." Here he looked troubled, however, and the motion of his pen stopped. "He'll come to a bad end, though. I very much fear it."

Lenox leaned forward, so that Rodgers might not hear, and said, "Do you think he could be involved—"

"No, he lives on a farm far out of town. Little chance of him taking a horse back and forth half the night to do it, even if he could take a horse without being noticed. Which is unlikely. It's DeMuth's land, too, and he knows where his crofters are. That much is sure. Rodgers, nod the next one in, would you?"

The cases were always heard in order of ascending seriousness, and there was little doubt of the guilt of the man who came in now, from Oates's testimony, a French laborer named Fontaine, very large and very strong. He had beaten his common-law wife badly one morning, apparently unprovoked by drink, which was unusual, and then gone to Bath by coach, where he passed a night spending money very freely before the police hauled him in. Dr. Eastwood—who along with the squire and a few others was one of the great men of Plumbley—came in and testified to the woman's wounds. Fontaine himself was silent but stared unerringly, some might say threateningly, at the magistrate, even when other people addressed him.

"Where did you come by this money?" asked Frederick.

Fontaine was silent, his face expressionless. Even when Rodgers tried to bully him into speaking the Frenchman remained that way, perhaps secure in the knowledge that the law could not compel him to speak, and finally Frederick sentenced the man to thirty days in jail without the option of a fine, for the violent mistreatment of his common-law wife. He would be tried in Bath for his crimes there. When he had gone out, Lenox asked Frederick if this was about the usual run of cases he saw.

"Lighter than usual, perhaps," his relative said.

"Exceeding light," said Rodgers with great firmness.

"But this next one is a bit novel. Call him in, then, would you, bailiff?"

A very handsome, dark-eyed young man came in, willowy and with flowing dark hair. He wore a bottle-green blazer made of velvet.

"The lady in question is here?" asked Frederick of Rodgers.

"Arrived half an hour ago, Your Worship." Then he added, "In a curricle, too." This was a very quick, superior sort of conveyance, two horses for one or two passengers.

"Bring her in, please."

"Very good." Rodgers leaned out into the hall, made a beckoning motion, and then announced, as a beautiful young woman came in with a footman for company, "Miss Louisa Pershing."

"Miss Pershing," said the magistrate, rising. "May I introduce myself, and my cousin. My name is Frederick Ponsonby and this is Charles Lenox. May I ask you to sit, here, yes, just near me, and give me an account of this little matter?"

Miss Pershing was only too happy—it was dreadful what a dishonest man could achieve. The trust of a young person—society today—and so Miss Pershing, who looked perhaps better in repose than in conversation, nattering as she did, eventually produced her tale. One morning she had been walking in the flood meadow near her father's property with her small dog, a toy fox terrier, when a brutish man, passing by, had simply picked up the dog and stormed away. Miss Pershing's grief was evident and real as she recalled this, and Lenox, who loved his own dogs, felt a pang of sympathy for her.

Two mornings afterward a handsome young man—and here she pointed to the accused—had come to her house, saying that he had heard of her misfortune and, admiring her from afar for so long, taken it upon himself to find the dog. He had achieved this, and now it would only take three pounds to recover the animal. If he had *had* three pounds, of course, even his final three pounds on the earth, it would have been his pleasure, his signal honor . . .

It was a familiar old story. In the end the handsome fellow and his brutish partner extracted eighteen pounds from the young woman.

The man himself only spoke once. "We returned the dog!" he cried, when Miss Pershing had broken into fresh tears. "It was a service well rendered!"

Here Oates stepped in. "Sixth dog they've caught 'em taking, here and around. It's a pretty living, too."

"Set him to gardening," Rodgers muttered, unsolicited.

The young man looked heartbroken at this suggestion. Frederick, with a thank-you to Miss Pershing, said that he had better wait until the Petty Session to sentence the man, the matter lying as it did somewhere between blackmail, extortion, and dog-theft. (For many years this last had been the most serious of those crimes, when rich men's dogs could cost as much as workhorses.) With that decision he thanked Oates, Weston, and Rodgers, and adjourned the court, looking relieved to be done.

For his part, Lenox's mind kept returning to the strong, silent Frenchman, to what secret precisely he might have been keeping, and to why he had so much money to spread around Bath.

CHAPTER FIFTEEN

That afternoon Lenox walked into town to see the grain merchant, Wells. The shop, not far from Fripp's, was a big, shiny affair, with a bright coat of hunter green paint on it and in the windows an enormous iron scale with counterweights for measuring large quantities of grain, seed, and flour.

Nobody was inside at the moment, however, except for a man behind the counter.

"Mr. Wells?" said Lenox.

"I am. Who's asking?"

"My name is Charles Lenox, sir." He shook hands. "I'm staying with my cousin at Everley, at the moment."

Wells's manner shifted just slightly toward the deferential. "Oh?"

"I'm also trying to help him—and Mr. Oates and Mr. Weston—discover who's been vandalizing the town. Including your shop, I understand. Your window was broken?"

"We'd string the lout up by his thumbs, if I had my way, who did this," said Wells.

"What happened?"

"It's a short enough story. Old Fripp, down the road, had his window broken, and along about six or seven days later they did mine. Same kind of rock, same picture wrapped around it."

"Do you have the picture?"

"I gave it to Oates."

Lenox looked around. "Your shop seems to thrive."

"Thank you, sir. It's not been easy."

"Does Captain Musgrave shop here?"

Wells was a purposeful-looking man. He had a dark mustache and was dressed in a black apron with a bow tie. He betrayed no real emotion at Musgrave's name. "Not any longer."

"He did once, then?"

"He doesn't have much in the way of livestock or farmland," said Wells, "but he stopped his cook buying her flour and corn here." The word corn, here in Somerset, referred to any kind of grain—oats, barley, wheat.

"And the clock that was stolen from you—who knew it was here?"

"Anyone who'd been in the shop the last fifteen years, I suppose. That's all, if you want to round them up."

Lenox looked at him levelly. "Thank you." He had noticed that in a small back corner of the store, next to a padlocked door, there was a narrow band of lighter, newer floorboards, mismatched with the timeworn ones they lay alongside. "And this is your expansion?"

"Yes. We can keep more stock with the new shelves there," he said. "It's been a good year for business."

"Would you mind if I examined the place they took the clock from?" said Lenox.

Wells gestured toward a shelf over the door, now empty. "Be my guest. Do you want to stand on a stool?"

"If you wouldn't mind."

As Wells brought a stool over, Lenox asked, "Did the thieves come in after the rock, through the window?"

"They reached through it and unlocked the door. Left it standing wide open."

Lenox ascended the stool. "How did they get the clock down? Was this stool standing here?"

Wells nodded. "The same one."

"It's very rickety—I wouldn't like it if you let go at the moment. Makes me think there were two of them. Was it heavy, the clock?"

"Yes. Why?"

"It would require a man taller than I am or stronger to fetch down a heavy object from this position. You have a high-ceilinged place here, and I don't doubt most men would have dropped the clock, including you. It would have been difficult for one man to take it away very quickly."

"True enough," said Wells, his voice grudgingly impressed.

"What I wonder is why they risked it, knowing the town must have been watchful after the first incident."

"They're scoundrels."

Lenox tested the shelf's sturdiness, decided he trusted it, and then hauled himself up, rather laboriously, so that he was resting on his forearms, feet off the stool. "Hold steady down there," he called.

"Be careful," said Wells, sounding alarmed.

There was nothing interesting on the shelf, except the lighter-colored wood where the four feet of the clock must have stood for many years. As he was coming down to the stool, though, and drew eye level with the window, he saw something: In small lettering in the windows it read F. W., PURVEYOR. It gave him pause. He filed the information away for later.

"Who do you think did these things?" asked Lenox, when he was on the ground again. "Captain Musgrave?"

"I wish I could say."

"Are you afraid?"

"No," said Wells, but his eyes shifted slightly—or so Lenox thought.

"There's no shame in fear."

"I said I wasn't, thank you."

Lenox was silent a moment, looking around the shop. "Very well, then," he said. "If you think of anything further to tell me, you can go through Oates, or you can find me at Everley. I hope we may catch him for you."

"Here's Mr. Oates, now," said Wells, gesturing toward the door, behind Lenox.

Lenox turned just as the constable came in. "Hallo, Oates," he said.

"Mr. Lenox, sir. How about that last chap?"

"The dog thief?"

With more animation than he had possessed before in Lenox's company, Oates launched into the story of Miss Pershing and the dog thief to Wells. The detective, as soon as he politely could, left the shop.

It was just darkening, now, the sky a twilight pink above the rising hills in the distance. A feeling of sweet melancholy filled Lenox's chest as he gazed out upon it. He looked forward to the evening, the wood fire in the dining hall—his uncle still abjured coal, one of the last stubborn few—the good night to Sophia, the civilized and quiet supper, still served, out here in the country, *à la francaise,* with the dishes on the table where anyone could scoop themselves a potato when they wanted one, rather than, as all over London, *à la russe,* the Russian style, with the footmen serving from the left. Much more companionable that way.

In the still evening air he realized that what he felt was a sense of being home. Beyond a certain age one made a home for other people—for Jane, for Sophia—and lost that childhood sense of refuge and security. Perhaps it was because Frederick reminded him of his favorite person, his mother . . . but no, Lenox pushed that thought back, painful as it was. Even ten years later he didn't like to think of her being gone.

He and the dogs stopped on their way into the post office. At any rate it was what Plumbley called a post office; as so often in the country it was the front room of the home of an older woman, who in exchange for a small stipend received the mail and passed it on to the postman. (A funny quirk of the language, as the *Times* had pointed out recently, that in Britain the Royal Mail delivered the post, while in the United States, the Postal Service delivered the mail.)

Lenox knocked on the door and was called in. The dogs were welcome here—there was a bowl of water set by the door for them, which they took turns lapping at—and they tumbled in alongside him. "Hello, Mrs. Walsingham," he said. "Any post for the Hall?"

"Nought but a telegram. But that is indeed for you, sir," said the redoubtable old specimen sifting through a pile of letters.

Idly Lenox wondered whether she knew all the gossip in town—so easy for a wax seal to fall open!—or whether she was honest. Surely the latter. They would have perhaps taken the job from her otherwise. Telegram in hand, he thanked her and left.

He was sure it would be his brother who telegrammed him, with further advice, but here he was out. In fact it was from his friend Thomas McConnell, a sometime Harley Street physician of Scottish descent, married to Jane's cousin and dear friend Toto. In other times he had helped Lenox with his cases, an impromptu medical examiner, but those days were long past. What could he be writing to say, urgently enough to wire rather than write a letter?

The telegram answered that question.

DALLINGTON MAKING A FEARFUL ROW ABOUT THE WEST
END STOP THOUGHT YOU SHOULD KNOW STOP TALK
OF THE CLUBS STOP STARTED AT THE BG TWO DAYS AGO
STOP SHALL I TELL THE DUKE OR WILL YOU STOP NO
WISH TO CAUSE THEM PAIN STOP REGARDS MCCONNELL

Lenox's step slowed as he read this, and his heart fell. The BG would be the Beargarden Club, a haunt of many young and debauched aristocrats. Not coincidentally it was where Dallington's letter to Lenox—perhaps his final piece of professional duty on the murder of Arthur Waugh—had been sent in. So.

Lenox went back to Everley with this telegram in hand, much preoccupied, thinking the entire way about what he should do. When he arrived he went straight to see Jane, who was writing at her desk, a curl of hair fallen fetchingly over her absorbed, concentrating face.

"Ah, Charles!" she said, smiling and looking up when she realized he was in the doorway. "How are you?"

"Unfortunately I think I shall have to go up to London," he said, and handed her the telegram.

CHAPTER SIXTEEN

In the end it took a very short while for detective to find detective: Lenox ran Dallington to ground ninety-odd minutes after the train from Bath arrived in London. Now he was walking down Villiers Street, a slim cobblestoned lane that lay directly in the shadow of Charing Cross station. It was dark and cold out, with a bitter, penetrating rain.

He stopped at a dim, unmemorable little doorway with a sallow lantern flickering above it, the name GORDON's stenciled in black on its glass. Another hundred steps on he could see the Thames and the lights of Hungerford Bridge, and the intrepid small craft that even at this hour, in this weather, were out on the water, scavenging, ferrying, on whatever mysterious errands their pilots had in mind. Lenox had always felt more comfortable in stately, leafy, daytime London than in its dark and secretive nighttime brother. He had had his adventures in both.

Gordon's Wine Bar was down a stairwell, and Lenox had to stoop to take the steps one by one. By the bottom his eyes had adjusted to the candlelight. The ceiling was formed by a succession of low, steeply curved vaults, so that some parts of it left five feet above your head and some five inches, rather like a cave or an old Roman bath. Its stone walls and columns were smudged black here and there with smoke. Everywhere—under and around the scratched tables and uneven chairs, beneath the bar, above the bar, hung from the ceiling—there were pallets of red wine in clear bottles marked only with a few swipes of chalk.

The bartender, a saturnine, white-haired man with a large belly, was backed by seven great oak casks, marked AMONTADILLO, MADEIRA, PORT, and so on. (Why was it all Portugese, the wine? Many years before a canny British trade envoy had agreed that his country would buy solely wine from that country if she bought her cloth solely from England. It was one of the most unbalanced bargains ever struck, and the reason that every stolid insurance man in Lambeth drank something as exotic as Port, or Portuguese, wine.) Occasionally one of the quiet customers would sidle up to the bar with his glass and the bartender would fill it from a cask. At the small tables there were men sitting alone, others playing chess, others reading newspapers, the majority of them with the eyes and the complexions of the committed drinker.

This quiet was broken, however, by occasional shouts and laughs from some deeper recess of the place. Lenox followed the noise to a stooped semicircular door, very heavy, which he opened to reveal a group of ten or eleven men and women in a brilliantly candlelit room.

The scene was one of loud debauchery. There were empty bottles by the dozen, women sitting on men's laps, cards, dice, and cigars flung across every surface.

"The chap with the wine! Capital fellow!" shouted a carrot-haired young man, who happened to be near the door. Then, drunkenly, he said, "But you've forgotten the wine. Foolish thing to do, it was your only job."

Dallington hadn't turned, yet, but Lenox could see his profile. He looked far gone. His eyes were barely open, and the two women on his lap—prostitutes, almost certainly—couldn't coax him to awareness. Occasionally with great effort he would stretch one eye open and murmur something incomprehensible, and take a sip of a greenish liquid in a small, bell-shaped glass that never left his hand. Even at this advanced remove from his senses, a carnation stood fresh in the lad's buttonhole.

Lenox set back out into the main room after a moment. His stomach flipped when he thought he had seen someone from Parliament, a young secretary, but upon closer examination the resemblance was only vague. He walked straight to the bartender. "How long have they been in there, in the back room?" he asked.

"Who's asking?"

"Have they paid?"

"Very regular."

"And the women!"

Here the bartender assumed a look of almost total, blank stupidity. "Don't know."

"Lord Dancy and William Lawrance can drink themselves to Gehenna, for all I care," said Lenox, and registering the bartender's surprise, added, "Yes, I know them all, the idlers, and half their parents. But I do need one of them out. The dark-haired one, with the carnation in his buttonhole."

"John Best."

"Yes, why not." The bartender stared at him for a long moment, and then Lenox realized that he was waiting for the transactional element of the conversation to begin. "Do you have anyone to roust him out for me?"

"And who are you?"

Lenox took out the brown, calfskin billfold that Lady Jane had given him two birthdays past, and removed a pound note. "Get me two strong men and have a cab waiting at the top of the stairs."

"They're good for that in the next two hours," said the bartender. "Don't want to disturb their group."

Lenox doubled the amount now. The sum was what a housemaid might make in a month of work. "Haste, please," he said. "I'll wait here."

The bartender paused and then, imperceptibly, nodded. He swiped the notes into his waist—for a panicked moment Lenox wondered if he was simply going to steal them—and then, by way of consecrating their deal, poured a glass of red wine from a bottle under the counter. "My finest," he said.

"Thank you." Lenox took a grateful draught of the wine.

Fifteen minutes later two men appeared, looking grim, and it only took them a moment to drag a dark-haired young man up to the bar.

It was the wrong one. "For the love of heaven," said Lenox and, leading them and the bartender—and a few mildly interested onlookers—back to the door, said, "That one."

They pulled Dallington out. He couldn't stand under his own power. Lenox liked a drink, now and again, but this looked like something different, very like illness. He was glad to have dispatched a message, when he arrived in London, to McConnell, asking him to come to Hampden Lane.

Dallington just opened his eyes enough to register Lenox's presence. He didn't seem surprised. He put up a token resistance against the men dragging him upstairs—enough to make them pause, though they could have carried on—and said, with titanic effort, slurring badly, "The one in the red dress, the red dress."

Lenox nodded. "Wait at the cab for a moment, if you would," he said to the men.

He went once more to the back room and found the girl with

the red dress, gave her a bill folded in half, and left the room. He felt no sense of judgment, only one of fatigue and sorrow.

Lady Jane's two closest friends on the earth, once she had married her closest, were Toto McConnell and the woman she called Duch, the Duchess of Marchmain, Dallington's mother. It was a new and rather shiny title, three generations old, and both the Duke and Duchess disliked it—but it made them public figures. Beyond that, they were both so wildly happy, so immensely obliged, at the change in John . . . it was no surprise to him when Jane had agreed he should come to London and handle the lad himself, rather than telling the boy's parents.

At Hampden Lane Lenox had time, before the servants had recovered from their surprise at seeing him, to see his own house dark and uninhabited, and whether because of the rain or the kind of evening he had had, it struck a chord of deep sadness somewhere within him. He shook it away and, with the coachman, Staples, dragged Dallington into the study and laid him, half-crumpled, upon the couch.

Soon McConnell arrived, full of authority and good sense. In truth he had had his own battle with alcohol, but they had been far more private than this, had indeed occasioned relatively little notice beyond his friends. This made Lenox angrier: there were people's reputations at stake besides the young detective's.

McConnell forced Dallington to sit up and examined him very carefully, splashing water over his face, asking him questions. Lenox retreated a discreet distance, though not far enough that he couldn't hear. Well.

At last McConnell finished. "He'll be fit enough in a week's time, with rest," he said. "If he had gone on drinking much longer I would have worried, however, about poisoning. His liver is in a fragile state to start with, and he's feverish. We must hope it doesn't progress."

Together they managed to get Dallington into a bed upstairs, loosening his tie and removing his shoes. Then they sat together in Lenox's study for a long while, speaking in the hushed, comfortable tones of old friends called out on some unexpected duty together late at night, smoking their short cigars. Finally, at two or three in the morning, McConnell said he had better return to Toto—and of course to George, his daughter, was what went unsaid, for it never did to care too much about one's children. Lenox understood.

The detective went to sleep in his own bed then, and stayed there very late into the morning.

He subsequently wished that he had risen before he did. For when he finally went to his study, it was to discover upon a silver salver on his desk a telegram that turned his heart to ice:

CHARLES YOU MUST RETURN IMMEDIATELY STOP THERE HAS BEEN A MURDER STOP ALL SAFE AT EVERLEY THANK GOD STOP TOWN IN A STATE OF PANIC STOP EARLIEST TRAIN POSSIBLE STOP PONSONBY

CHAPTER SEVENTEEN

Six hours later Lenox stood on Plumbley's town green. At his side was Oates, the police constable, who was much shaken.

"Are you sure you can carry on?" Lenox asked.

"I can," said Oates.

"If you need to retire for a few hours—"

"No, no, nothing of the sort."

"So he was lying upon this spot."

"And a knife between his shoulder blades, as dirty and cowardly a way—" Oates stopped himself. "Yes, he was lying here, sir. The poor fellow."

Lenox had returned by the first train. Unsure what to do with Dallington he had simply dragged the young man—coherent but wan—from bed, had two footmen place him by the window in the first-class car, and brought him along. He was lying in a bedroom at Everley now. Dr. Eastwood was busy with the more serious matter of an autopsy, but had promised to check in on the lad that evening. In the meanwhile Lenox and Frederick—his face a mask of calm, his emotions, when you spoke to him, deeply disturbed—had come to the center of town, where they had found the corpse upon the green. A shock of red hair was the first thing visible, in full view of St. Stephen's church, of Fripp's, of Wells's, and of the rows of mild shops and houses that squared it off. Once he had brought Lenox to the scene of the crime, Frederick had left to go see the lad's numerous family members in their homes.

The green was not large—you could walk from end to end in perhaps a minute and a half, and easily have a conversation across it at a quiet moment—and Lenox was persuaded somebody in the houses must have seen something.

He restated this opinion to the constable now.

"I sent word around with the women. Nobody has come forward," said Oates. "And everybody loved the boy."

"Yet after the crimes of the past few weeks I would have imagined many open eyes, open windows."

"Nobody has come forward," repeated Oates stubbornly. "And everybody loved the boy."

The boy—his body found corkscrewed, knife in its back, his face, according to Oates, full of horror—was also one of the few people in town Lenox had known.

It had been Weston.

Lenox's first thought when he heard this news, arriving in Plumbley, was of the constable's rather winning description of his polling-day drunkenness. His second was of the victim's extreme youth. Nineteen! He had barely lived. It grieved Lenox powerfully.

Of course he knew that in all likelihood one day longer in Plumbley would not have altered his understanding of the case, or prevented the violent assault upon Weston, and yet he resented Dallington for fetching him back to London at such a crucial moment.

A sort of voluntary commission of deputies had sprung up now, men from across the town. Wells and Fripp, as well as the pub owners, usually implacable enemies, were among them, a group of ten or twelve. They ringed the square, answering questions from their neighbors and protecting the site of the crime from trampling feet. Lenox wished they had left the body for him to examine *in situ*, but understood why Oates had felt that to be impossible.

In the back of his mind, like the nuisance of a bee buzzing against a window, an idea or a thought was trying to come through, something that bothered him. Something about Weston? About the vandalisms? It had been there all morning, a low hum of agitation. There was no use doing anything but waiting for it to come out on its own.

Methodically, he began to circle the site where the corpse had lain, very slowly. "Where did he live?" he asked, eyes still to the ground.

"In a pair of rooms behind the police station," said Oates.

"Did he have any help?"

"A charwoman who came in mornings, fixed a few meals for him. She didn't live in, obviously."

"There's no chance she would have been there at night?"

"I shouldn't think so. We might easily ask her. She arrived to work this morning and found us all here, looking at his body. I half killed her, it did. She went straight home for a glass of malmsey."

Lenox stopped and wrote this down in his notebook, then continued, eyeing the ground in his broadening circles. So far he had seen nothing, but there was light left and he was a patient man. "Did he ever go out so late in the evenings?"

A dozen witnesses had confirmed that they had passed across the town green at 11:00, when the King's Arms closed, and there had been no body upon it then.

"I don't know," said Oates.

"But it wasn't part of his duties to patrol the village?"

"No, sir."

"Not even after the vandalisms?"

"No, sir. Perhaps it should have been."

Wells, Fripp, Weston, the church doors. What connected them? He had reached the outer perimeter of the town green now, and he went back to the spot where the corpse had lain. He began his circles again. "Then he must have been called out," said Lenox. "Have you looked in his rooms yet?"

"Not yet."

"If we're lucky there may be a message. If we're luckier still it may be signed." He made another note now. "I would also like to go through his effects." He didn't want to say the words, but there was always the chance, however out of character it might have seemed, that Weston had been the vandal. Drawings, paint, any of it might still be in his rooms.

"We can go directly after we finish here, if you like," said Oates. "It isn't a hundred yards."

"And his family?"

"He was my second cousin, of course."

"Other than you?"

"His mother is dead—which, thank God, if you don't mind me—and his father has been dead many years. Half of the doors in Plumbley were open to him, of course, by way of cousinship or friendship."

"Who was he close to?"

"The lads his age, of the Royal Oak, I suppose."

Lenox made another note. He was circling back inward now, slowly beginning to despair of finding any clue here on the green. "And the man who found the body . . ."

Here was the most interesting fact of the case. Oates's face, which Lenox glanced up to see, darkened. "Captain Musgrave, yes."

"He is amenable to being interviewed, I suppose, this afternoon?"

"He had damned well better be."

"Then perhaps we should go there directly. I can see nothing on the green itself of much interest. Unless—"

"Mr. Lenox?"

They were in the corner of the green closest to the church and the police station next door, meaning they were also close to Weston's rooms. "Where is his doorway? Does he have one from the outside?"

Oates pointed to a small alcove behind an iron gate in the police building. "Just there."

Lenox started to walk the line, examining the ground as minutely as he had examined the green. The deputies around this part of the green made way for him, men he didn't recognize. "Was he found in shoes, or barefoot? In nightdress, or in a suit of clothes?"

"In shoes, and in a suit of clothes."

"Suggestive." His eyes were glued to the ground. "Had anyone seen him at the pubs?"

"No, and I know that he went to his rooms after we knocked off, at six or so. Said he was tired."

"There you are!"

"Sir?"

Lenox was stooped over. Just by the iron gate was a small pile of cigar ends. Carefully he picked one up. "These are the cigars he smoked, as I recall—correct? Yes? He was in shoes and clothing, you say, at such an hour of the night. I think we may conclude that he was waiting for someone. For at least twenty minutes or so, judging by how much he smoked. On the other hand there are no cigar ends on the green. Either he stopped smoking or the meeting was short."

Oates seemed to go pale. "If Weston was waiting to meet someone—does that mean he knew his murderer?"

Lenox nodded. "I fear so."

"It may have been the vandal himself who asked him to meet," said Oates.

"The thought had crossed my mind. Come, I want a look at his rooms now."

"Yes, sir."

Suddenly, with a spark of comprehension, he knew what it was that had been bothering him all day, that vexing near-thought that had thrummed in his brain. "Oates," he said.

"Sir?"

"Something occurs to me. About Weston and the vandalisms."

"Yes, sir."

"The date today, do you know what it is?"

Oates's face crunched with confusion, until it dawned on him what Lenox meant. "That Roman numeral, the bastards," he said. "It's the twenty-second, isn't it?"

CHAPTER EIGHTEEN

Before they went into the rooms where Constable Weston had lived, Lenox had a thought. He walked toward Fripp, who was positioned in sight of his storefront. "Will you do me a service?" he asked.

"Yes," said Fripp immediately.

"You're here every day. Would you knock on doors in the square, whether you like the people behind 'em or not, and ask if they saw anything strange last night? Oates has already canvassed them, but a second try can't hurt."

The fruit-and-vegetable man nodded. "If they saw anything you'll hear of it."

"Thank you, Mr. Fripp."

The rooms Weston had occupied in life lay directly behind the police station, through a large walnut door or, alternatively, through the side gate where the cigar ends had been dropped. Lenox and Oates took this second point of entry.

There were two rooms, as bare and tidy as monks' cells, leading one into the other. In the first there was a small round table with three much-scratched chairs around it, a comfortable armchair by a grate, the coals in it half-gray, still usable, and along one wall a shelf of thirty or forty illustrated novels. Lenox flipped through these carefully, looking for odd scraps of paper, but Weston had evidently been too organized for that.

"I take it he liked these stories?"

Oates nodded toward the book Lenox was holding. "That one, there, was his favorite. Dick Turpin."

The illustrations were garish and violent. Dick Turpin had been England's most famous highwayman during the century before this one, and his tale was still widely told. Oates was right; the spine of this book was creased from use. "Most of the books are about criminals."

"He never wanted anything but to be a police officer," said Oates. He spoke stiffly.

"Then I am heartily glad he was able to do it, while he was alive."

"I suppose."

On the walls of this first room there was only one framed image, a mezzotint showing the cathedral at Salisbury. "Constable," said Lenox.

"Sir?" said Oates, who was standing behind him.

This play on words had been inadvertent; instead of trying to explain, he said, "Is there a kitchen attached? I see he has the leftovers of a meal here."

Indeed, there was a plate with lamb and peas sitting on the table, as well as half a candle and another illustrated novel, this one about the thief-taker Jonathan Wild. It was marked with a blank scrap of paper.

The second room, like the first, was largely vacant but not without its comforts. There was a soft bed, still made, presumably, from the day before—Weston had never gotten into it before his meeting in the small hours. Lenox knelt to the ground and looked beneath. Stored there was a stout low-slung trunk, which, when opened, proved to contain his clothes, nothing else. On the night-stand was another book.

"The world can ill afford to lose such a reader," Lenox muttered.

"Yes."

"And yet—"

"Sir?"

Lenox sighed. "I hope these tales of adventure didn't tempt him into some rash or reckless crack at heroism."

"Such as?"

"Meeting the vandal alone, for instance. Would he have come to you?"

"Oh, certainly. He was never a rebellious sort, you know. Very respectful."

"Mm."

The walls in this room were entirely bare, and the only remaining furniture in the room was a desk. It had no drawers, but on top was a stack of papers. "Shall I look through those?" said Oates. "Him being my cousin."

"I think we had better both do it," said Lenox.

The constable looked pained. "But it seems wrong, don't it, to—"

"Our debt is not to his privacy," said Lenox.

"But—"

To put an end to the objections Lenox sat down and began to scan, with great care, the first sheet of paper. It was only a note from a cousin in nearby Cramton, full of prosaic news, but the detective nevertheless read it over with great diligence. Then he moved onto the next note, and the next. In all he sat at the desk for perhaps twenty minutes, reading and passing on the papers to Oates when he was done.

His reward for all this was nil.

At last he stood up. "I suppose the rooms are a blind alley, then," he said. "Though it is sometimes valuable to learn about the character of the victim."

"His character?"

"I knew he was amiable, which these letters prove, but I did not know about his taste for adventure novels. I did not know about his tidiness—that cannot be attributable solely to the charwoman—and it makes me think he had a well-ordered mind for police work. I wonder how that reflects upon his meeting on the green last night."

Oates grunted as if to say that yes, plainly they were both wondering that. "Next, then?"

"Tell me, did he come and go as he pleased from the police rooms, on the other side of this door?"

"He had a key to lock it from the inside, but from our side it was never locked. He could go in and out as he pleased. Certainly I didn't mind."

"In that case let us look at his desk there."

"You could scarcely call it a desk—there aren't any papers in it. He did mostly footwork, to be honest, Mr. Lenox. I handle the papers, like."

"Nonetheless."

They went through to the next room. Lenox's mind was busy; that Roman numeral, XXII, was beginning to obsess him. The hanging men and the black dog, too. If one of them had been a threat—and if this was a coincidence it was rather a wild one—they all might have been threats. Were they to be read in conjunction, or separately?

The small, narrow table where Weston had sat in the police station was dishearteningly naked. Oates had been correct; there was nothing here.

Yet almost as soon as they had finished looking at it, news came of a fresh clue. It was Wells, the grain merchant, who knocked on the door and ducked his head in.

"Dr. Eastwood would like to see both of you. Says he found something in the boy's effects. Oates, did you hear that?" called Wells. "Eastwood found something!"

Oates, who had been at the far side of the room, back to the door, turned and said, irritably, "Yes, yes, one moment."

As he turned back, Lenox saw a glint of metal and realized the man was taking a nip from a flask. "Shall I go on alone?" he said. "If you have business here?"

He had been hoping to let the constable off after his horrifying night, but Oates's tone was sharp when he said, "No, I'll come along."

"He's right down at his office," said Wells.

"We know where he would be, thank you, Mr. Wells," said Oates.

"How far is it?" asked Lenox, when Wells had closed the door behind him.

"Not three minutes," said Oates. He took his coat down from the peg. "Shall we go?"

"Yes."

There was to be a delay, however. When Lenox and Oates came out of the door, Fripp ran up to them, his face alive with news.

"What is it?" said Lenox.

"It's Mr. Carmody, in thirteen," he said. "He saw something."

"What?"

"He won't tell me. Says he'll tell it to the member of Parliament. Come along, this way, this way."

CHAPTER NINETEEN

When they reached Mr. Carmody in number thirteen, and an upper maid admitted them to a sitting room to wait, Lenox's heart rose. From the armchair by the window, surrounded by snuffboxes and opened letters, it was clear that Carmody spent a great deal of time here, and the window itself offered a perfect vantage on the town's green. With luck they might discover the identity of Weston's murderer in the next ten minutes.

Carmody himself shuffled in, and Oates, Fripp, and Lenox rose to greet him. He was a gray-haired man, taciturn perhaps but not in bad condition, whose shape was rather like that of a snowman, with especial prominence to the roundness of his middle figure. Everything about his personage and this small chamber, with its japanned table of decanters, its piles of books, its soft furniture, indicated a life of ease and comfort.

"Mr. Lenox, I presume!" said the man. "Pleased to meet you, sir."

"The pleasure is mine."

"Yes, Oates, I see you. Hello. Tea, gentlemen?"

"No, thank you," said Lenox. "If you could tell us—"

"Of course it should be sherry, at this hour. Esmeralda, two glasses—no, four, why not, Oates and Fripp, it's not every day you sit with gentlemen, I know, but—"

"Please," said Lenox, "I thank you but I would prefer to keep my wits. If you could simply tell us—"

"Nothing sharpens the wits quite like a sip of something at six o'clock, I say. There she is with the glasses. No, not this sweet nonsense, Esmeralda," he said, taking a bottle from the maid. "Bring me the Oloroso, of course. No, hold that thought, the Fino, yes, I think Mr. Lenox will like the Fino. You may pour for Mr. Oates and Mr. Fripp from the bottle you have in hand, however. Mr. Lenox, you heard from Mr. Fripp of my occupation?"

"No, sir."

"I imported wine, for many years. Go to Covent Garden and see if they know G. F. Carmody, just you see."

"I've no doubt—"

"Retired fifteen years—"

"If—"

"Or was it sixteen, Fripp? How long have I been coming to your shop?"

"If we could just—" said Lenox, but was again interrupted, as Esmeralda returned with a new bottle of sherry.

Carmody watched its decantation greedily and then, not quite smacking his lips—but not not smacking his lips either, for what sense that makes—raised it to his mouth. The sigh he gave after swallowing a tot of the liquid was one of a man at peace with the world.

Lenox, out of politeness and exigency, took a large gulp, found it burned his throat, and set the wine down. "Thank you. Now—"

"What d'you make of that, Mr. Lenox?"

"Very nice," he said.

"Very nice! If I told the boys in Covent Garden that you called a twelve-year Fino very nice, one hand-selected by G. F. Carmody, I wonder what they would say." Carmody chortled at the possibilities. "My, oh my. No, but the palette, sir, consult the palette. Do you not find an oakish taste to it, something that lays off the sweetness of the first impression, something of the old—"

"Oh, yes, rather, just so," said Lenox desperately. "But about—"

"Yes, yes, the boy. Terrible pity." Carmody took another sip and then set about prying open a small, mother-of-pearl snuffbox, hideously inlaid with a pink tile outline of what appeared to be a donkey. "Ah, you see my snuffbox, sir? Presented me by Don Pedro Sousa himself, with an image of a Spanish stallion, representative of our mutual strength. Ask the boys in Covent Garden about Don Pedro Sousa."

Lenox nodded. "As to Weston—"

"Of course, you are all in haste. I understand. Let me just—" He took a moment or two—what seemed to Lenox like several hours—applying snuff to the inside of one nostril and inhaling it, then repeating the procedure on the other side. "Yes. Weston. Sadly I saw nothing of what occurred on the green. I would have been abed for an hour or two, at least, by the time I hear it must have happened."

This was a disappointment. "But you saw something?"

"Two things, in fact. I am of a rather stout build, you may see, Mr. Lenox, and I find a walk after supper a eupeptic diversion—most salubrious, in fact. Yesterday evening I was dining with a friend, Mr. Hugo Fish."

Oates, whose sherry had vanished, and Fripp, whose sherry was untouched, both nodded to indicate that they knew the gentleman in question. "Go on," said Lenox.

"Consequently my evening constitutional began much later than usual. I took the path to Epping Forest, a quarter of a mile east of here—"

"At what time of evening?" said Lenox.

"It must have been past ten thirty."

"What did you see?"

"I go by there rather often, two or three times a week, and I have never seen what I saw then—to be precise, two horses hitched up against a tree together, chewing from oatbags. Quite alone."

"You didn't recognize the horses?"

"No."

"Were they well saddled?"

"It was dark, you understand, but they appeared to be decently turned out."

"Were you close to the path, or off it?"

"Oh, I know these woods quite well, Mr. Lenox. I couldn't possibly get lost in them. And then it was rather a fullish moon. I was off the path."

So whoever had left the horses there had at least tried to conceal them. It was obvious why, if they had business with Weston, they hadn't wanted to come to town on the evening coach. It was not a busy route. A coachman upon his reguler route would have remembered two strange faces.

Why had they come so early, if they hadn't met Weston until well after midnight? What had they been doing away from their horses in the interim?

"You say you saw two things?"

"Yes."

"And the second?"

"Upon my return, I saw Captain Musgrave, stalking across the green with that great animal of his."

"Did he see you?"

"No."

"Was this before or after the pubs had let out?"

"I walked for an hour, or thereabouts."

"After, then. Did he seem agitated? Was he walking quickly, slowly?"

"There was nothing remarkable about his conduct, as far as I could ascertain," said Carmody. "He walked as men will walk."

"Did you see Weston?"

"I did not."

"Did you look to the corner of the green, next to the church, where he lived?"

"It's a small green, Mr. Lenox. I would have seen him. Ah, I see you find the sherry to your taste, now." Lenox had taken another sip, distractedly. "Esmeralda!"

"No, you're too kind, but I'm afraid we have urgent— Thank you, Mr. Carmody."

"Would you leave in such haste? Esmeralda! Please, I entreat you, sit, Mr. Lenox," said Carmody, "for one more glass."

"I apologize," said Lenox. "I must be on my way. Oates? Fripp?"

Both touched their caps to Carmody. When they were on his steps, Oates a ways ahead of them, Fripp whispered, "Wanted to tell Mr. Fish he had two glasses of sherry with you, I reckon. More social, less official, like. Does that help?"

"Enormously," said Lenox. "Thank you. Mr. Oates, which way is it to Dr. Eastwood's, from here? The light is going and I should still like to see both him and Captain Musgrave."

"Musgrave, this late in the day?"

"Yes. I should especially like to see him," said Lenox.

CHAPTER TWENTY

D r. Eastwood, whom Lenox's cousin had mentioned was one of the leading men in Plumbley, practiced out of a small, well-situated cottage along a brook close to the edge of town. The maid who admitted Lenox and Oates was quiet and respectful; they were in a gentleman's house. For many years physicians had fought hard against the old reputation of their profession—some grand doctors refused to tap a patient's chest or use a stethoscope because to do so would have brushed too closely against manual labor, a prejudice that had doubtless resulted in many deaths—and Eastwood was, perhaps, the beneficiary of this fight.

Unfortunately, according to Frederick, Eastwood was not entirely at home in Plumbley, having bought a practice here in the hopes that it might lead him to a happy life. He had found relatively few friends and, though unmarried, had no special favorite among the local women. It was surprising; when he greeted them, shaking hands, Lenox saw that he was a tall, handsome, chestnut-haired man, still at the tail end of youth.

He led them into his surgery. "The body is laid out here," he said in a soft voice. "It offers, sadly, little information."

"The time of death, perhaps?"

"I cannot say with any great specificity. Not after two in the morning, probably, because the hardening of the tissues was complete by the time I saw the body. Any time up until then, however. I fear that may not help much."

"Were there any wounds about the hands or arms?"

Eastwood shook his head. "I checked, having some acquaintance with the literature of police medicine, but no. He was taken quite unawares. Perhaps only turned away for a moment."

"What was the instrument that killed him?"

"There I can give you slightly more information. It was a knife with a blade of five inches, say, or six. There were no serrations in the wound, so I imagine the blade was smooth. Any kitchen knife might have done it. Then again it could have been a more . . . a more professional sort of object, too, a fold-down."

"And in his effects?" said Lenox. "You sent word—"

Here he was brought up short, because they had come to Weston's dead body, bare-chested, cleansed of blood but not of the muscles' terrible, wrenched contortion. The body's intense pain, so unmistakable from Weston's expression and position, was like a rupture in this cheerful work space—the table upon which he lay no doubt the same one where women with pleurisy and children with croup consulted the doctor every afternoon, the glass cabinets above, with their tidy rows of physic, mementoes of a less violent world.

Eastwood paused for a suitable moment, and then said, "Yes. His pockets had been emptied—or were empty when he came to the green, I suppose."

"I didn't see any money or keys in his rooms, did you, Oates?" said Lenox.

"Then he was robbed?"

"I feared as much," said Eastwood. "But they must have missed the ticket pocket in the dark."

This was the small pocket in the waistcoat just above the bigger, regular pocket, found only on the right side and just large enough for a rail ticket. "What was in it?" Lenox asked.

"This piece of paper," he said, and handed it to Lenox.

It was folded over three times. On the outside it read, CONSTABLE OATES. Lenox offered it to Oates, who took it and read aloud. "Eye on swell's basement. Come if you can."

"Once more?" Lenox said.

Oates repeated the phrase. "I don't know what it could mean."

This was obvious: The constable's eyes were dulled with fatigue, sherry, and sorrow. Lenox doubted whether he was fully aware of his surroundings. Oates's strength had already been frayed, and now seeing the body seemed to have destroyed it altogether. Looking at him, Lenox saw a few small details he hadn't before—a patch of hair missed on his shave, dirt under his fingernails—and realized, with a bolt of pity, that Oates must not be married.

Yet this was no time for weakness. "Think!" Lenox said sharply, trying to snap the constable to attention.

"I don't know."

"It might be a month old," said Eastwood.

"No, the paper is too crisp for that," said Lenox. Then, under his breath, he said, " 'Swell's basement.' Does the phrase connote anything to you, Doctor?"

"It does not, unfortunately."

"Oates? Think hard."

Oates, with great effort, screwed up his eyes and concentrated but it was no use. "Perhaps after I sleep," he said. "I feel muddled, just at the moment."

Eastwood looked troubled and said to Lenox, "Perhaps you

might carry on for the evening alone, if I see Constable Oates home? Here, Oates, sit down."

Lenox nodded. "You know where he lives?"

"Yes."

"I thank you, then. I'll be on my way."

Lenox knew from his uncle the location of Musgrave's house. He was tired and footsore—had it really been less than twenty-four hours ago that he was a few steps from Charing Cross, rousing Dallington out of that gin bar?—but determined. The meager clues that the past few hours had offered, the cigar ends, the horses in Epping Forest, the note Weston had scrawled out for Oates, had formed a kind of useful drone in his mind, their repetition a form of internalization.

"Swell's basement"—was it some kind of code? Increasingly Lenox thought so. Weston had been keeping a vigil by the town green, and perhaps he had written the note only if, by chance, someone came by who might convey it to Oates's house a few streets away. In that case a code would forefend any reward for nosiness. "Come if you can," he had written, too, meaning that he planned to stay where he was.

Suddenly Lenox realized that the whole thing—the night, the cigar ends—suggested perhaps not a meeting but a lookout. Weston had been spying on someone. Perhaps the men who had ridden their horses to the edge of town.

He felt he was making progress, now, but Musgrave brought a halt to that. Lenox arrived at the house, a rather grand one, and sent in a card with the butler, who bore it on a salver.

He returned, funereally expressioned and his tails impeccable, with the card untouched. "I'm afraid, sir, that Captain Musgrave is occupied."

"Tell him it's about this murder, if you would," said Lenox.

"If you wish to return in the—"

"Tell him now, please."

"Sir."

But Musgrave was unmoved. The butler was gone for some time and when he finally returned, looking deeply sorrowful, said that unless an officer of the law was present, his master had no wish to speak with anyone; it had been a taxing day; he would be very happy to meet Mr. Lenox on some other occasion; and so forth.

Lenox knew when he was defeated. He thanked the butler and left the hall.

Outside it was dark now. He had come out in a light sack coat, more suitable to an autumn's day than an autumn evening, and he regretted it, wished he had worn his tweed frock coat. It was the whistling country air: One could always find warmth of a sort in London, over a grate, in the motion of other humans, near the horses at the curb. One was more alone here. Poor Weston!

Unusually for a man of his station Lenox never carried a cane, that gentler descendant of the sword, but by the time he reached the gates of Everley he wished he did. His legs and feet were tired, and as he came into the hall he asked for warm water to wash his feet and his hands. He would have given anything for fifteen minutes of quiet repose, but then there was a great deal to do here: There were Jane and Sophia; there was Frederick; of course there was Dallington; and worse yet, they were meant to sit to supper in something less than twenty minutes.

Freddie, with his usual tact, had foreseen this. Bowing slightly, his butler said to the tired detective, "The master has requested we serve supper in your rooms, sir, unless you wish to dine more formally this evening."

Lenox did not.

"He would also like to invite you to the small study at your leisure, sir, and adds that he will be up very late—that you cannot come too late for him."

"Thank you, Nash."

"Yes, sir."

Jane's face, when he entered, was etched with anxiety, but she saw that he was, if worn, nevertheless safe. Slowly, over an excellent supper, they returned to more even tempers. They even got to see Sophie, briefly, before Miss Taylor took her.

At last, lighting a small cigar, Lenox said, "I think perhaps you should return to London, Jane."

"Nonsense."

"Until I know that it's safe to be in Plumbley—"

"I consult my memory and discover that we are in Everley, not Plumbley, Charles, and anyhow we Lenox women are made of sterner stuff than that." She put a few soft fingertips to his face. "You look very tired."

He smiled. "It may be that I'm not as young as I once was."

She smiled, too. "Almost certainly you are not."

"Are you sure you feel safe? Comfortable?"

"Charles, can you think I would leave? With the speech to come, and now this, not even mentioning poor John?"

He kissed her. In the end perhaps this was love: a balance of strength left over, just when you thought yours had all vanished.

CHAPTER TWENTY-ONE

Fortified by their hearty supper, Lenox went downstairs in slightly higher spirits to see Frederick. The older man was standing by his telescope, glass of wine in hand.

"Ah, Charles," he said when the door opened, not turning. "Put your eye here. Remarkably clear out."

Lenox looked. "Beautiful," he said. The stars, isolate and furious in the black of the night, were spread in a pattern unfamiliar to him. "What am I seeing?"

"Did you know that the Chinese—well, of course they wouldn't have the constellations the Greeks set out, the bears, the dippers, Orion, would they? I'd never thought of it before. Instead they have what they call the Twenty-eight Mansions of the Moon, I learned recently. Really rather interesting. At the moment you're looking at the White Tiger of the West. More specifically its neck, or at any rate what they call its neck."

"I can't claim to see the resemblance."

"No, and the Black Tortoise of the North is less like a tortoise than anything I ever gazed upon. With a little imagination the

Vermilion Bird of the South comes good, however." Freddie chuckled. "The Chinese. Funny to think of them, for the last few thousand years, seeing the stars we see, but spotting such different things there."

"They saw animals, too."

"Yes. I wonder whether that means it's a human need, the fact we all see animals in the sky."

"Or a human superstition." Lenox paused. "How were Weston's people, then?"

"He was well loved. What have you and Oates discovered?"

Lenox described, in brief, the series of interviews he had conducted. Frederick laughed at the encounter with Carmody. "I've always had half a mind to go meet these boys of Covent Garden, next time I'm at the flower show," he said. "I wonder if they've ever heard of him at all."

"Nonetheless his story is suggestive."

"Then you think it was outsiders who committed this terrible crime?"

"I can't imagine it likely that Carmody should take that route so often, two or three times a week, without great incident, and then on the night a lad is murdered on the town green, happen by sheer coincidence to find two abandoned horses to be standing in his way."

"It is a danger to confuse correlation with causation."

"Just so, and I don't rule out that it might be randomness at work. Especially because the motivation of these two horsemen is obscure to me. Why would they want to kill Weston? And what does it have to do with these petty crimes in the town?"

"I'm wholeheartedly glad you're here," said Frederick. "Though I fear it will do your speech little good, to investigate this crime."

"No matter." Lenox found that he meant this: Compared to the visceral urgency of the case, the noble, papery pursuits of Parliament seemed insignificant. He couldn't deceive himself that it was otherwise. "Tell me, Freddie, do you think Jane and Sophia should go?"

"To London? I think they'll be safe in the house and the gardens."

"Perhaps a word with your staff—"

"Nash has already spoken to them. All the verticals are to be on the lookout while they work, and the gates and doors are to be triple-checked by the horizontals."

The outdoor staff had vertical stripes on their waistcoats, the indoor staff horizontal ones. "That puts my mind at ease," said Lenox.

"What is your next course of action?"

"I mean to have a word with that man Musgrave. After that . . . well, I would like to see Mr. Weston's charwoman."

"Mrs. Simmons? I dropped in on her this evening, the poor soul."

That was Frederick Ponsonby: quiet, in his way, but full of surprising knowledge and of deep consideration for others. Lenox felt a burst of love for him, not unmingled with a burst of love for his mother, who shared those two qualities. "How did she seem?"

"Devastated. I think she mothered him. His own mother is dead."

"So I learned. Did you ask Mrs. Simmons if she knew anything, had seen anything?"

"Gently, yes. She kept repeating that Weston was in a very high mood yesterday afternoon—very excitable."

"I wonder why."

"She didn't know. It may be nothing. It's all the information she had, anyhow, though of course you have a better idea of how to speak to people when—in circumstances like these."

"Yes."

"Speaking of poor souls, by the by, you've provided me with a new houseguest?"

Lenox smiled ruefully. "I'm sorry for that, I am."

"I suppose it's all right. Can I ask—"

Lenox set forth, then, with straightforward honesty, Dallington's character and history. His cousin listened carefully, his stare growing hard. Lenox rather trailed off. "If you wouldn't mind, for a day or two . . ."

Frederick was kind, but he had the sharpness and shortness of a squire about him, too, on occasion. "Damned nuisance," he said.

"I know it."

"You're coming it a bit high, filling my house with the dregs of every London gin house."

"I can only apologize."

"Ah, well." Freddie showed the hint of a smile. "We can always set 'im to gardening, I suppose. Rodgers would like that."

Lenox's next stop was to see Dallington himself. The young man had sent him a note earlier in the evening, rather formal in tone, requesting a moment of his time. Lenox was in no hurry to see Dallington—still felt too vexed by the lad's behavior, and its timing—but he decided it was best not to spoil his sleep by putting the meeting off till morning.

As if by way of censure Frederick had chucked the boy into the house's least comfortable rooms. These belonged to an airless warren built many centuries before, when glass was a dear commodity, and were generally only just less warm than Hades. No question of a draught, anyhow. The ceilings, ancient and wooden, were the perfect height for even a small man to bang his head at every lintel. The fireplaces smoked.

Dallington sat up in an armchair, wrapped heavily in a dressing gown despite the heat of the room. His things had followed him down to Plumbley by the train—McConnell's work, very likely—

and he was reading from a novel, different perhaps in quality but not in kind of those beloved by young Weston, about an orphan who is discovered to be a countess.

"Hello, John," said Lenox.

"Charles, how can I—"

"Are you quite comfortable?"

"Yes, very."

"You've eaten?"

"Yes."

"And has Dr. Eastwood visited you?"

"Not yet, but I know my constitution well enough. There's no grave danger to my health at present."

"Very well. I shall bid you good evening, in that case, and—"

"Oh, damn it, Charles, leave off the stern fathering. I've had it from everyone a day or more older than since I was in short pants."

Lenox paused. "You've heard something of the case?"

The moral superiority in a conversation can shift very quickly. Dallington blanched, perhaps sensing that it had now. "Yes. May I help?"

"No, thank you. You heard of the timing of my trip to London, too, then?"

"You would scarcely have been on the town green at two in the morning if you weren't in London, Charles," said Dallington. Yet his voice was unpersuasive.

"It's impossible to say where I might have been."

"Come, now, I feel badly enough—"

"That is an easy way to feel after the fact."

Dallington sighed, and set his book down. He took a sip from the glass of water on the table next to him, then leaned forward, face earnest. "I am in your debt, I know," he said. "It was boredom, that was all. And seeing the wrong people at the wrong moment of boredom."

"And the women?"

"Charles. Please, let me help with the case."

"I'm afraid not," said Lenox. "And now I must say good night."

"Charles, I—"

"Good night."

CHAPTER TWENTY-TWO

Lenox went out riding on the house's chestnut hack again the next morning. He hoped it would be a full day so he only rode for thirty minutes or thereabouts, but the exercise and the crisp wind flushed all the commotion out of his mind, and he returned feeling vigorous, revived.

The groom, a dark-haired man named Chalmers nodded at him as Sadie ambled into the stables. "How far did you take her, sir?" he asked.

"There are orchards a mile or two west of here?"

"Aye, McGinniss's apples. Famous cider."

"She's a graceful jumper."

"Isn't she, though, sir?"

Lenox looked up at the high trees that fringed the gardens of the great house and circled the lake, all of them beginning to shift from green into orange and red. He could smell a fire. "I took an apple." He pulled it from his pocket. "The temptation was very great."

"You're not likely to be the last," said the groom, straight-faced.

Lenox smiled, handing the reins over. "Perhaps I'll go confess to the magistrate."

"See you again tomorrow, sir?"

"I hope you shall. If I've time I'd like to ride again."

He went inside, rabid with hunger; according to his pocketwatch it was still shy of eight in the morning. He heaped a shaky pile of marmalade onto a piece of toast from the toast rack and champed it, pouring himself coffee from a silver pot as he chewed. There was always the freshest milk at Everley, and just as he was thinking it was his favorite part of visiting, he remembered the riding, and the clear air, and the happiness of the tumbling dogs about his feet, and, though an ardent Londoner, found himself thinking: Is there any reason we should not live in the country?

Just as he was committing a violent attack on a second piece of toast Miss Taylor walked in. She was the last person in creation before whom one wanted to appear at any disadvantage, and hurriedly he brushed the crumbs from his lips.

"Good morning," he said. "I trust you're quite well?"

"Yes, thank you," she said.

"Will you join me for a bite?"

"Thank you, I will." She went to the sideboard and took a plate, nodding her thanks to the attendant behind the chafing dishes, and started to spoon decorous quantities of egg and kedgeree onto it. She paused when she reached the kippers, and turned. "Sophia is with Lady Jane," she said.

"I had surmised as much, but I thank you."

The governess permitted herself a softening kind of smile. "I didn't like you to worry."

"Most considerate."

She arrived at the table and sat down, Lenox standing to help her into her chair. "You take coffee, Mr. Lenox?"

"In the mornings, exclusively. I learned that aboard a ship. I used to take tea at every hour of the day, but nothing cuts the salt out of the air like a bracing cup of coffee."

"For my part I find tea too mild before noon."

"Will you allow me to pour you a cup of this coffee, then?"

"Oh, thank you."

Again she smiled and Lenox apprehended, with a sense of surprise, that he liked this young woman, her grave, quiet manner, her seriousness. She had arrived with a fearful reputation for seriousness—the rudiments of Hebrew, competent to teach dancing without a master—and had cowed him for some while, but in the past weeks she had slipped, unnoticed, into his affections. "Are you quite comfortable?" he asked.

"I am," she said, "and I feel singularly fortunate to walk Sophia in these beautiful gardens."

"D'you know, when we were children, my brother and I used to dig up the flowers, simply to annoy the gardener. He threw a trowel at Edmund once, with my hand to God I swear it. Nearly took his head off."

"It was too kind a punishment for the two of you, if the gardens were anything like this," she said.

Lenox laughed. "My uncle still might toss me in a cell, if he found out. Have you had a chance to speak to him about the flowers? I can promise you an uninterrupted monologue of three or four hours if you would like one."

"I haven't spoken to him, no," she said.

Governesses were often in a precarious position, Lenox understood, lying as they did somewhere between the staff and the masters, but now he perceived for the first time that Miss Taylor, whom he and Jane had striven to make feel welcome in Hampden Lane, might nevertheless feel that prejudice. "I hope you feel free to meet anyone here on—on equal terms," he said, haltingly and in truth without much tact.

"Yes," she said.

"I mean to say—" but he knew well enough now to stop himself. "I don't think I ever heard where you were from in the first place?"

"My family lived in Berkshire, just outside the village of Crowthorne."

"I passed through it once."

"It was a lovely place to grow up," she said. Then, perhaps sensing the question he hadn't asked, she added, "My mother and father died a year apart, when I was thirteen."

"I'm so very sorry."

"My father was a gentleman," she said, her voice rather rushed, "and I was raised as a gentleman's daughter, but unbeknownst to us he had financial difficulties—some peculiarities in a business dealing—and it left me with something under sixty pounds a year. With the help, I may say the begrudging help, of an uncle, my father's brother, I went to Miss Crandle's school, where I helped teach the younger children to earn my keep."

"How difficult it must have been."

"No!" Her cheeks were suffused with a red color. She took a sip of coffee to steady herself. "No, I was very happy there, indeed."

"And you learned much," said Lenox, smiling at her.

"Exactly so. No, I have been fortunate, very fortunate, and now I do what I love best and look after children."

"To happy endings," he said, and raised his cup.

She smiled and raised hers. "To happy endings."

Sixty pounds a year! What enormous strength this young woman must have had, to be left with such a pittance upon which she might live and to fashion out of it, through industry, through her natural gifts, the career she had! It filled Lenox with admiration, and, rather more obscurely, with guilt. The story also made him wonder whether it was primarily shyness and not severity that had held her tongue—though he remembered, too, being sharply checked by her when he did something incorrectly about his daughter.

They passed the rest of the breakfast in friendly conversation. Just as they were leaving the room, Dallington arrived; he bowed to Lenox, stiffly, and to the governess with slightly more ease. Seeing him, a shadow of worry passed across Lenox's mind. He wondered if he had been too hard on the lad, too astringent, and he wondered if it was in part because he didn't want to cede any of his claim to the case.

"May I have another cup of coffee with you, Dallington?" he asked.

"Certainly."

"Miss Taylor, please tell Lady Jane I'll cut along to see her and Sophia shortly, if you wouldn't mind?"

When Dallington had piled a plate high with food—his appetite was a good sign, Lenox thought—he came to the table. "First allow me to say—"

"No, drop it, leave it. Listen, though—there's a Frenchman called Fontaine, whom I met a few days ago . . ." Lenox elaborated for Dallington now upon the scant facts the lad had heard about the murder, telling him about the vandalisms, the two horses Carmody had seen, the note in Weston's ticket pocket, all of it. "But I can't shake this man Fontaine from my mind. Why did he beat his wife on an arbitrary Tuesday morning? Why did he have enough money in his pocket to run riot over half of Bath?"

"You think it's connected," said Dallington, ignoring his food.

"I don't know. But as I concentrate on the murder, if you could—"

The young man stood up. "I'll go now."

"No, no. Finish eating first. You need the strength. You still look pale."

"Well, just after breakfast, then."

During that meal Lenox, a man with a forgiving heart, forgave Dallington. But the juxtaposition of his self-indulgence, a young man who had been given everything, with the austere self-discipline, the breadth of spirit, that he discerned in the young governess, would linger in his mind through the days and weeks that followed. No particular sense of judgment obtained to the comparison: only that constantly self-renewing sensation all intelligent people feel, of wonder and surprise at one's fellow man.

CHAPTER TWENTY-THREE

Oates arrived at the great house not long after breakfast adjourned. "Have you that note?" he asked. "The one in Weston's pocket?"

Lenox nodded. "Has it rung a bell?"

The constable, stoutly, said, "I don't know that I was myself last night. Perhaps if I could see it again."

"Yes, sit and have a think while I speak to Freddie."

Lenox had expected his cousin to look exhausted, but perhaps the local certainty of his fragility had been overblown; he looked galvanized, ready to fight. "Shall we collar him today, Charles?"

"I hope we may."

"How can I be useful?"

"You know of Carmody's tale, about the two horses?"

"Yes."

"I should have asked him for a more detailed description. Perhaps you could have someone do that, while Oates and I inspect the spot in the wood to which he referred. After that we shall call on Musgrave, but if you would spread the word about, to see if two riders have been spotted at any of the coaching inns—perhaps, for instance, the cart drivers who frequent these roads might have noticed them."

"Very well."

"On top of that I would like another canvas of the town green. Someone, besides Carmody, must have seen something, someone who had been in the pubs, perhaps. I can do it myself, but it will take time. Would the pub owners help us?"

"They will," said Frederick.

Lenox rose. "Good."

"The vandalisms—they must be linked to his death, mustn't they?"

"I think so, yes. I think they were darker in nature than I suspected." He nodded decisively. "Very well. We'll reconvene here this evening."

When Lenox went back to find Oates, the officer was sitting, brow knitted, the note loose and forgotten in the fingertips of one hand. "Anything?" said Lenox.

"No. And yet I feel so sure—the meaning seems so close."

"Take your attention off of it," said Lenox. "Sometimes that helps. Here, let's go see Carmody's clearing."

Not quite half an hour later they stood there, a treeless ridge at the center of a dense wood. At some points the trees had been so close together it was hard to imagine horses passing between them, but there had certainly been horses here, and men, too. The ground was scuffed with hoofprints and kicked-up sod—it was damp still—and there was evidence of a makeshift fire. Perhaps the two murderers had grown cold, but would they have risked someone stumbling upon them?

There was one further remnant of their occupation of this site; Lenox, as he had at the town green, inspected the site minutely, but the only clue he found had been visible from the start, a brown glass ale bottle, empty but with an alcoholic odor. A stiffening drink before they had met Weston, perhaps. The name on the bottle was Grimm's—according to Oates a brewery that was popular throughout Somerset. No lead there.

Oates, the inspection complete, was ready to leave—it had started to drizzle—but Lenox stayed him. "Is this clearing well-known in Plumbley?" he asked.

"Fairly so. The children will play here from time to time, and Weston and I have rousted our share of vagrants and fruit pickers, itinerants, like, from it."

"If I passed along this road and by this wood for the first time I would never have known it was here."

"No."

"And it's some ten minutes' walk in. Hardly an intuitive place to stop."

"I don't understand."

"Do you not find that strange, that our out-of-town visitors knew of it?"

Oates shrugged. "There are plenty've folk who know this switch of the countryside by heart."

"From outside Plumbley?"

"Perhaps."

Lenox stood, thinking, for a moment. "I just wonder," he said.

"What?"

"Nothing. Let's carry on."

They were on foot, and it took them ten minutes to get back to the road and, from there, another fifteen to walk to Musgrave's house.

This time the butler admitted them without demur to a handsomely furnished drawing room, long and rectangular. On one of the room's long walls, painted directly onto the plaster, was a series of French paintings—not quite to Lenox's taste, cherubim chasing each other through pale blue and pink landscapes. Between each painting in the sequence stood a plinth with a marble bust upon it. Opposite this long wall was a range of windowed doors, showing off a serene little stretch of garden.

Lenox took a spot on an ornately carved cherrywood sofa with blue cushions, and Oates balanced himself on the very front edge of a chair nearby. He seemed better today, his face calm again. Both men soon had cups of bone china placed before them. In ten minutes they held only the dregs of some excellent coffee; Captain Musgrave was making them wait.

It gave Lenox time to ponder the man's character. What to make of a person who came to Plumbley and furnished a house this way—the butler, the coffee, the cherubim? When Dr. McGrath had lived here in Church Lane this had been a comfortable, unspectacular place. Now it looked like a Parisian drawing room. Was Musgrave a cruel epicure, particular in his tastes, unkind to his wife when she failed to meet them?

Most soldiers would not answer to such a description. There was also something that had left Lenox uneasy from the start. If Musgrave were truly the type to act such a tyrant, if his exertion of will over his modestly born wife was so total—even to the point that the village suspected him of some violence against her—why would he ever have acceded to move to the place of her birth? A place to which he had no connection himself?

Finally they saw him approach the French doors from the garden, a great bounding dark bloodhound at his side. Oates and Lenox both stood.

"How do you do?" Musgrave said. "Please excuse me for keeping you."

"Not at all," said Lenox, bowing slightly at the waist, hands behind his back.

"You are Charles Lenox, I presume?"

"Yes."

Musgrave extended a hand. "Captain Josiah Musgrave."

He was a very pale, red-cheeked, slender man, with black hair and dark eyes. No doubt he was considered handsome, though a critical eye might have quarreled with the set of his jaw, thrust slightly too angrily forward.

He had yet to acknowledge Oates, who was standing in front of his chair. Lenox, making a rapid judgment of Musgrave's character, decided on an appeal to class. "You see now, Captain Musgrave, that I may summon the law enforcement if you wish me to do so. But perhaps it would be better to speak as two gentlemen."

Musgrave inclined his head. "Just so."

"Oates, my uncle is at Mr. Carmody's house. Perhaps you might go there and aid him?"

Oates, to his credit, shot Lenox a look of canny comprehension, and nodded his way out of the room.

"Would you like more coffee?" Musgrave asked.

Best to preserve the tone of a social call. Lenox assented.

He would have to tread carefully. There were men in Scotland Yard now trying to raise this art of detection to a science, and much of their concentration had been devoted to the art of interrogation. Lenox admired and respected their efforts—in fact wished that he might donate some of his own time to such studies—but he had also found that too rigid and systemic an approach to this sort of interview could be counterproductive, hindering rather than helping the interviewer.

For instance: The wisdom of these men at Scotland Yard dictated that the first step in such an interview was to begin by attempting to shock one's interlocutor into confession. So that Lenox should, by rights, have said to Musgrave without preamble, "Why did you murder Weston last night?"

He suspected that this might not work with Musgrave, who

seemed self-protective and perhaps slightly brittle in his temperament, liable to suspect effrontery even where none was intended. Lenox had a great many questions, and he didn't want to scare Musgrave's coolness away.

He began, therefore, by saying, "You have heard of the murder two evenings past?"

"Yes, a terrible thing."

"It is *pro forma*, but I must ask you some questions."

"Why me?"

"You were seen walking upon the town green an hour or so before the murder."

"Surely you cannot suspect me? An officer in the military?"

"No," said Lenox, and then, making his voice confidential, "we believe we may apprehend the criminal sooner than we had dared hope, in fact."

"Ah. Good."

It was difficult to tell what emotion passed through Musgrave's face now, if any. His black dog, which had been sitting upright, slumped into a curled shag at his feet.

CHAPTER TWENTY-FOUR

"Perhaps you could begin by telling me something about yourself," said Lenox.

Musgrave shrugged. "There is little enough to tell. I was born to two excellent parents in Bath, who purchased me a commission in the Tenth Regiment of Foot when I was still in an Eton jacket. I took up my commission some twelve years ago, and sold it out in 1870, just before it looked like being worthless."

Parliament had decreed the year after that, in 'seventy-one, that men could no longer buy or sell their way into military office. "And subsequently settled here?"

"My wife is of a delicate constitution and wished to live near her childhood home."

"You met in Bath."

"Yes," he said shortly.

"Are your parents there?"

"They are both deceased."

"And how have you found Plumbley?"

"It is not to my taste, I confess to you."

"But you stay?"

Musgrave was silent. "You may see that plainly enough for yourself, yes."

"You do not find the people of the town congenial?"

"I never met a more tired social circuit in my life, and—excepting your relation, I mean," said Musgrave, realizing his solecism. "I have not had the pleasure of much of his acquaintance but he seems a capital fellow."

"And the shopkeepers, the men and women in church?"

"Am I expected to take notice of them?"

"What did you make of the vandalisms?"

Musgrave smiled maliciously. "Foolish superstitions of a foolish village."

"Then you do not ascribe to them any connection with Mr. Weston's death?"

"I had not thought of it."

"It has been noted in the village that you have a black dog, of course."

"I wonder whether there are ten thousand black dogs in the county? More, very likely. No, it is because I am new here that people do not like me. Have you noticed, Mr. Lenox, the intense moral pressure that a village feels it has the right to bring to bear upon any of its members? That is why I take joy in their panic over these childish symbols in the windows. It serves them right, the yattering halfwits."

Lenox—who felt fairly confident he had a sense of the captain's character now—said, "Let us turn, then, to the evening of Mr. Weston's murder. The accounts we have received place you upon the town green at half past eleven. Is that accurate?"

"It may be. I did not have a close eye upon my pocket-watch."

"Did you cross the green at the beginning or at the end of your walk?"

"Both. I went to the Yew Walk. The town green lies between the walk and Church Lane."

"And you would not care to venture a guess as to whether you were going out or returning, at half past eleven?"

"Returning, I should imagine."

Lenox made a note in his mind—important not to introduce the formalizing element of the notebook, just when they were talking so easily—to ask Carmody which way Musgrave had been walking, toward or away from Church Lane.

The dog was an alibi of sorts.

"Was your wife with you?"

"No. She would have been retired for several hours by then."

"Is it a custom of yours, to walk at that time?"

"There is no specific time of day when I walk him." He gestured toward the dog. "When the fancy takes us."

"What is he called?"

"Cincinnatus. Cincy, inevitably."

Lenox nodded. "I have my dogs with me, from London. They prefer the country air."

"He has never known anything else."

"Did you see anyone while you were walking the dog, Captain Musgrave?"

"One or two people, yes."

"Did you know them?"

"I saw Mr. Fripp. Mrs. Tolliver, a widow who lives in Gold Street. One or two others, to nod to. In London of course I wouldn't know them, but in a small village, you see, these civilities . . ."

"Were any of the people you saw behaving suspiciously?"

Captain Musgrave pondered this quickly, then said, "No."

Lenox thought of the clearing, the horses, the bottle of ale. "Did you recognize all of them?"

"Yes. By face, even if I couldn't place their names." A footman came in from the hall, to pour more coffee. "Not now," Musgrave said sharply.

The footman blanched, his visage transformed by fear, and quickly withdrew. Ten minutes of conversation with him might be valuable. Or with any of the servants. They still hadn't spoken about Musgrave's wife.

Almost as if by prearrangement, at that moment a piercing scream went up in a far corner of the house. It was a woman's voice.

Musgrave stared steadfastly ahead, pretending not to have heard it. Good manners dictated that Lenox do the same, but his investigative instincts did not, and he made a point always to sacrifice the former for the latter when they came into conflict.

"It is impolite, but necessary, to ask whether that was your wife, Captain."

"There is no other woman in the house."

"She does not keep a lady's maid?"

"No."

That was unusual. Perhaps it was to keep her isolated. "I understand that she has not been well?"

"She is receiving excellent care."

"From Dr. Eastwood?"

"From a doctor who comes from Bath. None of these countrified barbers when it comes to the health of my wife."

"May I see her?" Lenox asked.

"Certainly not."

"If I were to return with Constable Oates, he—"

"Was she seen upon the town green? Is she a suspect?"

"No."

Musgrave's face was dangerously composed. "In that case, nothing short of legal compulsion shall grant you an audience with her."

Lenox had asked the questions he wished to ask. Now he risked a gambit of the kind that Scotland Yard might approve. "You keep her a prisoner, from what I understand?"

Musgrave stood up, his rage near to overflowing. "You should be ashamed to repeat the lazy gossip of stupid women, Mr. Lenox. You will see yourself out." He strode to the door, Cincinnatus on his heels—such a pompous name for a dog!—before turning back. He was shaking. "Would that it were a different age, that I might see you at dawn tomorrow with a pistol in hand," he said, and then left the room.

Lenox, quite unperturbed—he had been glared at by men with a dozen murders to their credit, in gin mills east of the Isle of Dogs, so it was unlikely that Musgrave's genteel ire would much frighten him—sat for some moments, considering the interview.

This man was certainly capable of violence. He had been in the military and he had a temper, but why would he have killed Weston? Were his answers, straightforward and occlusive at once, evidence of any larger concealment?

At length Lenox stood, pocketing a couple of the macaroons from the plate on the table, waved good-bye to the cherubim, and walked out.

There was a snarl of inconsequential, linking facts that he felt confident lay at the heart of the case. The question now was to order them for himself, if possible to add to them, and to reduce them, finally, to their common element. He was closing in, he knew. It vexed him that for the moment he could not see how, or if, Musgrave fit into it all.

Outside the rain had intensified and steadied, and he regretted not bringing an umbrella. He hunched further under his coat, lit a small cigar, and puffed it meditatively as he began the short walk back to town.

CHAPTER TWENTY-FIVE

Lenox had no real plan, now, except for a period of calm reflection—perhaps he would have lunch at one of the town's public houses—but found himself walking in the direction of the village green.

Frederick was there, outside of Fripp's shop. Honoring Lenox's request, he had arranged for a further canvass of the houses that had a view of where the crime had taken place—there were men knocking on doors. It was obvious from his face, distracted and with a dissatisfied clench around the eyes, that his efforts thus far had been unavailing.

"Charles," he said. "Oates is speaking to Carmody now."

"Excellent. I have a question to add to his."

"Was Musgrave a help?"

"I don't know, yet. Have you turned up anything here?"

"Not yet. I spoke to Jones, at the Royal Oak, however, and asked him to direct any coach drivers who come along toward me, before they leave again."

"Have there been any yet?"

"No, but there should be a flurry soon. I mean to have lunch there, so that I may catch them."

"I was about to do the same—with regard to lunch, I mean."

"Then we shall go together."

A small, murmuring crowd had gathered on the steps of the church, Lenox noticed. He shot a quizzical look at Frederick.

"Gossip," the older man said. "Nothing more."

"Still, gossip may be useful."

"Oh?"

"I'm going to speak to them, and then to Carmody. Shall I see you in the Royal Oak in half an hour?"

"Half an hour," Frederick responded with a nod.

Fripp was standing among the people on the church steps. As he walked toward them Lenox heard the name Musgrave spoken.

"How do you do, Mr. Fripp?" said Lenox.

"Charlie. Do you know these ladies, my boy?"

"I don't."

Fripp said a flurry of names, which Lenox immediately forgot. "What are you speaking about?" he asked.

"These women are afraid, unfortunately," said Fripp. "They feel—"

"Last night I locked my front door for the first time in fourteen years," said a stout middle-aged woman, a child braced under each arm.

"Why did you lock it back then?" Lenox asked, curious.

"Rabid badger roaming the town," the woman answered immediately.

There was a chorus of gratified concurrence at this recollection. Lenox just managed to stop himself from asking what the difference between a locked door and an unlocked door was to a badger. "You suspect Musgrave?"

All of them did, vocally. "Why would he want to harm Mr. Weston, though?" Lenox asked.

"Mischief-making," said a woman, thin as a flagpole and with a great beak of a nose emerging from a tightly tied bonnet. "And what he's done to that poor girl I shudder to think. As was Cat Scales, I mean."

"His wife," Lenox said.

"That's her."

Wells's grain shop was very close by, and so after Lenox had doffed his hat he stopped in. The shop was empty, its fine bronze weights and barrels of grain awaiting their next customer. Wells himself stood behind the counter, jotting in a ledger. He looked up as the door opened.

"Mr. Lenox," he said. "Have you found my clock yet?"

"Soon, I hope. I wanted a quick word."

Wells laid his pencil down. "By all means."

"I take it you saw nothing from the shop, late last night?"

Wells sighed and shook his head. "I was home several hours before Weston died. I dearly wish that I had been here."

"You live . . ."

"Three streets south, on the corner of Maiden Lane. A large white house. My servants"—this word delivered with an inflection of pride—"can attest to my presence there yesterday evening. I was up rather late, past midnight, working on my books, and at least two of them stayed up with me, fetching drinks, managing the fire. They'll tell you I never left my study."

"Is anyone else in the village accustomed to passing time here in the evenings?"

Wells narrowed his eyes thoughtfully. "Perhaps the vicar," he said. "Or his curate. They have keys to the church at any rate."

Lenox paused, now, uncertain of how to ask what he wished to ask next. At last, he said, "Your incident with Captain Musgrave—"

"Yes?"

"Was it possible as you saw him to gather anything of Mrs. Musgrave's mental state?"

Wells shrugged. "You might say as she seemed unhappy—but then with tales passing around the town like 'flu, it leads to an active imagination."

"Confidentially, what have you heard of her mental state?"

"Nothing of her mental state. Only that she is unhappy—fearfully unhappy—and kept captive in that house." Wells looked troubled, and Lenox remembered Frederick telling him that Wells had been one of Catherine Scales's suitors, before she met Musgrave.

He wondered, as well, if he was duty bound to investigate that scream. Perhaps he would return with Oates.

For now, though, he bade Wells good day, lifted his hat to Fripp and the women on the church steps—still yattering away, to Musgrave's bedevilment—and walked to Carmody's. Carmody provided Lenox with a great deal of unasked-for information about the gentlemen in Covent Garden, as a sort of tax upon entering his home, before finally condescending to hear his question.

"Which way was Captain Musgrave walking when you saw him at eleven thirty—toward Yew Walk or home, toward Church Lane?"

"Toward Yew Walk," said Carmody without hesitation.

So. It was not a lie, perhaps, but it was an infringement upon the truth. If his walk had been very long he might well have seen—spoken with—even murdered Weston on his way home.

"Did the bark of a dog ever wake you, that night?" Lenox asked.

"No," said Carmody, "and I am a very light sleeper."

"Thank you," said Lenox. "Oates, I shall stop by the police station later today to speak with you."

"Sir."

He could feel that he was circling closer to the truth. His mind went to Dallington, who would perhaps return that evening with some account of Fontaine's behavior. Might that prove the key?

He walked to the bar in a meditative disposition.

Frederick was sitting at a table in a private room upstairs in the Royal Oak. It was a friendly pub, full of highly polished brass and gleaming oak, with glasses and tankards hung above the bar and a worn sign that said DUCK OR MUTTON—the diners' options, presumably—hung from two chains between a pair of bow windows, and swaying each time the front door was opened or closed.

They spoke for some time of the case but the facts, Lenox felt, were beginning to become stale to him, his energy growing inward and sterile.

"I think the solution will come to me more readily if we turn away from the subject," he said.

The mutton had just arrived, ringed around with heaps of peas, potatoes, and smashed turnips. There was a bottle of claret on the sideboard. Frederick nodded. "Very sensible," he said. "Occasionally when I have been too long at my desk, describing the properties of the *Hyacinthus sylvestris* or sketching a dried *Spiræa ulmaria* that I have picked—meadow-sweet, you would know it as, or meadow-queen—I can become rather muddled, and when I feel it, I immediately make the decision to go three or four days without once looking at or thinking of flowers. In general I spend the time off wandering about the house, finding things that need to be patched up or painted. Drives the servants mad, I'm afraid."

Lenox took a sip of wine. He paused before he spoke. "Can you really be thinking of leaving Everley?" he asked. "Your gardens?"

Frederick, whose mood had been light only a moment before, scowled. "None of that, Charles."

"I remember coming here with my mother, in 'fifty-four, and—"

"No, no reminiscing, either. I love Everley, and for that reason I must do my best by her."

"The best she could have is your presence, Uncle Freddie."

"Sentimental nonsense, Charles. There is no sense in resisting time, or change. Both will come to all men, whether they accede gracefully or kicking. I'm old, now, and let that be an end of it. There, eat some peas, you need a bit of greenery, you look tired."

CHAPTER TWENTY-SIX

After their mutton Lenox took himself back to the house, while Frederick packed his pipe, unfurled a newspaper, and waited with the last quarter of the bottle of wine for his foot soldiers to report to him. He invited Charles to stay, but the younger man declined, restless still, a bit befogged from being in the warm public house on this cool and wet day, in need of the clarifying brace of the outdoors.

He made the walk back to Everley quickly. At the gates, and passing down the broad, tree-lined avenue, he gazed at the house, at its beautiful reflection in the rain-scattered pond. It was difficult to imagine it without Frederick inside. The thought reached some sorrowful place in Lenox, bound up in his mother's early death, in his own advancing years . . . but it was better not to think of that. He decided he would go and find Sophia.

In fact, once he had so decided he felt a primitive need to lay eyes on her. In the activity of the past few days, dating back to his trip to London, he had gone longer spells without seeing the child than he had since her birth.

He went to the nursery. The door was pulled-to but not closed, and he hazarded a gentle tap of two knuckles against the frame. "Miss Taylor?"

Her nearly silent footsteps came to the door. "Yes, Mr. Lenox?"

Her face was forbidding, steadied for rejection, Lenox saw. "Could I see her, do you think?"

"I think just at the moment, since she's sleeping—"

There was a faint sound behind the door, something between a cry and a yawn. "She's stirring," said Lenox.

A polite governess could not roll her eyes—but it must nevertheless have been a very great temptation to Miss Taylor, standing in the doorway, having anticipated a quiet forty minutes in which she might read or knit. "Come in, then," she said.

Lenox approached the bassinet and looked down over it with love in his eyes. His daughter was stretching out her arms and legs upward, languorous with rest. "Shall I take her out?"

Miss Taylor looked through the window at the gardens. "Let me change," she said.

"No," said Lenox quickly, "you sit and read here. I shall take her—I'm dressed for it anyhow. You can watch me from the window if you like, to make sure I haven't spilled her." He looked up. "Or introduced her to tobacco, or whatever paternal vice you might suspect me of."

The governess finally smiled now. "I'll just prepare her, then."

Lenox watched as this was done—as Sophia was bundled like a bag of flour into warm clothes, layer upon layer of them, and then into her bassinet—before asking, "Has Lady Jane been in to see her, already?"

"Oh, several times."

"Perhaps while I find an umbrella to cover us both and put her in her perambulator you could cut along and ask her if she cares to walk with us?"

The governess went to do so, and Lenox, very carefully, fetched Sophia—who was gurgling pleasantly upon his shoulder, wide-eyed now—down the curved main flight of stairs. He settled her in her contraption, a buggy they had ordered especially from a workman in Kent, upon the advice of Toto McConnell, and then found two umbrellas, one of which he jimmied in between the handle and the bassinet so that it hovered above the child and one for himself.

Lady Jane sent word back that she was busy at just that moment, but would see them when they returned, and so Lenox and Sophia went along on their own into the gardens, accompanied by Bear and Rabbit. He insisted that Miss Taylor return to the nursery as a respite from her duties.

The dogs, restive after a day of sitting and staring at the rain, bounded ahead of their humans and then came back in tearing sprints, breathless, rendered simple by their excitement. After they settled they began to show signs of wanting to dig, and Lenox had to remonstrate with them, having been on the receiving end upon his arrival of a sharp, just barely respectful speech from Rodgers about dogs and gardens.

There were miles of paths extending out from the house at Everley. Lenox picked one at random, a long thin meander with sunken gardens full of Somerset flowers on either side.

"Well, Sophia, though your Uncle Freddie didn't care to hear of it, perhaps I shall tell *you* of 'fifty-four.'" He spoke conversationally, trying not to use that near-universal tone of loving condescension with which most parents spoke to their children, the same one men and women would use with dogs, though he had moments of weakness.

She looked up at him, big-eyed, clutching occasionally at the air with her small fist. The rain had stopped and he removed the umbrella from her pram so that she could look out at the world.

"I would have been, what, twenty-three, twenty-four, I suppose. I thought I knew a very great deal about life."

She laughed.

"Yes, it is rather funny, though you will be civil to your papa, please.

"My mother and I came here for two weeks at Christmas, your grandmother. How she would have loved you! It's a pity you never met, but then I daresay you will like Jane's brother very well, and Jane's mother, and Edmund, and of course your cousins.

"Where was I? I suppose I was going to remind Freddie about the widow McReary, but perhaps he wouldn't remember. I do. It was a cold day, there may even have been snow. McReary was the wife of a farmer who lived four or five miles south of here, upon a little allotment, two acres, perhaps three. He died, a cataleptic fit as I recall."

How many years had it been since anyone discussed Frank McReary? Lenox wondered as he pushed Sophia along. Yet villages have long memories, and he had, no doubt, had cousins and nephews and uncles in Plumbley and the countryside around it. Look at Weston.

Sophia sent up a fidgety noise, not quite a cry, perhaps because her father had fallen silent. He resumed his story. "Shall I tell you something about the widow McReary? She was a thief! I don't know if she became a thief before her husband died or after—she was childless, so she must have had a terrible time with the farm—but she was known in town to be a thief.

"Freddie was magistrate back then, too, you know, and could have put her in the dock with a dozen witnesses against her—she stole at the Sunday market, which earned her no friends, picked vegetables that weren't hers, for all we knew stole from the church plate. And in fact my mother—who was a very gentle soul, not much for punishment—advised Freddie to have Mrs. McReary up in court."

He could see miles and miles of westward country rising upward away from him as he walked along slowly, hedged into tidy squares and rectangles, mostly a lovely shamrock green but with lined fringes of red and orange and golden trees. It was the kind of vista that reminded you that you were in England, that lifted your heart. He thought of Parliament and his place there with a flash of solemnity and deeper comprehension. The world was a larger place than one ever seemed to remember.

Sophia started to squirm and her father, in his calming voice, began to speak to her again. "What Freddie did, however, was something more intelligent. He enquired about her condition. He spoke to her younger sister, who lives still in Plumbley I believe, and to her brother, whom I know must be dead by now—he was well beyond sixty then. Though perhaps not, perhaps I'll ask Fripp if he's still alive, since Freddie doesn't want to hear it.

"He asked her friends. The people who had been her friends. They weren't any longer. Which is one of the many reasons you must never steal, Sophia." He frowned at the child, comically, and she smiled up at him. "And what did Freddie learn? That she was close on starving, the widow. She was perhaps too proud for help, or it may be that she simply liked to steal. I don't claim that she was any saint, of course.

"So he . . . ," Lenox looked up at the skyline, eyes narrow, contemplating his visit of all those years ago. "It was one of the first times I had an understanding of justice, of its fluidity," he said. "There have been more than a few times when I looked the other way, during a case, you know. It was Freddie who taught me that lesson."

His eyes were still up, and he had come to a stop. He glanced back at the house, some ways off now, its beautiful yellow stone, the white paint around its windows.

He shook his head briskly, as if to clear it, and began walking again. "So he put her in the way of something good to steal. He visited her—stopped in on his way to a nearby farm, he said, to ask if she still had any quince preserves laid down that he might buy, for Christmas supper—which she didn't—and he left behind a billfold and, so that it might not seem like charity, a pair of gloves. I was with him, if you can credit that. Seems like yesterday."

They were some ways off from the house now, the pace of the dogs slackening, and Lenox decided he would go in. As they set back toward the house, he said, "I know she didn't return the billfold, or the gloves, in the next week. After that I was gone. I don't know what became of her."

He thought back to that time with a quick, piercing sorrow. How strange to be forty-five and miss one's mother, like a child in nursery!

As they returned he told Sophia other stories, allowing his voice to float soothingly over her, not especially listening to himself. He was thinking. It was a pleasure to walk with his daughter, but perhaps more importantly he understood, without acknowledging the feeling, that the facts of the case were revolving in the back of his mind, latching together, leading him somewhere. He was almost there. It wouldn't be long now.

CHAPTER TWENTY-SEVEN

Upon his return Lenox learned from Nash that Frederick was waiting to see him in the drawing room of the house. As he and Sophia entered the room, his cousin was having a quiet word with Miss Taylor.

"You must give me a tour," she was saying.

"With great happiness. We have some flowers blooming even this late, Rodgers and I. The autumn snowflake in the bay by the east window is especially beautiful, though very, very delicate. *Leucojum autumnale.* We picked them up in Chelsea this spring, the bulbs. They're Iberian by origin."

As Frederick was delivering this short lecture the governess had nodded and, at the same time, gone to Sophia, taking her up in her arms. "Did she enjoy the walk?" Miss Taylor asked Charles.

"Tolerably well, I daresay. It started raining again toward the end, but a little damp shouldn't harm her too much, should it? And she was covered for all but a moment by the umbrella."

"I will listen to her chest. I have a device. Though I've no doubt she's fine—blooming, like your uncle's flowers."

She was worth the money they were paying her, Lenox reflected. "Thank you. And, Freddie, you wished to see me?"

"Yes, come and sit down here." Both men stood until the governess had left, and then sat, silent, while a footman wrestled the pram back into some discreet corner of the front hall. "It's about the coach drivers."

"Oh?" said Lenox.

"We've asked about half of the drivers who were along the roads last night if they saw two riders a-horseback. None of them did. We'll ask the rest as they trickle in this evening."

"Would you have expected them to?"

"They all seemed fairly definite that they would have spotted anything out of the ordinary. Then again it is possible to sneak on and off the roads, ride across open country . . ."

Lenox shook his head. "No, standing in that clearing, I felt—I think those were Plumbley horses. I think perhaps they were even left there to be found. How many men in town, and in the surrounding country, have two horses?"

"At least thirty, in all likelihood closer to forty. Several just in the town of Plumbley, for a start. Many of those old houses have stables attached to them—Dr. Eastwood's, Musgrave's, even Fripp's."

"Could you make a list of the names of all these men?"

"I'll ask my groomsman to do it. He'll know a sight closer than I would who has what in the way of horseflesh."

"Excellent. And the canvass—"

"Nothing, I'm afraid."

"It was still worth the try. Did you see Oates?"

"He was off to meet with a representative from the police force in Bath, last I saw him."

Lenox furrowed his brow. "Is that common?"

"If there's a murder in these parts one of the larger constabularies will usually check for themselves the proper steps have been followed." Frederick looked pensive for a moment. "Charles, do you feel you have any idea of who killed Weston, the poor lad?"

"Nearly," said Lenox.

"And who do you think—"

"I cannot say, yet, even to you. I'm not sure myself what I think; it is only an intuition. I should not like to stake anything to it."

Frederick looked set to protest this, when Nash entered the room. "Your wife requests a moment of your time, Mr. Lenox," he said.

Lenox rose. "I shall go back into town, soon. I'd like a skulk around. May I speak to the publican, as he speaks to the coach drivers?"

"Yes. Ah, but before you go, I promised I would remind you that the cricket match is in only a few days. Fripp is in a lather for you to play."

"They're going on with it?"

"Oh, yes. There will be a moment of silence, I expect, but it's the last weekend, the pavilion has been erected, yes, we must have the cricket. It's the fifth match of the summer. And the decisive one, this time—for the first time since 'sixty-eight the sides have split the first four matches."

"King's Arms against the Royal Oak, as in the old days?"

Frederick laughed. "When that changes, England will be no more, Charles."

"Have you played this summer?"

"Oh, I'm too old."

"If I play you must, Freddie."

"I wouldn't pin your hopes to it."

Lenox left his cousin and went upstairs. Jane was seated at her desk, surrounded by piles of books and papers. Now that Lenox thought of it she had been spending a great deal of time here in the past few days.

"Too busy to come along on a walk with Sophia?" he asked, sliding in through the open door.

She turned in her seat, her face bright. "There you are!"

"What are you writing?"

"This and that, letters. Tell me, will you be able to come to supper tomorrow evening?"

"I should think so. Why?"

"It would be nice to have a little company, I think. I told Freddie as much and he agreed, but I wanted to sure you'd be here. It would be nicer for Dallington and Miss Taylor, I think, to have a few fresh faces around here."

From the indifferent tone of this last utterance, Lenox detected its primacy. "You cannot be matchmaking, Jane, can you?"

She had stood up, and she took him by the lapels of his jacket and kissed him on the cheek. "No, no, of course not. Though have you observed how often they're together, in the gardens and the drawing room? Fast friends."

"Jane, not two days ago I was dragging John Dallington—"

"Yes, dear."

"I cannot imagine his mother would congratulate you on that match, either, considering—"

"No, I know, dear."

"Even if it is true that she would wish to see him settled, a governess, over thirty, without more than what she makes by the sweat of her brow, with parents who—"

"Yes, dear, you're quite right," said Lady Jane. "Let's talk of something else."

"Who will you be inviting to supper?" said Lenox crossly, unfooled.

"Oh, I've had a word with the housekeeper and Freddie."

"Is that what you were writing?"

"No!" she said. "Something very different. You shall know before too long."

He saw that this, anyhow, was true. He changed the subject. "I'm to play in the cricket."

"Do you have the whites?"

"I shall have to borrow them, but there are always a few spare sets lying about Everley. Will you watch?"

"I suppose my nuptial duty dictates I must."

Lenox laughed. "Hardly, no. You ought to come if you like the sport as a general proposition, however."

She frowned. "As far as I understand you play by attaching mattresses to your legs and waddling back and forth between two sticks, while occasionally gesturing with your own personal stick at some sort of red ball. But then I don't call myself a great sportsman."

"You do yourself an injustice there."

"Still, I should like to see you bat."

"And my friend Fripp is a great bowler, even at his age, I expect," said Lenox. "You can come around during the breaks, if you prefer. They'll have tea and cakes, the wives of the players."

"I should be involved in those preparations, then?"

Lenox pictured Lady Jane, as he had seen her many times, closeted in private conversation with the great and good of the royal court, of London society, and was tempted to laugh. Then he realized she would be just as comfortable in the pavilion, and felt a flourish of love for her. "If you like. Freddie can tell you which of the women in Plumbley to consult about it."

Miss Taylor knocked at the door then; this was the hour, customarily, just before tea, when they took Sophia—but if they wished to skip it today, Mr. Lenox having taken the child on her walk, then—

Of course they did not want to skip their half hour, and played very happily with the child, showing her rattle to her, making faces over her bassinet, and generally making fools of themselves until the bell rang for the afternoon repast.

CHAPTER TWENTY-EIGHT

Dallington had still not returned by five that evening. According to Frederick, who presided over the cakes and the sandwiches—in addition to Lenox and Lady Jane an old and unmarried woman of the parish, Miss Wilson, was in attendance, as apparently she was each Thursday—that morning the duke's son had asked the kitchens for roast beef on a roll, tucked it into his pocket without so much as the benefit of a napkin to wrap around it, and been off before seven.

When they heard a footstep in the hall, then, all of them looked expectantly toward the door for him.

It was Oates, however. Lenox and his cousin went out to greet the constable, who had taken off his helmet and stood, rather drenched, in the hall. "It's Musgrave, sir," he said. "Sirs."

"What of him?" asked Freddie.

"He's done a scarper."

Lenox raised his eyebrows. "He's left town?"

Oates, who again looked and spoke as if he had taken a few drinks in the King's Arms that afternoon—not quite enough for full impairment, but hardly a professional quantity either—pulled a notepad from his pocket. "Reported by Mrs. Flora Criscombe, Musgrave and his household in three coaches, with equipage, headed on the road to London."

Lenox turned to Frederick. "Does he often travel?"

"Oates?"

"Not since he moved into Church Lane, in my memory, and what it is, I reckon he's done poor Weston and—and now—and knows we're getting close to him," said Oates, slurringly.

Lenox felt badly for the man; at the same time he wished for a more professional ally. "To so incriminate himself would be exceedingly stupid, and Musgrave did not strike me as a stupid gentleman."

"No," said Freddie. "Has his wife gone with him?"

"Only a footman was left behind," said Oates. "He was covering the furniture when I knocked on the door."

"Where did he say Musgrave had gone?"

"He didn't know. He—"

"I say it would be foolish of Musgrave to leave," Lenox interjected, his chin in his hand, arms folded, eyes cast down with concentration, "but if there is some devastating piece of evidence soon to arise it would, perhaps, be wise in him to go to the continent."

"And he took poor Catherine Scales, too," Frederick murmured. "I dread to think of the life he's leading her."

Lenox turned to a servant. "Fetch me my hat and coat, please, would you?"

"Charles?" Frederick asked.

"We must look over the house. If he left in haste perhaps there is some evidence to parse. Oates, will you come with me?"

"Of course."

Frederick was looking rather askance at Lenox, who smiled, reading his thoughts. "We cannot stand upon much refinement in this business," he said "Certainly Musgrave has not."

They directed the carriage to Church Lane, and were there only a few minutes later—luckily the horses had been warmed already, from their evening exercise. The house was dim.

"Does the footman you met live in?" asked Lenox.

"I don't know," said Oates, and thumped the door with his nightstick. "That should rouse him if he does."

There were no footsteps inside, and the doors were locked. Oates, tapping his nose, went to work on the lock with a small metal rod he took from his pocket, and soon had the door open.

"It's an interesting brand of police work," said Lenox, disconcerted.

"If he killed Weston it's better than he deserves."

They went inside. The rooms already looked as if they had been vacant for months, drop cloths on the furniture and over the paintings, that peculiar stillness of an unlit and uninhabited house. Each man took a candlestick and lit a candle, and they started their way into the place.

The lower floor revealed nothing to them, despite an extended survey of it, and finally Lenox, with a mixture of compunction and determination, suggested they seek out the sleeping quarters. They went upstairs.

These rooms, too, were disappointing. One of them quite evidently belonged to Mrs. Musgrave—its wardrobe full of women's clothes, its dresser scattered with bottles of scent and old scraps of ribbon—but whatever evidence it might have offered of her daily life beyond these objects had already been scrubbed away.

It was Oates, to his credit, who remembered that they ought to look in the basement. They went down the narrow staircase with careful steps, Lenox for his part made slightly uneasy by the dark, the close walls.

"How many servants did Musgrave have?" he asked, in part to break up the eerie silence.

"At least four," said Oates. He seemed more sober now. "Here are their bedrooms. Shall we look in them?"

"Yes, certainly."

The servants' bedrooms were to the left of the stairwell, down a thin hallway, while the enormous kitchen, dominated by a vast oven, was off to the right. They turned left, tipping their own candles to spark the candles in sconces along the walls, providing further light.

These rooms, too, were cleansed of any sign of their former occupants, though Lenox and Oates inspected them all carefully, ultimately finding a few small pictures, a child's toy, and a great deal of bed linen. It wasn't much help.

"The kitchen," said Lenox.

The pantry was still full—and here, at last, he found something. Oates was sifting through stacks of plates on the other side of the room, and Lenox called him back.

"This was next to the tea chest," he said.

"What is it?"

Lenox held up a small cloth bag. Written on a tag, hanging from its drawstring, was *Mrs. Musgrave's sugar, one teaspoon to be included with her morning pot of tea.*

"Her sugar?" asked Oates.

"Yet here is a fat jar of sugar, as you can see," said Lenox, gesturing toward the open cupboard.

They both stared at the bag for a moment, indecisively, until Oates, too quickly for Lenox to object, dipped a finger in and tasted the bag's contents.

"Not sugar," he said shortly. There was a pitcher of water standing nearby, and he swirled his mouth and spat into the sink. "Bitter."

Lenox nodded. He drew the bag's string tight and put it in his jacket pocket. "We shall have to see what it is, then. Dr. Eastwood might help us. Certainly my friend McConnell could. In fact I may send a little of the powder to each of them."

"I hope Cat's life isn't in danger," said Oates. "Such a pretty girl, she was."

Energized by their discovery, Lenox and Oates continued to look as closely through the kitchen and the rooms around it—the servants' dining room, the washing room—as they had upstairs. It must have been ninety minutes they had been here now, perhaps longer. They traced each other's footsteps to double their work.

Nothing new came up, however, for all their looking.

"Shall we leave, then?" asked Oates.

Lenox looked around. "Have we looked everywhere?"

Oates pointed at a bucket of slop underneath the sink, old carrot peelings and the like, and said, smiling wearily, "Not in there."

Lenox sighed. "Perhaps we should, just to be thorough. It's as good a hiding place as any. Will you start on it? Don't worry, I'll do the other bucket in a moment."

"I suppose," he said. "This stuff's only fit to give to pigs anyhow."

As Oates dug into the slop, Lenox closed the cabinets he had opened, then began to extinguish the candles in the hallway.

He heard a yelp from behind him. Oates. He ran back toward the kitchen.

"What is it?" Lenox asked him.

Oates was standing over the bucket of compost, his hands filthy; in one of them he was holding something. It was too dim, with the candles gone, to tell what.

Oates had inspected it over his own flame. His eyes were wide. "It's a knife," he reported. "I nicked myself. And I think where there's older blood on it, too, sir."

CHAPTER TWENTY-NINE

Lenox quickly took the knife, laying it in a white handkerchief. "Well done," he said, "very well done."

Both men peered down toward the object, dipping their candles better to illuminate it. "Is it the murder weapon?" asked Oates.

"Wash your hands and we'll take it back to the station," said Lenox.

Fifteen minutes later they were there. In the station were bright lamps, of long residence it would appear from the greasy black circles that had formed on the ceiling above them. Now they could inspect the knife more minutely.

Its smooth, nonserrated blade was perhaps four or five inches long, its haft about the same. Lenox asked for a tape measure to be sure. Yes; it was just a shade over five inches long, the blade. Which meant that it conformed to the description Dr. Eastwood had offered of the weapon that had killed the young police constable.

"Let's have a look at the bucket," said Lenox.

Oates had carried the slop bucket with them from Musgrave's, and now he tipped it over and spread its contents thinly upon a long table, which the two men had covered with old newspapers. Wearing white cloth gloves, he and Lenox went through the mess.

They were looking for anything maroon and sticky, at the detective's suggestion, for that was what covered the blade, and Lenox wanted to be sure that it wasn't beet juice, colored meringue, discarded grapes, anything of that nature. Satisfyingly, none of the slop bucket's contents, not its potato eyes, not its cauliflower stalks, looked likely to produce a red liquid.

"I think it is blood," said Lenox at last, as he and Oates cleaned up.

"Have you seen blood on a knife before?"

"I have. Have you?"

"No. It's what I imagine it would look like, though."

"Quite."

With a faintly chastened feeling they went back to the knife.

"I don't like to look at it," said Oates.

Lenox's face was pensive. "What I cannot figure is why a man of military self-possession, or even a man of rudimentary intelligence, would have left the knife behind. Why not take it with him?"

"Fear of it being found among his possessions, I suppose?"

"Why not wash it, then!" said Lenox. "Why not wash it and leave it in with the other knives? He might have called for hot water at any time and attracted far less notice than his presence in the kitchens would have."

"For that matter, why not leave it with the body?"

Lenox shook his head. "No, I believe such a knife might have been traced back to his kitchen, if it is part of a set. We will have to see about that. Although it may be that we are getting ahead of ourselves. Perhaps it was used to dress a chicken or a pheasant, after all. It's the correct size for the job."

"But if that was all anybody used it for, then why—"

"Why was it in the compost pile, hidden," said Lenox impatiently. "I understand the situation, Oates."

"Apologies, sir."

Lenox looked up. "No, I apologize. If only it made sense! Either way we must send word along to Bath and Taunton that Captain Musgrave is wanted for questioning, in connection with Mr. Weston's death."

Oates's face had a shadow upon it. "Do you think he did it, the bastard?"

"I think it's too early to reach any conclusions. We must send our telegrams now, though, even if it means fetching the dispatcher out of bed."

It was Oates who committed to do this job. Lenox took the knife in his pocket, for safekeeping, bade the constable good night, and—having dismissed the coachman and his horses when they dropped him at Musgrave's house several hours before—began the walk back to Everley.

When he reached the hall there were still lights on in the rooms of the ground floor. They would have had dinner without him, in all probability. His own hunger had vanished when he saw the knife; even as he took a step now he could feel its weight in his coat pocket swing away from his body and then return with a thump against his hipbone. He didn't like it.

He found his cousin and his protégé smoking a pipe and a small cigar, respectively, in the large library.

"How do you do, Charles?" said Frederick. "I was on the verge of asking your friend here whether he was much of a hand at cricket. Are you, Lord John?"

"Oh, none at all," said Dallington cheerfully. "In school I forged my own sick notes."

"Ah, excellent," said Frederick, "we can give you to the King's Arms. They're a bowler short."

Dallington looked prepared to object to this recruitment, but Lenox said, rather sharply, "You'll enjoy it, John."

Looking as if he doubted that assertion, the young man nevertheless said, "Yes, of course."

"Do you have a report to make on Fontaine?" asked Lenox.

Now Dallington's face brightened, exchanging the ease of an after-dinner smoke for a new sharpness. "Yes. Would you like to hear it?"

"Certainly. First, though, I should show you what I found at Musgrave's."

He unwrapped his handkerchief, now stained with a faint rust, to reveal the knife. His uncle gasped. "At Musgrave's? Is that blood?"

"Yes, on both counts."

Dallington, with the procedurally sound method that Lenox had taught him, used his own handkerchief to turn the knife over and examine it from every angle. "Fingerprints?"

"I am hopeful. I propose to send it to McConnell, in London, along with another little parcel." He had almost forgotten about the white powder, but patted his breast pocket, took out the bag, and showed it to the men. "I'm rather curious what it was that the kitchen staff fed Mrs. Musgrave every morning and afternoon."

Frederick was still absorbed by the knife, however. "Fingerprints, you mentioned? What does that mean?"

"It is a technology in its infancy, but quite useful," said Lenox. "The whorls and ridges of each fingerpad are quite distinctive, from man to man—"

"I once read that Babylonian potters used the impress of their fingers to identify their work," said Frederick, "but surely Musgrave wouldn't have pressed his finger against the knife. It isn't wet clay, either."

"It doesn't matter. Herschel's son has been using them as a means of identification in India for years."

"John Herschel? The astronomer?"

"Yes. Apparently with careful dusting one may 'lift' them, as the terminology has it, from any object. If Musgrave has held this knife, McConnell may be able to tell us. He has a very expensive kit, one of his own design, that he uses. He's become rather a hobbyist, in fact. Offered the thing to the Metropolitan Police and they declined, with a typical deficit of imagination."

"Where did you find it?" asked Dallington.

Lenox described the slop bucket and their retreat to the police station. "In the meanwhile Musgrave may be on a ship to Calcutta, for all that we know."

Frederick frowned. "Perhaps I can rouse the authorities in Bath faster than Constable Oates," he said. "I have one or two friends there. Will you excuse me, Charles?"

"By all means, though if you lack the energy to—"

"No, not at all," said Frederick, and indeed he had a steely look in his eye. He tapped the ash out of his pipe, gave it a quick swab with a ball of cotton that had been left on a silver tray nearby for that purpose, and left the room, calling for his coat and his horses.

Dallington and Lenox were left alone.

"Cricket, then?" asked the younger man with a smile.

"I expect you'll quite enjoy it."

"Miss Taylor and I had been planning to watch from the sidelines," he said.

"I would appreciate your playing."

The compact young lord merely nodded. "Will you hear about Fontaine, then?"

"In fifteen minutes, if you wouldn't mind. I would ship these things off to McConnell."

"I'll return with my notes."

CHAPTER THIRTY

The library in which Dallington left Lenox was one of the glories of Everley, built at the end of the seventeenth century by a student of Wren's. It had white plaster walls and a white plaster ceiling, with intricate moldings where they met, and vast, cathedral-like windows, flat at the bottom, where each had a bench, and rounded at the top. Down the center of the library—which was tiled black and white, striking especially in the sunlight—was a long oak table, while mirroring limewood bookcases receded to a fireplace at the end of the room. In these bookcases were treasures: old incunabula still chained to the shelves, folios from the early part of the 1600s, and long leather-bound rows of philosophy, a hobby of Frederick's father, their bindings well worn.

Dallington and Frederick had been sitting in armchairs by the fireplace; now Lenox took their spot, though not before pouring himself a healthy tot of whisky from the table of bottles nearby. He rang the bell and requested a spoon, some small boxes, and some string, and when they arrived he carefully apportioned a small amount of the powder into two separate parcels, writing a note to go with each, one to Dr. Eastwood, which he would send down in the morning, and one that would travel to London and McConnell. The notes asked if either doctor could identify the powder. He had more faith that his friend would arrive at the answer, but of course Eastwood was closer by.

After he had accomplished this he took the knife and made up a second package for his friend, and included a note, on a piece of blue-bordered Everley writing paper, that said, simply, *Fingerprints, urgent. Lenox.*

He rang again—for Nash, this time, the butler—and handed him the parcels. When this was just done, Dallington returned to the library. He sat down in the other armchair, eyes on his notes, without as much as a glance at the table of alcohol. Funny, that. Lenox had known men who were saintly fathers and husbands but couldn't be within fifteen yards of a quarter pot of beer without becoming different creatures, while Dallington, if he had work in front of him, seemed entirely indifferent toward his intermittent vice.

"Where shall I begin?" he asked.

"First of all tell me what you did when you left this morning," said Lenox.

"Did Oates tell you I sat with Fontaine for a while?"

"No. Did Oates himself let you in?"

"No, he's got a temporary constable, a man named Hutchinson who has a small farm nearby. Apparently his son can operate the place for a few weeks without much disruption."

"Did Fontaine speak?"

"Not to me. I tried all of the old tricks you taught me," said Dallington. "I told him about myself. I misstated a few facts about Paris, where I've been—to see if he would correct me."

"Did you have a pack of cards?"

"Yes, and I dealt out a hand of Beggar-Your-Neighbor, thinking he had to know it. I even started playing for both of us, and he looked down at the cards but he refused to take the bait."

"That was a dry well, then."

"Quite so. I had a bit more luck on his background, however."

Lenox took a sip of his whisky. "How did you proceed?"

"I went out to the farm where he worked. There were half a dozen Frenchmen there, and when I saw them I can tell you that my heart fell, thinking that they would all be mum on their compatriot's behalf. As it happened, they couldn't talk quickly enough. His wife was first in line."

"Why?"

"They dislike Fontaine. He came over because his cousin worked here, a man named Theodore Celine. Celine died last winter of consumption, but Fontaine stayed on. He was a good laborer, apparently, and in the early stages anyhow, a good husband. Lately he's been cruel to her, however, sullen and violent with the others, and skived his work."

"But he had a great deal of money when he was arrested, didn't he?"

"That's what's odd," said Dallington. "Six months' wages, easily. Some of it was bad coin, some good—that's one of the charges they have him up on in Bath, in addition to disturbance of the peace, a row with the constable, refusal to pay his bill at a chop house, and public indecency. Apparently he had a prostitute out with him in one of the nicer streets in Bath and was trying to redeem his payment then and there. She was—let me look at my notes—'quite a decent one, too,' according to the man in Bath, which I think is a testament to her long standing in town and relative modesty rather than to her professional skill. I laughed at that nevertheless."

"You went to Bath? Very thoroughly managed, John."

"Thank you," said Dallington, with a diffidence that seemed to betray, to Lenox at least, an ardent hope for redemption. "Shall I tell you what they said in Bath, or shall I—"

"No, tell me what they said on the farm."

"They didn't know why he had such an unusual amount of money, but they were certain that he came by it foully. He spends his wages the instant he gets them apparently. As do they all, in fairness."

"None of them had an idea how he got them? His wife?"

"She only said that he was absent more than usual."

"It's a wonder he wasn't fired."

"It was for-hire work, not a permanent position."

"Evicted, then?"

"His wife and her two cousins, also French, live in the house. A hovel, really, you would call it. I felt badly for them with the winter coming up. Not a switch of wood to be seen."

"Who is the landlord?"

"Yates."

"Yes, I always heard he was a hard man. Did they give you any other information?" Lenox asked.

"I asked whether he could ride a horse. He could."

"Well done."

"I also asked whether he spoke of any business in town. He hadn't. On the other hand they knew that he came into the money on the morning he was arrested, some three weeks ago, because he had been boasting about it for a few days beforehand quite brazenly."

"So it's a recent job. How do the dates line up with the vandalisms?"

"He was arrested after the first, before the second two. So he might have been involved, but he wasn't the chief actor, I suppose you could say."

"Still, it's telling."

"Do you think so?" asked Dallington hopefully.

"Money and crime are rarely cohabitants of the same neighborhood at random. What did they tell you in Bath?"

"Not much, sadly. I asked around at the places he spent his money, too, hoping that the alcohol had loosened his lips, but no such luck."

"Well, it's inconclusive, then."

Dallington mastered a look of disappointment on his face, and said, "I thought so, too. I had hoped it might dovetail with something you learned."

"It still may. I think it a promising lead, don't you?"

"I don't know enough of the case to say. Perhaps you would fill me in."

Lenox stood up and poured himself another splash of whisky. "Would you like a glass?" he asked.

"Not just at the moment," said Dallington.

Lenox sat down again and described the stages of the case to his apprentice more comprehensively than he had before. Just as he was reaching Carmody's account of the horses, his story was cut short by the door of the library flying open.

It was Frederick.

"It's happened again," he said.

Lenox and Dallington both rose, alarmed. "Not another murder?" Lenox asked.

"No, no," said Frederick. "Another vandalism has happened, and they nearly caught the man who did it. Come with me, I'll tell you on the way."

CHAPTER THIRTY-ONE

Lenox realized he hadn't seen Jane or Sophia since he came back to the house, and as Frederick led them through the front hall he asked for word to be sent up that he had come and gone again already. Part of him—the part that had consumed three fingers of whisky, in all likelihood—yearned to stay in, to stall the adventure by a few hours of sleep. It had been a long day.

Of course he went, though.

"There was a great commotion when I got into town," said Frederick as the carriage began the short drive. He faced Lenox and Dallington from one of its two plush benches. "I still managed to arrange about the telegrams with Timothy Milton, then I went off to find Fripp—"

"Is it his shop that has been vandalized?" asked the member of Parliament.

"No. It was the police station."

Lenox's eyes widened. "Really, though? I was there not an hour ago."

"I know it. I'm glad you were gone."

"What did they do?"

"It was the same again, a rock through the window—though this time there was a constable's helmet tied to it, with a white X painted upon it. Oates isn't taking it well."

"You say the culprits were nearly apprehended?" asked Dallington.

"Yes. It was Wells who saw them—as you know his shop is just at the edge of the green, there, where the station is and where Weston was killed. The fellow is distraught because he fears that the men saw his face, and will return to silence him. He and his wife are at the station house with Oates now."

"What did he see them doing?"

"The whole thing," said Frederick. "There were two of them, and he raised a cry as soon as he saw them. Dozens of people came flooding out of the King's Arms, and they gave chase down the Main Street. There were fresh prints from horseshoes there."

"What was his description of the men?"

Frederick shook his head. "Oates took them down. I don't know."

Suddenly, there in the carriage, Lenox did.

The pieces had clicked together in his mind now, the deductions made sense. A stray morsel of information from Dallington, another from Musgrave, one from Wells, one from Fripp, one from Frederick, one from Carmody: these ratcheted into place and he understood it all. Or so he believed.

He thought he knew the murderer's name.

"When we reach town," he said, "perhaps I can leave the two of you to interview Wells and Oates. I have a brief errand I would like to run."

Frederick looked at him queryingly. "If you like," he said.

"Call it a suspicion."

It was only twelve minutes or so to the village green, which was ablaze with light and jostling with Plumbley villagers.

"Look at this. It's like the first of November," said Freddie.

Dallington shot him a quizzical look, but Lenox understood. "You've heard of soul-caking?" he said.

"No," said Dallington.

"Spoken like a Londoner," Frederick said, though his eyes were fixed on the people congregated near the police station.

They stepped out of the carriage. Lenox said, "It's a custom in many villages, though I've never seen one take it as seriously as Plumbley. They do it differently here, too, because in most villages the children beg for cakes, but here the children make them. They spend the whole last week of October doing it, out of raisins and flour, nutmeg and cinnamon, perhaps a little ginger, that sort of thing.

"Then on the first of the new month the whole village opens itself up, lights on in every house, a glass of wine exchanged among all the neighbors, very friendly, and the children trade the cakes they've made for toys and candies. It's lovely to see. Old feuds are set to the side for an evening. At the end there's the first Christmas carol of the year on the town green, along with a hymn or two, by candlelight. Each cake that's eaten represents a soul freed from Purgatory, they say."

"Sounds rather like guising."

"No, there's nothing mean-spirited in it. There wouldn't be, in Plumbley." As he said this Lenox felt a surge of fondness for the little village, and simultaneously an anger at the men who had put it in a state of fear, had fretted the faces he saw in conversation around the town green. "You two go. I'm off to see Carmody."

That won their attention. "Carmody?" asked Dallington, eyebrows raised.

"I'll see you before too long."

As he approached Carmody's house there were clusters of people talking, in the low murmuring gossip of village life. In the window of the man's sitting room, Lenox could see that the curtains were parted and the lights were on. He knocked sharply on the door.

"Good evening, Mr. Lenox," said the housekeeper. "Unfortunately Mr. Carmody has retired. Would you care to leave a message for him?"

"Please rouse him, if you would."

"But—"

"It's a matter of some moment, ma'am."

"Very well. Wait here, please. I would invite you in, but at this hour—"

Lenox, standing on the stairs that led to the front door of the row house, pivoted so that he could survey the green as Carmody would have. He wondered where on earth Captain Musgrave might be.

The door opened again. "He will see you in his study, sir," said the housekeeper.

"Excellent."

Carmody was in his seat by the window, in a vermilion-and-gold dressing gown, a glass of port wine—no doubt of a vintage deemed acceptable by the boys in Covent Garden—in his left hand. "Mr. Lenox," he said, "I take it your visit pertains to this latest incident?"

"Would you dress and come with me on an errand?" Lenox asked. "It would only take fifteen minutes."

"At this time of the evening I fear I cannot—"

"Really, I must insist, Mr. Carmody," said Lenox. "The next murder could happen this evening."

"The *next* murder, Mr. Lenox?"

"Will you help me?"

"I do customarily take a walk in the evenings, as you know—but—well, yes, I shall come along, I suppose. Give me a moment, give me a moment," he said, with the flustered annoyance of a bachelor interrupted in his routines.

Soon they were walking down the dim, moonlit streets of Plumbley. The short white houses, with their stooped green doors and friendly brass door-knockers in the shapes of horses, dogs, coronets, any such thing, looked completely innocent of malevolence.

"Where are we going?" said Carmody, trotting alongside Lenox.

"I'm taking you on a circuitous route to avoid the town green."

"But where—"

"I'd like you to look at a pair of horses."

After a short walk, not more than eight minutes, they stood before a large house with stable adjoining it. Both were silent. "This is the place?" asked Carmody.

"Yes. Help me open the top-half of the stable door, if you would."

They creaked these open, Lenox trying to be quiet in case there was a boy who slept above the stalls. Nobody emerged, and soon three fine horses were at the window, open breast-high. It was just like Plumbley to have an unlocked stable so close to town. Or had been, perhaps, until the recent crimes. Who knew what precautions people would begin to take if it didn't stop; how the town would change.

"Are these the horses?" said Lenox.

Carmody looked at them very carefully. It was a piece of good fortune that the moon was bright. "Yes," he said at last, very slowly. "They are, these two to the left here, beyond a shadow of a doubt."

"Good. Help me close the door."

Carmody was dumbfounded. "Stay a moment. Can that mean—"

"I must entreat you to hold your tongue, Mr. Carmody. Soon enough it will all come out, I assure you, but until then your discretion is crucial."

CHAPTER THIRTY-TWO

The two men split apart now, Carmody for his evening walk—though he seemed apprehensive about venturing anywhere too far out of town, and said he would avoid the wood—and Lenox back to the town green.

Dallington, standing on the church steps, hailed him. "Charles!"

"How are you?"

"Well enough. More important, how was your errand?"

Lenox nodded slightly, his face grim. "I think the facts are settled in my mind. I shall wait until the morning—until this has died down—to make the arrest. First I must go to one of the public houses and have a quiet word with a man, as a final verification. Perhaps you and Freddie might come with me, and I shall explain."

Freddie was speaking in consoling tones to a group of woman who were standing in front of the police station. When he saw Lenox, he asked, "Do you need to see the constable's hat, the rock, Charles?"

The detective shook his head. "No, at least not at the moment. As long as Oates has retained it as evidence."

"It is in the station's safe."

"Will you come along to the Royal Oak for a few moments? I should like you to point out Weston's friends to me. We are close to the end."

Frederick looked hopeful. "You have it?"

"I think I may," said Lenox. "It is a pitiful reason to waste a life, if I am correct."

They trudged across the village green toward the King's Arms, a dark, low-slung Tudor pub without much cheer to it, full of quiet voices and lit only by a few swinging candles. The cider was reckoned to be some of the best in Somerset, however. Lenox ordered three pints of it at the bar.

"Which of these is Weston's friend?" he asked Frederick.

"Several by the back wall there, that young man, for instance, Michael Robe. Then there's Edward Carfax, just next to him, holding the glass of shandy."

"Which one can keep a secret?"

"Carfax, I would say."

"I'm going to ask the publican for a private room. If you could bring Mr. Carfax back to see me, I would be grateful."

Soon it was done, and in a few, low words, sealed with a promise of silence, the young man confirmed Lenox's suspicions.

Dallington and Frederick came in again when Carfax had left. "Well?" asked the old squire.

"Could you have a constable here from Bath, in the morning?" asked Lenox.

"Very easily, yes."

"And could you write up a search warrant?"

"Again, very easily, yes."

"Then I will ask you to do those two things—and for a modicum of patience with me. Tomorrow when the policeman from Bath arrives it shall all be clear."

Dallington objected. "Come, you must tell us now."

"No. I think my uncle would want to make an arrest, Oates is agitated, it is late, we have need of support, of a search warrant . . . and then there are a few final details I would like to ponder before I lay out the entire case before you."

"But—"

Frederick put a hand on Dallington's shoulder. "Come, we must permit him his methods. Charles, can I tell Oates when to meet us?"

"I would prefer if you did not. The murderer must not think himself closed-in upon."

"Is it not Musgrave, then?" said Dallington.

"I have my suspicions of him, perhaps, but let it wait until the morning."

They went back to Everley, then, the hour not much before midnight. It had been one of the longest days Lenox could remember.

Jane was still sitting up, however, a pair of lamps upon her desk, her head bent low over it.

"Still writing?" Lenox asked as he came in.

She turned. "Charles! You've been gone for ages, you poor soul. Did you ever eat?"

"Come to think of it, I did not."

"Let me call for something."

She moved to ring the bell-rope, hanging in the corner of their sitting room. "No, no!" he said. "I'll have a ginger biscuit and wait for breakfast. In truth I am out of my appetite."

"Is it your speech?"

"No—this murder."

"Come, sit and tell me all of it."

She beckoned him to a small, comfortable sofa near the window. The whole western gardens of Everley were visible under the moonlight: their precise graveled geometries, their intricate plantings and effloresences, their trimmed trees, all of Rodgers's and Ponsonby's many hours of mutual work. As Lenox gazed upon it he thought at once of how frivolous these country-house gardens could seem and how noble, what an achievement of man.

The tin of ginger biscuits (a present from Toto) was opened and raided, a glass of Madeira poured from a half-full bottle upon a side table, and soon Lenox felt less like a wraith, more wholly human.

He explained the entire sequence of events, as he saw them, to Jane.

"It is a gamble to go in blind, tomorrow," he said. "If the machine is not there I shall feel very foolish indeed. Yet all of the arrows—Weston's note, Fontaine's actions, the vandalisms—they seem to point in one direction, do they not?"

Lady Jane, for her part, had no doubts that he was correct. Her legs were tucked under her, her hands on his shoulder as she gazed at him. "Of course they do," she said. "And I think you're brilliant."

He laughed. "If I could just thank you to get that statement notarized, then I might show it to you the next time we need to settle a debate about the color of the carpet in my library."

"I said that you were brilliant, not that you were in full possession of your eyesight."

"Very funny." He gave her a kiss on the cheek. "Now tell me— what have you been working on, so assiduously? Is it for the charity ball in December?"

"Have you noticed that?"

"It would have been difficult to miss it."

She smiled. "I've had my head down, it's true. I'll tell you why in a day or two."

"It's too late to peer in on Sophia, I suppose?" he said.

"Far too late. Not fair on the governess, either. Incidentally, you can still sit for supper tomorrow evening?"

"Barring a catastrophe."

"Don't speak like that," she said, frowning. "I don't like it."

Though he ought to have been mortally tired, he found that when it came time to go to sleep he was more awake, more alert than he would have expected. It was often this way at the end of a case. Small details returned to him. Then thoughts about his speech. Then distant memories of Frederick, of his mother, of Everley . . .

Just after the great mahogany clock downstairs tolled one o'clock in the morning he realized that he was not likely to fall asleep soon. He got up and with soft footsteps made his way to the kitchen, a place to which he had made many unlicensed late-night visits in his early years of life, and made himself a pot of tea.

This, along with a few more ginger biscuits, he set on his desk, then lit a soft light, sat down, and set to work on his speech. It came to him effortlessly. Almost as if in a dream he filled line after line, sheet after sheet, pausing only for sips of the hot, then luke-warm, and finally cold tea, deaf and blind to the world around him.

By half past two he had written nearly the entire thing. With a contented exhalation he put down his pen and returned to bed, where he fell asleep instantly.

CHAPTER THIRTY-THREE

He slept later than usual the next morning, dressed quickly, and went down with Jane to breakfast. The room was empty, however: Dallington was walking in the gardens with Miss Taylor and Sophia, apparently, while Lenox's cousin was in his study.

After downing a cup of coffee Lenox looked in on him. The older man was sitting in a shaft of sunlight by the window, engrossed in a journal.

"Anything interesting?" asked Lenox.

"A history of the tulip in Brabant."

That was a kind of answer. "Do I have time for a quick ride out?"

Frederick took his pocket watch from his waistcoat. "The constable from Bath will arrive on the eleven twenty-seven, so if you're sharp about it I think you might have time. I don't suppose you'd prefer to sit and tell me who you think killed Weston?"

"Soon, soon," said Lenox, his voice apologetic.

"By all means, leave me in suspense as long as you wish."

It was colder than it had been in the past few days, but as he rode, jumping stiles and puddles, Lenox quickly warmed. After half an hour of pacey travel across the fields circling the village, startling birds and small game as he tore along, he was sweating.

It was refreshing to be in the country: He slowed the hack down with a tightening of the reins and turned her halfway back to gaze out at the course they had been running at Everley, set below them in its swale of land. This was the distance from which many artists had painted the house, and indeed it looked wonderfully serene. So, too, did the village, with its spires and its curvingly crossed lanes.

He took the way back at a canter, not a gallop, and handed the horse over to Chalmers feeling energized. As he was washing his face and arms, Nash, the butler, came in and said that the carriage was waiting downstairs.

It was with a feeling of some solemnity that the three men, Dallington, Ponsonby, and Lenox, gathered there at a little after eleven o'clock. They picked up Oates, who was silent after his greeting, then as a group met the train, where a tall, solid-looking constable named Archer, his face dominated by an enormous mustache, was standing on the platform with a small satchel. He did not require a bite to eat, no; he would prefer they made the arrest directly.

"Where shall we go, Charles?" said Freddie.

"To Fripp's, please."

"Fripp's!" said Oates.

It was a short, tense ride. The squire, who had lived on the same meridian as Fripp for these sixty years, kept glancing at his cousin uneasily.

The fruit-and-vegetable man was tidying his stalls, occasionally offering a stray word to one of the women prodding his goods. He looked up when the carriage stopped at the corner, and the men walked toward him along the white-stoned path that lay between the buildings and the green.

"Gentlemen!" he said. "Have you caught 'em yet?"

"Hello, Mr. Fripp," said Lenox.

"Charlie."

He turned to the three men. "You observe the sign in the window, gentlemen?" he said.

"W. F. Purveyor," said Archer.

"This was the location of the first vandalism," said Lenox. "Now—moving along."

Fripp looked confused. "Excepting what is that to mean?"

"You may come along if you like," said Lenox. "We're only walking ten doors down. I think your shop was vandalized by mistake, Mr. Fripp."

"To Wells's?" asked Frederick quietly.

Lenox nodded. "The location of the second vandalism."

Wells's shop was empty, though the man himself was behind his counter, apron on, barrels of seed full and gleaming, a pencil stub in his hand and a ledger before him. He looked up just as the bell, strung tightly to the door, clanged.

"Gentlemen," he said. "Can I help you?"

"You observed the sign in the window, as we came in, Mr. Archer?" said Lenox.

"F. W. Purveyor," said Archer with a nod.

"Outsiders, nervous about a job, knowing they're to commit a violation of a property on the east side of the village green—it is a mistake I understand. They came back a second time to do the job correctly, and took a clock, too."

There was a sudden strain, an airlessness, in the room. "What is the meaning of this?" asked the grain merchant.

"Mr. Wells," said Lenox, "I have come into your shop three times now, including this visit."

"I recall," said Wells coolly.

"On none of those occasions have I seen a single customer. Yet what was it you told me, Freddie—that he has changed it all out of countenance from the sleepy shop that it was in his father's day, that he had a gold watch chain now, a carriage for his mother. Is that correct?"

"My customers buy in bulk, not in dribs and drabs. But then I would not expect a politician to understand the ways of business."

Lenox laughed. "A point fairly taken, though I've seen grain shops busier than this. No, I grant you that—if it was only the watch chain, the carriage, then I would be on an unstable footing." He went silent. The laughter left his face. "But your expansion," he said. "The expansion of your store."

"What of it?" asked Wells.

"Are we to arrest this man?" said Archer. Oates murmured his concordance with the question.

Only Dallington knew Lenox's methods. He was quiet. "How long did the expansion take, Mr. Wells?" asked Lenox.

"Two months."

Lenox gestured at the narrow strip of new flooring in one corner of the room. "I noticed this when I was here before. Two months! It is a very small return on a very great investment of time and, I presume, money. Freddie, you called it a hellish noise, didn't you?"

"Yes, I did."

"And—I thought this was telling—he brought in men from Bath to do the work, too? Despite the town railing against Captain Musgrave for taking his custom to Taunton."

"I confess that I am still in the dark, Charles," said Frederick. "May we come to the point? Did Mr. Wells kill Weston?"

"Never!" said Wells, and indeed his face was filled with a convincing outrage.

Lenox strode toward a door at the back of the room. "Dallington, it was something you said about Fontaine that finally tipped me."

The junior detective's face—paled with guilt for these last few days, so eager to be of aid—seemed to flush with happiness now. He restrained it long enough to ask, in a casual voice, "Oh? Which was it? Glad to help, of course."

Lenox stopped at the door. "Mr. Wells, may we visit your cellar? As I remember there appears to be a heavy padlock on this door."

"Can that surprise you, after this shop was vandalized and a prize clock taken?" said Wells. "Am I accused of some wrongdoing, sirs?"

"I suspect the padlock predates the vandalism—but never mind that, may we see your cellar?"

Wells's face was, for a moment, reluctant, but then he said, "By all means. I have nothing to hide."

"Take us down, if you would."

There was a ring of keys tied to Wells's apron string. He selected a large iron one and opened the padlocked door, then led them along a short passage and down a flight of stairs, single file.

The cellar was disappointing. There were sacks of grain, old bits of machinery, a few papers.

Lenox felt the tide of the room turning against him; indeed, he was puzzled.

Then it came to him: The room was too small.

"Why is the cellar only a quarter of the size of the house?" he asked. He turned to Dallington, Archer, Oates, Frederick. Fripp had stayed upstairs, evidently. "Help me find the concealed door. It will be on this wall."

Now at last Wells broke. With a cry of fury he flung himself toward the stairs, but it was Constable Archer of Bath, as strong as an oak tree, who blocked his way and, with Oates's help, put handcuffs over his wrists.

"A concealed door?" said Dallington. "Concealing what?"

"Help me look," said Lenox.

They spent ten minutes going over the back wall minutely until, at last, it was Fredrick, puffing slightly from the exertion of stooping and crawling along the floor, who found the small latch. "It needs a key," he said. "There's a keyhole in the floor here."

Archer took Wells's ring of keys. It was the third key that worked, releasing the door in the wall a quarter of an inch. It was obvious now, in retrospect, where it had been all along.

"Here is the reason for your Bath workmen—your two-month renovation," said Lenox. "Dallington, it was the bad coin you mentioned that finally tipped me, one of the charges against Fontaine's in Bath. You recall, too, Uncle, Jack Randall, passing false bits. I suspect both of them worked for Mr. Wells. This room is the reason for all the trouble Plumbley has had."

All of them surged forward around the door as Lenox opened it, except for Wells, who was leaning, forlorn, against the stairs.

Lenox knew what he expected, but even he gasped when he saw it; the others went slack-jawed. Within a long chamber stood an enormous bronze machine, gleaming under lamplight, and even now pumping out row upon row upon row of counterfeit coins.

CHAPTER THIRTY-FOUR

The Plumbley police station had a back room with a table and chairs in it. The transfer of Wells from his shop's cellar to that room—a distance of perhaps fifty yards—took place quickly, in under a minute. Still it wasn't quick enough to prevent people from seeing. Freddie had ventured outside and found a bedlam of people pressed up against the windows of the police station, hoping for a glimpse of the suspect.

Now he returned to the room and sat with Archer and Lenox on one side of the table, Wells on the other, a pitcher of water and several glasses between them. Oates stood in the corner, watching.

Dallington was out looking for the farmhand Jack Randall, with the aid of Oates's temporary subordinate, the farmer, Mr. Hutchinson. As Lenox pointed out, Randall might have been involved or there might simply have been an uncommon quantity of false coin passing around Plumbley. Meanwhile Archer had sent a telegram back to his headquarters to report of the arrest and to ask that Fontaine be questioned about his relationship with Wells.

"Tell it from the start, please, Mr. Lenox," said Plumbley's constable. His wits seemed sharper today, uninterfered with by any morning tipple. "I still don't claim to understand it all."

Lenox shrugged. "Mr. Wells can recount the story better than I can."

Wells was silent.

"Help him along, perhaps," said Frederick. The squire looked heartily disappointed to be in the room, even in his relief at having caught the criminal.

"It was greed, I suppose. The grain shop Mr. Wells inherited was not as prosperous as he would have wished, and when he took control of it he must have been on the lookout for a new way to create income for himself. Only he can tell us how he came to acquire the machine, though I suspect it was from someone in Bath. The police in the big cities are so alert to coining now that the shofulmen in London have moved their business entirely to the country. Perhaps he had a smaller machine at first and the expansion of the store—so minimal on the ground floor, but enormous in the cellar, and permitting the creation of a secret space—only came after he had saved enough money to build it. But I suspect that he borrowed the money."

"The vandalisms," muttered Freddie.

"Yes. I think his partners in Bath were unhappy with his payments to them. Did they take your clock in partial payment, Mr. Wells?"

Wells was silent.

"Why should he lack for money to pay them?" asked Archer. "We saw what he had down there!"

They had inspected the machine in Wells's cellar for some time—an elaborate miniature processing plant of tools and dies, crucibles, melting pots, bars of copper, brass, and silver, coal fire, and machinery. It would send Wells to prison for life on its own, the murder charge aside.

"Most counterfeiters are caught," said Lenox, "because they circulate the false coin too freely. I imagine Mr. Wells owed his money in the Queen's true coinage, and perhaps didn't feel like paying. Or perhaps he was frightened to take too much of it to the bank at a time."

"But the third vandalism, Charles?" said Frederick. "The black dog?"

"Mr. Wells? No, you do not wish to speak? Anyhow I feel I can say with some assurance that he murdered Mr. Weston."

"How?" said Freddie.

"Last night Mr. Carmody and I paid a visit to a certain stable in town. He identified the horses he had seen in the clearing, the ones that were intended to make us believe the murderers had come in from out of town. The stable belonged to Mr. Wells.

"And in fact I had my suspicions about the horses in that clearing. It is not a location, in my opinion, that a criminal from beyond Plumbley's borders would know—so much easier to hitch your horse to a post on a country fence that a rich man's steward might check once a week. Those woods are much walked-in by locals, however. Including Mr. Carmody, nearly every night."

"Carmody," said Wells, with a derisive snort. It was the first word he had uttered.

All four men were silent, hoping he would go on.

"Yes?" said Archer at last, but Wells had remembered himself.

"Then there was Carfax," said Lenox.

"The young man at the Royal Oak," said Freddie. "I wondered what you might have asked him."

"What nickname have they taken to calling you, with your carriage and gold watch chain, Mr. Wells? Around Plumbley?"

It was Oates, smacking his head, who offered the answer. "Swells! Of course! How daft have I been!"

Lenox nodded. "Weston used the slang his friends did, writing that coded note. But why murder him, Mr. Wells? Did he see you making a payment? Perhaps you were bringing coins out of the cellar? I know that he had a good vantage of your shop from where he stood, smoking his final cigars."

Oates was pacing now, angry. "Is that what it was, Frank?" he said. "Did my cousin catch you?"

No response was forthcoming.

"I don't understand," Frederick said after a moment. "The vandalism. Why not write him a note? Why go to the trouble of smashing windows?"

"That would introduce all sorts of unnecessary risks," Lenox said. "The handwriting might be matched, the note might fall into the wrong hands, Wells himself might have held it back for blackmail. The vandalisms achieved the same end without the possibility of incriminating the vandals. Or their boss."

"But smashing a window in a small town—that has its own risks," said Frederick.

"Yet they did get the clock, the closest object of value, before they went. If they hadn't made the mistake with Fripp's the town would still have been sluggish."

Oates stood up. "So the vandalism yesterday—the police station . . ."

Lenox nodded. "I was coming to that. I don't think you saw them after all, Mr. Wells, did you? Didn't you break the window with the rock and the helmet yourself? Another diversionary tactic. To try to pin it all on a gang of outsiders. Clever, in an insular village like Plumbley."

"I didn't do it," said Wells. "None of it."

Frederick stood up, then. The room went silent, in anticipation, and as if to prolong this sense he slowly poured a glass of water for himself. Then he offered to pour some for Wells, with a gesture, but the prisoner declined.

"I knew your father well," said Frederick, still standing. "He was a good man."

"Oh?"

"And you have a son, do you not?"

"You know I do," said Wells.

"Is he—what, sixteen?"

"Yes."

Frederick shook his head. "Sad. Very sad."

Wells looked uncertain for the first time. "What?"

"Your father kept the shop in his name and yours, in case he should die, did he not?"

"Yes."

"Have you done the same for your son?"

"What of it?"

"A life sentence in prison, for a boy that age."

The terrible truth seemed to come alive in Well's eyes as they widened. "No!" he said. "The boy had no idea about the dimmicking—had no—Mr. Ponsonby, play it fair with me!"

Frederick shook his head. "Justice demands that the owners of the store that held that machine come to trial, Mr. Wells. You and your son, both of you."

Oates, his face unhappy, said, "Weren't as if you gave Weston a chance to have much longer than sixteen years, either."

Lenox weighed in now. "But Freddie, if Mr. Wells confessed to the murder—you're a magistrate, you might have a word with them."

Frederick took this in, as if the thought hadn't occurred to him. "Yes, that's true," he said. "Mr. Wells? What do you think of buying your son's freedom back?"

There was a brief thrust of defiance in Wells's face, but as he looked at the four men surrounding him—all of them free to return to their hearths now, their happy families, their own children—something gave way.

"Yes, then," he said. "If you're willing to drag a sixteen-year-old boy to prison for it, you can have my confession. I was there when Weston died."

CHAPTER THIRTY-FIVE

Y ou stabbed him?" said Oates.
      "No," said Wells. "That was an Irishman named McCutch-
eon. He came to collect payment from me. We usually met in
Taunton on Market Day, but he was to return my clock to me, too,
and apologize, because I was back on schedule. I hadn't fallen behind, only tried to pay them with some of the dimmicks. I tried to
warn Mr.—I tried to tell my friend in Bath that his people should
never come to Plumbley again, after the vandalisms, but McCutcheon showed up unannounced."

"Who was McCutcheon's boss?" asked Archer, keenly interested.

"It's worth more than my life to tell."

"Your son, Mr. Wells," said Frederick.

Yet here Wells was adamant. Both he and his son—all his extended family—would be at risk, should he divulge that particular
identity.

Archer seemed nevertheless to have some idea of who it might
be, testing out a few names on Wells. None of them drew a reaction.

"And Weston confronted you?" Frederick asked, when this exchange had finished.

"Go back for a moment," said Lenox. "How did McCutcheon arrive in town, if not by horse?"

"He took the train to Forstall"—this was one town over—"and then walked here. He was the one who spotted Weston, watching us."

"Was it his idea to put the horses in the clearing?"

Wells shook his head. "I sent round word to my groom to take the two horses to the clearing, and a few beer bottles, after McCutcheon was so hell-bent on killing the witness. I liked Weston, for myself."

"Liar," spat Oates, full of rage.

"I did."

"You weren't worried that your groom would give you in?" asked Lenox.

"He's loyal," said Wells, shortly.

Frederick elaborated. "Simple is more like it. Joseph Thatcher, he had his head stoved in by his father when he was a lad, and hasn't been the same since."

"I knew Carmody or some-such would find the horses," said Wells.

Archer was taking notes. "And you'll testify against McCutcheon? If it saves you the rope?"

"Why not? But the other one—no, not the boss. My skin wouldn't be worth a counterfeit groat if I did."

This was one of the coins that Wells's machine had produced, worth four pence, along with a shilling—that was worth twelve pence, the most valuable coin he could manufacture—and a ha'pence. These were the most easily replicable, apparently. A sovereign, a pound coin, worth twenty shillings, was too valuable to counterfeit, according to Archer. The penny itself had been counterfeited so often that it had been redesigned, and was more difficult to copy now.

It was now past one in the afternoon, and Wells, looking haggard, asked if he might have some food, or even a word with his wife.

The men all looked at Lenox, who consented to the first request, but not the second. "I will not have her destroying evidence," he said.

"She knows nothing about it," said Wells.

"Oh?" Something in Wells's voice persuaded Lenox that she was not a conspirator. Later he would have to question her.

For now he sent a small boy hanging outside of the station—part of the undiminishing crowd—to the King's Arms, to fetch hot food and beer. Lenox handed him a few coins as payment for the favor, and realized he had almost passed off one of the false ha'pennies. How easy it was!

They ate in one room, Wells in another, and then they returned to interrogate him again, but in truth there was little more to discover. Teams of men from London and Bath had been sent for already, and were no doubt steaming along the rails toward Plumbley, desperate to analyze the contents of the grain merchant's cellar: For both police forces counterfeiting was of primary importance.

The murder was simple, terribly simple. Wells had approached Weston, while McCutcheon waited in the shadows for the young man to turn his back. A cowardly killing, in that regard.

Lenox went on probing, however. "Why did you clear out his pockets? You could not have imagined that he would go unrecognized, if you took his identification."

Wells shrugged. "Greed."

It was Oates who said something—Lenox would have waited until they searched Wells's house—about the weapon that killed his cousin. "What about the knife? What did you do with it?"

"McCutcheon took it," said Wells. "At least as far as I can re-call. Certainly I never handled it myself."

Oates and Lenox exchanged looks, each wondering, perhaps, to what purpose the knife in the slop bucket had been used—and where Captain Musgrave, late of the Tenth Regiment of Foot, might be. Wells couldn't help them, however.

At half past two none of the men had any questions. Archer, the constable from Bath, wanted to take Wells right away, but Wells wanted to stay in Plumbley.

Frederick agreed in principle, but demurred. "I scarcely feel comfortable leaving Mr. Wells with Oates, whose cousin has been murdered by this prisoner."

Oates shook his head slightly. "I respect the system of justice, sir," he said with some self-mastery. "He shall not be in danger under my care."

"I trust Oates not to do me any harm," said Wells, his voice cold, "and should take it as a great kindness to be permitted to stay in town, near my family. Bath is a city I do not know."

Lenox and Archer, then, went to inspect the shop and Wells's house more closely, and Frederick—still holding strong, despite his age, though slightly wan—sat down with the merchant's wife to tell her what had happened. How she told her son and daughter was her own decision, he said.

With that duty discharged he said that he thought he might go back to Everley. "You've solved it, Charles, thank you."

"It never feels quite as triumphant as it ought, does it?" asked Lenox.

The old squire looked at him with a half-smile. "No, it doesn't," he said. "D'you know what's funny, I feel worse knowing than I did not knowing, though I'm glad the danger has passed."

"You've been doing too much. You need rest."

"Yes, it will be a relief to return to my books, my flowers. I think I shall take my tea alone today, if it won't bother you and Jane."

"Never."

Wells's house and his shop were both barren of further clues as to his villainy; from all appearances he was what he claimed to be, a prosperous seller of grain and corn. Only his ledgers—his real ones, which showed a certain recent slackness of business—offered any hint to the contrary. That and the monolithic machine in the basement.

Dallington returned at 4:00 that afternoon, arriving at the police headquarters with Hutchinson and a meek-looking Jack Randall, the man Frederick had fined only a few days before for passing bad coin.

"He'll talk," said Dallington grimly. "It took two hours to chase him down to an apple orchard and another two to get him to say a word. None of the words he said after that were very pleasant, but he's as scared of prison as anyone I've ever met."

Randall's hooded eyes went up when he saw Oates. "Couldn't come arrest me yourself?"

"I was busy arresting Mr. Wells," said Oates. "Coiners, in Plumbley. You should be ashamed, Mr. Randall."

"I don't want to go to prison," he said.

"I'll help you if I can," said Oates. "I've known you long enough, and your family, but you must be honest with us about Wells."

Randall, looking slightly more confident, took a seat opposite Lenox, who had returned from inspecting Wells's house and shop to speak to Archer. The constable from Bath was on the verge of leaving, but, looking at the clock, must have decided to stay until the 4:49 train.

He would have been just as well going; Randall's tale was useful but unexciting. Once every two weeks he was to take fifteen pounds' worth of coins and, through trades and small purchases, return with a minimum of ten pounds for Wells. Any of the false coins he had left over he could keep for himself. That was how he had been caught: His entire payment was in false coins, and naturally he wanted to spend them.

"Did you ever come up short of the ten pounds?" asked Lenox, more out of curiosity than anything.

"No, no. Usually cleared a pound or two for myself, and then I got to spend the other three—musicals, the best seats, ladies . . ."

"Where'd you usually go?"

"Mr. Wells made sure I went to different places—Bath, Salisbury, twice London, each time with thirty pounds . . ."

"That's a great deal of money to spend in one day in London."

"I was there three days. I found coffee shops worked well, put down a pound coin and pick up nineteen shillings and sixpence. Problem is you have to drink a great deal of coffee, then."

"Public houses?"

"They're suspicious of a coin there," said Randall. "As I learned."

"Did it never attract notice when you left Plumbley?"

The farmhand shrugged. "I work day shifts when I like."

Lenox wondered how many such emissaries Wells had sent out into unsuspecting England, how much the man had enriched himself. "Do you know of anyone who did the same?" he asked.

"None such."

"Fontaine?"

"That Frenchie?" said Randall, with the sort of dim-witted confidence that made it seem unlikely he was lying or concealing anything.

CHAPTER THIRTY-SIX

There was a distinguished and (locally) famous lady in Plumbley, who had lived there for many, many years, named Emily Jasper. She had been married when the century was still young to a barrister in Taunton, widowed at thirty, childless, and, betaken herself back to the village of her youth, where her sister and her sister's husband and her sister's seven children became the primary concern of her days. As she was much richer than they were she could take a pretty active hand in their lives, given certain inconsistently timed contributions to their budget, and the children had been schooled at her expense, while her brother-in-law, a painter of great talent and little enterprise, had been made to show the world his work, in London. Though it had brought him a small measure of fame he did not thank her for the headache it gave him—which was a gratifying state of affairs to Mrs. Jasper, because it made her both correct and inconvenient. She still wore black crepe.

Now ninety years old, she lived in the finest house on what villagers called the Hill. With her lived a niece named Lucy, who was certainly past thirty-five and had never married—but who, rather surprisingly, had a sweet and lovely temperament, a great deal of patience, in fact, true love for her aunt, and a talent at the piano that Lenox remembered vividly. The result of that schooling, perhaps.

It was Emily Jasper who was to be the guest of honor at the dinner party that evening—the trumped-up dinner party Lady Jane had devised. When Lenox arrived home, just after seeing Archer onto the train back to Bath, he recalled for the first time that day that the house had committed itself to such an event. He groaned.

"It's hardly an auspicious time for it," he said, "just when we—"

Lady Jane, away from her desk for once, came and kissed him on the cheek, one earring in, the other held between her middle finger and her thumb. "I heard, the maid told me! Congratulations, Charles. That evil Wells, would you believe it?"

"This dinner—"

"Does my hair look passable?"

"Lovely. But I say—"

"Dr. Eastwood will be here. And we have Mr. Marsham coming, too, of course."

This was the vicar. "Nash had better lock the wine cupboard."

"Charles!" she said, not at all scandalized. "Anyhow Miss Taylor is dressing. She even asked me what I thought of a gray dress, which I consider a positive sign, given that I usually skulk around her in fear."

"Oh, she's not so bad," said Lenox. "Did you approve the gray?"

Lady Jane smiled. "I recommended something more vividly colored, if she had it. Charles, could you see her with young John?"

"Enough of that, please. Where is Kirk? I need my shirt pressed."

They prepared for the party together, in the comfortable rhythm of a couple that by now had done so together many times. Lenox told her about Wells and the coining machine.

"Your uncle must be relieved."

"He is primarily exhausted, I think. His strength is not what it once was."

Jane stopped what she was doing. "Perhaps it's not a bad idea, him moving into the village. A smaller house."

"How can you say that?" he asked. "It would be such a loss—for the village, for you, for me, for Sophia. Not to have Freddie in Everley?"

"You did not say that it would be a loss for him."

"Of course it would be!" he said, his voice rising with anger.

"You have the luxury of coming here when you like. He must manage a great estate all on his own, year-round. I can understand why he might want to leave that responsibility to his nephew."

Now Lenox became positively vexed and she, usually so good-natured, said a word or two back to him—and the result was that when they finally went downstairs to the guests, they were thoroughly fallen out with each other. It happened rarely enough, though they had been married several years now. Still, Lenox remembered with a sort of resigned dread, this sort of argument often lasted a day or two when it finally arrived.

Dallington, despite his exertions of the day, seemed fresh; by contrast Frederick looked squinty and out of all sorts, and when he was addressed responded only with a few short words, occasionally even with silence. He needed a good night's sleep, thought Lenox, and then perhaps a day or two of quiet recreation in his small study, with his books, his manuscript, his telescope, his evening wine. His routine.

For her part, Miss Taylor had dressed up very finely indeed. When she came into the drawing room the three men stood and bowed, all, to one degree or another, dazzled by the transformation that had come to her face simply from loosening her rather severe plaits of hair. She looked pretty now, less ascetic, softer. Her dress was a vibrant blue color, and cut slightly lower than they might have been used to in Somerset, though it would have been modest for London. She smiled graciously when Dallington offered her a glass of champagne.

The conversation at dinner was not, it must be observed in the hopes of maintaining the strictest honesty, very sparkling. Still, Lenox was genuinely glad to see Lucy—he had known her in other years—and sat next to her, laughing softly with her throughout dinner about the people in town that he had met and re-met in the past few days: Carmody, Fripp, the women on the church steps. Mr. Marsham told Dr. Eastwood a few hoary anecdotes from his days at Clare and Emily Jasper was content to be kept company by Lady Jane, being something of a snob. This left Dallington and the governess to talk, with occasional, now more spirited interjections from Freddie, who had recovered something of his color with a glass of wine.

Inevitably conversation turned general, however, when Wells's name arose. Dr. Eastwood said, his face grave, that he thought it was a very bad thing for Plumbley, whose name now would be bandied around the county, possibly even the country. "Such associations tend to linger," he said.

"I am an old woman," said Emily Jasper—a statement that it would have been impossible to contradict—"but I cannot see why he was not apprehended sooner."

"He was concealing his activities, Aunt Emily," said Lucy, voice gentle. "I think it was very clever of Mr. Oates, Mr. Ponsonby, and Mr. Lenox to catch him."

"Hm! I like that. Did he think of us at all?"

"I doubt it, ma'am," said Dr. Eastwood, and Lucy laughed.

By the time dessert was being served Lenox had to stifle a yawn every thirty seconds or thereabouts. Coffee perked him up, however, and when the men withdrew to smoke, he was alert enough to pull Dr. Eastwood to the side.

Lenox glanced over at Dallington, Marsham, and Frederick, who were discussing cigars, though the young detective, with his usual keenness of perception, plainly had an ear bent toward this conversation. "Did you receive the parcel I sent you this morning?"

"I did. I didn't mention it before supper because you've caught—"

"I'm still very much curious."

"Unfortunately I cannot say what the powder is. I have a friend in Liverpool, from my days at St. Bart's, who might be able to help. I can tell you it is nothing in the ordinary way, not flour, not sugar, not arrowroot. I did one or two basic catalytic reactions to determine that much."

"Could it be poison?"

"Yes, I suppose it could. Would you like me to send it to Liverpool?"

"Thank you, no, I have a friend in London who is already looking into it."

"Please tell me what he finds."

"I shall, of course," said Lenox.

The men and women reassembled soon therafter and heard Lucy play, ate walnuts and apples from a silver tray, and drank port. At eleven, finally—too early for some, including the indomitable Emily Jasper, too late for others, including Lenox, whose entire determination it took to keep his eyes open—the party broke up.

It had been another surpassingly long day, and Lenox felt he might sleep without any trouble until the same time the next evening. He gave word that he didn't need to be awakened at any particular hour.

Soon he and his wife were alone in their room again, and he could let himself give way to exhaustion. He loosened his tie and slumped into a soft armchair by their window.

Throughout the evening Jane had been affectionate with him,

but now, alone again, she was silent, undoing her hair and removing her jewelry.

He granted her the right to silence, not doubting that he had been too harsh in his speech before supper.

At least he spoke, trying to make her smile by teasing her. "I would not call it your most successful party." She didn't respond, and so after another moment he added, "But did you see Dallington speak to Miss Taylor?"

Here was bait she could not help taking, though she knew it was offered for precisely that reason. "They were barely apart for the last hour of the evening," she said. "So there, Charles Lenox."

"Freddie was on the couch with them, dear."

"Mark my words, it will be the making of him, to marry that young woman. She has a great spirit."

"There we agree."

They were quiet again for five or ten minutes after this, Lenox at his desk very casually looking over his speech, Lady Jane finishing a letter to her brother, in Sussex, that she intended to send in the morning. Yet their interchange had left them feeling more inclined to softness with each other, and when Lenox apologized she circled his neck with her arms and said that she, too, was sorry—and so they made it up.

CHAPTER THIRTY-SEVEN

"You hear of the calm that comes before the storm," said Frederick Ponsonby two mornings later, "but I find I much prefer the calm that comes afterward."

"Alas, the storm usually causes enough damage to make the aftermath unhappy," said Lenox.

"Yes, you're right of course—poor Weston."

They were sipping coffee at a small wrought-iron table on the veranda outside the library. It was the warmest day since Lenox had arrived in Plumbley, brilliant with golden sunlight, though it was still before eight o'clock in the morning. Off a quarter mile into the gardens they could see Lady Jane, Sophia, and Miss Taylor walking, the dogs barking them to order when they slowed.

The men did not wear their customary clothes—Ponsonby his quiet gray flannel and subdued cravats or Lenox his more metropolitan dark suits and ties—but instead were dressed identically in whites, ironed white pants, white sweaters, and snub-nosed white caps. The day was ideal for cricket.

"It seems somehow more and less tragic at once, that he has no close family," said Lenox.

"There is Oates."

"Yes, there is Oates. Who knows what condition he is in, however," said Lenox.

The constable had been drinking heavily in the King's Arms the past few nights, according to the gossip that had worked its way up from the servants' quarters. True to his word, however, Wells, in the Plumbley jail, remained unharmed. Oates and a series of reliable townsmen took shifts watching the prisoner, always in pairs.

"Oates will have himself dried out by the time of the funeral," said Frederick.

This was to be the next afternoon. "I hope so, certainly."

In fact the murder seemed already as if it had happened a long time before. The past few days had been wonderfully peaceable, the kind Lenox had looked for when he decided to visit his cousin. Freddie had retired to his study for the whole period, other than meal times, and looked better for it, while Jane, in between stretches at her desk, was helping to plan the refreshments they would have at the cricket. For his part Lenox rode out upon horseback at nine in the morning and at three in the afternoon, and otherwise worked with steady application at his speech, which was all but drafted now. He was proud of it. As he had written to his brother in a letter that morning:

I imagined that what I needed to focus on the writing of the speech was time away from London, in the country. In fact what I needed was this case—the matter of the coining you have no doubt read about in the papers—to free my mind from the task at hand. It has worked beautifully. My hope is that this speech shall shame the other side into doing something for the poor—something more. It is past time.

The case had, as Lenox learned almost immediately, made the London papers. In general he preferred to keep his name away from the investigations in which he participated, retaining, as he did, some sensitivity to the sneers of those members of his caste who believed his work was beneath his station—it was this that drove him to privacy, and not, as he would have preferred in himself, modesty.

Nevertheless it was sometimes impossible to keep his name out of things. There had been a raft of telegrams congratulating him on his role in the case's solution, including one from his friend Inspector Thomas Jenkins at Scotland Yard, who was chasing a criminal in the gin bars of Brussels (and drinking a fair bit of the stuff himself in the process, from the sound of it) but took time to write; another from the head of the Royal Mint; and several from colleagues in Parliament, all of whom managed a joking reference to his speech. No doubt they thought he had been neglecting his duties. On that count, however, his conscience was entirely clear. The speech was in excellent fettle.

A team of men from Scotland Yard was, even now, dissecting the great coining machine that Wells had stored in his cellar. Apparently it was of an uncommon type, producing the kind of fraudulent coins that tended to pop up in the western part of England, which led them to believe that a great deal of coining was centered in Bath—peculiar, given that town's affluent reputation. There was a fresh excitement and endeavor to their efforts: here was a new lead, a chance at halting the production of hundreds of thousands of pounds of illegal money. They were mildly grateful to Lenox; he had solved the murder, and discovered the coining only incidentally, and for these men, who had something of the air of obsessives, the latter was a more serious crime.

The only loose end the case had left, as far as Lenox could discern, was Musgrave's behavior. There had been no report of him in Bath, which meant that he must have switched roads in the miles of road between that city and Plumbley, but why had he left? Why had his new wife been so decidedly homebound since their wedding? Lenox hoped McConnell might provide the glimmer of an answer, if he could identify the powder that had been marked as Mrs. Musgrave's "sugar." The doctor had written in a telegram that he hoped to have some idea in a day or two, not longer.

As they sat on the veranda the men did not discuss any of this, however. They talked instead of the cricket, and then of old matches they had played in, many years before, when Lenox was a school-boy permitted to stand in the field for the last few overs, never to bat. By the time he reached the age of sixteen he was the Royal Oak's second to last batsman (both men always played for that side, for reasons lost to history), desperate to overcome the invincible King's Arms side. The KA, as they were called, had then boasted a blacksmith named Millington—dead now, kicked by a horse he was shoeing—who had seemed like Hercules himself, back in the fifties. It wasn't until Lenox was past twenty-two that he saw Mill-ington go out for less than a half-century.

"Have you played at all recently?" said Lenox.

"Not for five years. In honor of your return, however, I may let them stick me at the end of the queue to bat. I expect the game will have been called for dark well before then. Hopefully, that is."

Lenox smiled. "Have you got the same bat?"

"Oh, yes, though she's a bit yellow now." Freddie's bat was made of an old Everley willow tree that had been struck dead by light-ning. He had made it himself, many years into the distant past.

"I'd have brought mine," said Lenox, "though it was only store bought."

"Fripp will have you sorted."

Lady Jane was wandering in their general direction now, and waved at them, her soft smile visible even from a few hundred yards.

Lenox felt a flash of love for her. He stood and started toward her, to say they ought to leave soon.

Indeed by half-eight they were at the cricket pitch, an enormous expanse of closely shorn meadow just beyond Musgrave's house on Church Lane. (Dallington had been spared, there being enough players for both teams, and was left behind at Everley.) It was an absolute carnival already when they arrived, though the match wouldn't begin for another half an hour; there were men in their whites striding everywhere, calling out hearty taunts in each other's direction, and women congregated around a white pavilion, cloth-topped and erected the week before. Jane went in that direction, greeting Mrs. Richards, the wife of the local butcher, as an old friend and enquiring as to the state of the tea, which was being brewed in frantically large quantities, by quite what method nobody could entirely agree—tea being a substance that provoked sharp and definite opinions in nearly every person present. Off in the distance four men shifted a sunscreen, white and as tall as a two-story building, so that the batsmen of the morning hours should be able to see.

Nominally the captain of the Royal Oak side was a man named Symes, who owned the public house. He was an ill-natured fat person, generous, and above all desperately and misguidedly in love with new technology. His most recent acquisition—which he rode with quiet dignity around Plumbley, despite near universal derision—was a penny-farthing. This was a kind of bicycle with an enormous front wheel and a small back one, in proportion roughly the same as a penny and a farthing sitting side by side upon a table.

Symes had an ugly cut on his forehead.

"The high-wheeler?" said Frederick sympathetically. "Well, well. You can only improve at it."

Symes scowled. "It is very difficult to mount, Mr. Ponsonby, but once the position upon the front wheel is ascended, is achieved, it is a marvelous—I assure you a very marvelment of—well, yes. I don't like to hear a word against the machine, myself. That is my own prejudice I grant you."

Even Symes, who ran a pretty rigorously decorous public house, could not commandeer Fripp: here the fruit-and-vegetable man was absolutely and entirely in his element. He walked off the boundaries, double-checking them, with the captain of the King's Arms, Millington Junior, the town's new blacksmith, whom Lenox had never seen—the dead spit of his father, though perhaps even larger in the arms. Fripp, wiry and brown as a nut, looked miniature next to his opposite number, but he exuded a kind of calm authority that made the mismatch seem, obscurely, to lie in favor of the Royal Oak; even the tea debate subsided when he went round the pavilion to check that all was in order for the midday break.

After that errand was complete he returned to his team and spotted Lenox. "Charles," he said, with a tight smile.

"Mr. Fripp. Are you—"

Just then the umpires arrived, gentlemen imported at some expense from Taunton, and the cricket ground went silent, somber. Fripp and Millington hurried toward them. The Royal Oak side said good-bye to their wives and their children and assembled at their benches, many of the men nodding deferentially—perhaps uncomfortably—at the two aristocrats in their midst.

"Are we taking anyone's places?" asked Lenox of his cousin, swinging a bat to loosen his shoulders.

Frederick said, "No, Tolbert took a bad leg, Walcott inherited a piece of land in Devon, and someone else—oh, yes, Crockington is in London, for who-knows-why. I wouldn't have played myself, if we didn't need a final batsman. Fripp made me swear up and down or I should be in my gardens, now." He nodded toward the coster-monger, who was arguing vehemently about the state of the wicket. "I hope nothing is riding on my innings, either," Freddie said. "Fripp looks liable to give someone a hiding."

CHAPTER THIRTY-EIGHT

The Royal Oak won the coin toss—Lenox wondered in passing whether it was truly one of her Majesty's ha'pennies that the umpire flung into the air—and Fripp, in consultation with Symes and a beefy farmer named Truelove, elected for his side to take the field first. So much in cricket depended on the patch of grass between the two boxes where the complementary batsman stood, and Fripp claimed it would be more favorable as the day warmed, that the bowls in the afternoon would come in harder but truer, with less spin. Besides, everyone knew the KA was a shabby place and if they didn't show Millington and Apswell that the Royal Oak was superior they should be ashamed of themselves, properly and heartily ashamed. Oh, and welcome to Mr. Lenox, the member of Parliament.

The squad cheered their assent to this rather lamely concluded motivational speech as if it had been delivered by Leonidas upon the brow of Thermopylae, and Millington Junior in fact Xerxes Junior: Fripp's passion was so evident that his words were secondary to his purpose.

Lenox took his place rather shy of the boundary on the covering side, shielding his eyes against the sun. He watched their bowler—Fripp's cousin Thorpe—toss a few lazy practice balls. A new cherry! How long had it been since he had seen that brilliant red, soon to be dulled by bats and dirt!

In cricket, of course, an out is a rare thing—hours may pass between them—and the goal of the batsman is simply to stay alive, often unspectacularly. The batsmen of the King's Arms were steady and merciless. Lenox came to loathe their opening batsman in particular, who stroked short, sharp balls in every direction, none of them ever coming within five feet of the outstretched arms of a Royal Oak man. At last the KA lad made out on a spectacular curve of the ball from the bowler, Thorpe—Fripp's shout of glee might have been heard in three counties, and all the men crowded around to congratulate him.

The next batsman was equally consistent, only once hitting the boundary rope on the bounce—for a four—and never hitting it over the rope altogether for a six, but stringing together one run, one run, two runs, one run, until the score began to mount.

So the morning wore on. The Royal Oak changed bowlers from time to time, switching over from Thorpe's wicked spin to the straight, hard bowling of a groomsman with an enormous mustache called Gibbs.

Though it seemed as if it would take years for their ten to go out, gradually the men of the King's Arms fell. One, standing stockstill, had his wicket nicked by Gibbs, another was caught out by Fripp, and Lenox, too, made one sharpish catch, one-handed and with his body fully elongated, so that he landed painfully on his ribs. That was for the seventh out, and he felt a flush of joy—perhaps the purest joy he could recall—as it was his turn to be crowded about and receive the plaudits of the team, even Symes, his wound flaring under the sunlight, grinning like a baboon.

Then, just after noon, it ended very rapidly. In ten minutes two King's Arms batsmen were dismissed—one stumped, one bowled—after many of their compatriots had each batted for well over an hour.

Frederick, who had taken a shaded and obscure spot and seen nothing of the cherry as he fielded, waved to Lenox. "What are they out for?" he called.

The two men converged near the wicket, and walked toward the side of the field together, after congratulating their teammates. "Two hundred seventy-seven," said Lenox.

"Rather steep."

"We shall have our chance to respond," said Lenox. The Royal Oak's ten would bat now, until they were out or the sun fell.

Frederick looked doubtful, and it was true that twenty-eight runs per batsman was a high number. If one or two of them went out for a two or three—or even a duck, a turn at bat with no runs—then that number could rise quickly, too, demanding thirty runs from each remaining batsman, thirty-five.

Fripp was having none of it. Just as his dourness before the match had brought the men's lazy cheer—a day of cricket!—into line, now, when they were feeling somewhat downtrodden, he was all high spirits, we shall get at 'em, the pints tonight shall taste sweet (the victors by tradition receiving theirs from the purses of the losers), have your tea and then prepare yourself to bat as you've never batted.

He sidled up to Lenox just as the detective was setting out toward the pavilion. "You shall bat fourth," he said.

"Are you sure?" asked Lenox.

"I remember how excellent you were with a stick, my boy."

"And Freddie?"

Fripp shook his head. "Won't bat anywhere but last. We shall have gotten to three hundred before then, anyhow! Go on, find your wife. Good catch, though, Charles—I thought for sure it was going for a four, and just when they had all the momentum! That saved us."

Lenox, pleased as a schoolboy, found his wife. "Did you see my catch?" he asked.

"I did, and I must say I thought you should have run faster, so you didn't have to dive."

"I—"

"And you've gotten your sweater covered in dirt!"

"But Jane—" Then he realized, from a slight slyness in her eyes, that she was teasing him. "You're rotten," he said.

She laughed and squeezed his hand. "It was well done."

People tucked into their tea now—tea being an appellation in this instance not confined to that brew alone but encompassing cold beef, jam sandwiches, scones, pressed apple cider, toast with marmalade, suet pudding, cold fish pie, and cakes of every imaginable flavor and quality (some of which were of the same general edibility as one of the cricket bats). Lenox and Frederick split themselves, almost as if by silent consent, among their teammates, Lenox congratulating Thorpe and meeting his pretty young wife, Frederick making the rounds.

Just before the Royal Oak was to come to bat they rejoined. "Thank goodness the fielding bit is over," said Frederick.

"No, you never liked it."

"Terrible bore. Look, Symes is going up to bat. I do hope he shall stay up for a while, chip away at their number."

Symes, however, almost immediately struck a lofted, harmless ball, which landed with a feathered *thwock* in the hands of a King's Armer. A groan went up from the boys who were supporting the Oak. Symes looked furious.

When the next batsman up, a farmer called Winton, went out after only eight runs, things began to feel hopeless. Lenox, who was next after Fripp, felt his heart thud: they were going to lose! He hadn't even thought about the possibility until now. But here Fripp came into his own. With Thorpe managing to stay alive across from him (for two men always batted at once), Fripp offered the spectators ranged along the boundaries, in their chairs, a clinic on batting. He might have been old but his body was still obeying his commands—he sprayed the brilliant red ball, so striking against the blue sky, the brown woods, the green field, in every direction, a two, another two, and then, to thunderous applause, two consecutive sixes. The King's Arms changed bowlers to no avail: a four, a four, a one, a two, a one. Even in the force and anger of his batting he seemed strangely still, as alert as a hunting animal.

When he finally went out, bowled, it was for a score of seventy-three. As one, the men and women around the field, irrespective of their public house allegiance, stood and cheered.

Now Lenox was to come on.

The bowler was Millington Junior, who, despite his size, was a spin bowler. Lenox preferred that style, actually. He walked to his spot slowly, sizing up the light, tentatively loosening his wrists with the bat. He watched the first ball sail high. The second he cut cleanly, and though it didn't go far it was a pleasure to feel it come off his bat. He realized that he could do this—that the old, cultivated skill still lingered somewhere in his arms.

In fact he fetched Millington's third ball a tremendous wallop. *That will go for a four, easily,* was his first thought, when he realized, with a sense of dismay, that the KA's annoying batsman, who had refused to go out, was sprinting pell-mell toward the boundary. At the last moment he dived.

And caught it. An enormous cheer gusted up from the crowd; it had been a spectacular catch. Lenox felt his chest go hollow. He looked up and saw Jane, whose mouth was pursed up in sympathy and sorrow. The walk back to his bench was the longest he had ever taken.

"Hard luck," said Fripp, straining to be understanding. "Very hard luck."

"No, I should have played for safety. Foolish grandstanding of me," said Lenox.

"Never mind it," said Frederick, and if he hadn't been the squire the looks of disapproval at this casual attitude would have been sharper.

Lenox felt cruelly disappointed. The odds had lengthened against them again. He and Symes had both done badly, very badly. The next batsmen worked hard, getting out for twenty-six and thirty-one, but that great number, two seventy-seven, seemed far away still. They had barely cleared two hundred runs, and it was getting on toward dark.

Soon the eighth batsman had gone up, and despite a couple of booming sixes, been retired relatively quickly. Lenox, somewhat recovered, looked at his uncle, who was deep in conversation with the curate, fifteen paces off.

"Freddie!" he called out.

"Oh, dear," said the squire, after he had turned and assessed the situation. "I suppose I had better go up, Mr. Lanchester."

The team cheered him, dutifully, but there was a feeling of defeat along the bench. Frederick walked toward the box, plump and unhurried, waved a friendly hand at Millington, stood, waiting for the ball—and when it came immediately and with great authority cracked it wide and right, for two fast runs.

This drew a murmur of surprise in the crowd, and from opposite ends of their bench, Fripp and Lenox caught each other's eyes and smiled; they knew, or at least had suspected, for age's ravages are unpredictable, something that the others didn't, that perhaps only a few of the older men and women in the crowds could recall.

It was this: that Freddie with a bat in his hand was a man reborn. He grew taller, surer. Lenox had to admit that his swing was slightly different—now the squire had a way of curving the arc of his bat around his paunch that was unlike his old batting style, but it was just as graceful, just as effective. He smacked ball after ball for a run, two runs, a run, rarely hitting one for four or six but never, ever looking in danger of getting out, either.

In fact, once he had swung a second time, proving that his first attempt was not a fluke, the outcome of the match never seemed in doubt. The men of the King's Arms tried to gee each other up, shouting encouragement, telling the bowler that it was an easy one, but even to them it was as plain as day: Freddie wasn't going to make an out anytime soon. Twenty minutes later, the light still not quite faded, his face red but grinning, he stroked a calm single, and had posted the forty-four runs—"the famous forty-four," as Fripp and his friends at the pub would come to call them—that the Royal Oak needed to win.

CHAPTER THIRTY-NINE

W hen do you imagine we shall return to London?" asked
Lady Jane, late that evening.

"It has been on my mind, too," said Lenox. "The speech is a week
from today and I still need Graham to read it, as useful as the notes
you gave me were."

He was exhausted. The celebrations at the Royal Oak—
attendance mandatory, Fripp insisted—would go on all night, but
for he and Freddie an hour there, after a long day in the sun, had
been enough to drive them home, amid good-spirited jesting about
their lack of vigor. Freddie, of course, had been the real hero of the
hour. The men of the King's Arms had lined up to shake his hand
after the match. The blacksmith had offered him a pint at a time of
his choosing, which Freddie, whose loyalty to the Oak was strong
only in matters of cricket, generously suggested that they might
take at the KA. There had been more tea, more sandwiches, after
that, in the pavilion. Only Lady Jane remembered Lenox's failure,
squeezing his arm and smiling when she saw him.

"For my part, I could stay a while longer," she said. "Sophia rather enjoys it."

"I'll send a telegram to my brother in the morning and ask when he thinks I should return. It needs at least three or four days of preparation, the speech. I shall have to run it by one or two of the ministers."

"Must you?"

"Can't be avoided," he said.

"Mm," she said. She was sewing something or other.

He was sitting by the window, warm in his quilted red evening jacket, smoking and gazing out at Everley's gardens under the moonlight. His eyes felt pleasantly heavy, his skin pleasantly warm. Parliament seemed a very long way off; though metropolitan to his bones, he understood at least to some degree why his brother always felt vexed at being in the city, away from Sussex and Lenox House.

"Perhaps a few more nights," he said. "They cannot positively expect me before the Monday. And then I am curious to see Wells one last time."

"And the funeral tomorrow."

"Yes," said Lenox.

In the morning he was dreadfully stiff in his arms and legs from his few exertions, and realized that it was a piece of luck that he had been caught out so quickly. He dressed himself gingerly.

The funeral was at St. Stephen's, which was jammed with townspeople. Frederick had a pew, but he had given it over to Weston's closest cousins, so that they might be near the front. All of the Somerset superstitions were in place: the clocks had been stopped at two o'clock, as close as possible to the time when Weston had died as they could guess; there were boxwood wreaths and candles lining the walls of the church; and along the pews were laid funeral cakes, wrapped in butcher's paper and sealed with black wax.

As they were finding their seats, Lenox said to Lady Jane, "Did you know they consider it bad luck, in Plumbley, to wear anything new to a funeral? Hats in particular. Funny."

"Of course, in Sussex they think that everything means you're about to die—an owl in the daytime, the smell of roses when there aren't roses nearby, the wrong fold in clean linen."

He smiled. "I had forgotten one or two of those."

The vicar Marsham gave young Weston an admirable eulogy, and it was Oates who stood by the door afterward, dressed in black and with a black armband, shaking the hands of people who left— walking out, in fact, to the very green where Weston had met his murderer. At the graveyard just by the church door was an open rectangle of earth, tidily excavated.

As the casket came out of the church (feet forward, always) it began gently to rain. There was a murmur of happiness among the guests at that: For it was thought to mean that Weston was in heaven, as promising an omen as rain on a wedding day.

When the funeral was over Lenox shook Oates's hand, met Weston's aunts and cousins, and then, with Frederick, Dallington, and Jane—Sophia and Miss Taylor having stayed at home, of course—said good-bye and returned to Everley.

That afternoon he sat in the great library, poring over his speech, slicing apart certain paragraphs to see where they were soft, tightening, tightening. After a few hours he stood up, suddenly sick of seeing these particular words in this particular order. It was a sure sign that he needed a fresh set of eyes.

The teatime post brought two letters to divert him.

The first was from Edmund, and had anticipated his telegram of that morning. It filled him in on the news from London, and added that Lenox had better come back Sunday evening or Monday morning, both to meet with the cabinet ministers who would like to check that the speech gave no ammunition to the other side, and—though it was unfortunate—to be seen in London. A retreat was one thing, invisibility another.

Still, that gave them three nights more in Everley. At tea he mentioned as much to Frederick, who had spent the past hours showing the governess his flowers between spells of rain. Both of them were full of chatter about what they had seen—apparently there was a budding yew tree they both found especially fine—but Frederick was brought up short by Lenox's news.

"I had hoped you might stay longer," he said.

"We shall return soon."

"I've no doubt of it," said the squire stoutly. "Come any time."

His expression troubled Lenox.

After they took their tea Lenox motioned to Dallington. "Come through to the library. I've a letter from Thomas, you can hear the news if you don't mind watching me read."

"With pleasure. Did I mention, by the way, that I had word from Bath just before tea?"

They were walking along a dim corridor now, oak-walled and lined with paintings. "No. What's happened?"

"Fontaine admitted that he worked for Wells. Apparently he did the same as Randall, but he was given much more than usual on the day he had his spree. Wells needed the money and didn't care about the potential for exposure, I suppose."

"To pay off his connection in Bath," said Lenox.

"Yes. At any rate Fontaine will testify against Wells, too."

"I mean to go see Wells himself in the morning, if you'd like to come."

"Of course."

They reached the library and went to sit in front of the fire.

Lenox read the letter, throwing out the pertinent bits of information as he came across them. It said:

Dear Charles,

Thank you for two very interesting problems. The powder was the trickier of the two. I shall come to that in a moment.

As you suspected the only fingerprints on the knife belonged to Constable Oates, who of course picked it up. They matched the second set of sample fingerprints you enclosed, which I believed to be his, though you didn't mark them. (Sloppy science, Charles.) The more interesting discovery: The blood on the knife is human, not animal blood. I think it not much older than the parcel you sent me, certainly not more than a week or two.

Now the powder. It took a great deal of work in the laboratory on the second floor—and a fair few bangs, which made me glad Toto and George are out of the city—to determine that it is a common enough compound of magnesium, calcium, and arrowroot, a mixture that some doctors prescribe during difficult pregnancies. (Its medical value is doubtful—it may perhaps be what the Romans called a "placebo," that is, "I will please.")

Has it occurred to you that Musgrave's wife may simply be in her lying-in period?

Let me know if I can be of any further assistance—I can put anything else aside, needless to say, should you need my help as your friend,

   Thomas McConnell

PS: I should add of course that I send my best along to Jane and to Sophia. As I mention, Toto and the child are out of town, and have been for rather a long time. Perhaps Jane told you. I trust that John Dallington is not too badly off. Give him my best if he's stayed in Somerset, otherwise I shall see him soon. TM.

CHAPTER FORTY

For a moment McConnell's postscript diverted Lenox's attention. He re-read but found that it was impossible to discern whether Toto's absence from London was innocent or not, because in the earlier years of their marriage, when the doctor had been drinking heavily, their separations were so frequent and long. Certainly things had been better in more recent times. McConnell had finally come to terms with giving up his practice, as Toto's more aristocratic family had essentially forced him to do, and in place of that work had gone deeper and deeper into his chemical and botanical studies. Yet Jane and Charles alike always feared a relapse on the part of either of their friends—in McConnell his drinking and sullenness, in Toto her immaturity and wrath.

Dallington snapped him out of these thoughts. "So Mrs. Musgrave is with child," he said. "Is that all it was?"

Lenox grimaced. "I feel very stupid. Also rather ashamed, if they left Plumbley because of her health. I imagine they have gone to London."

"How long ago were they married?"

"Six months, I believe. We might ask Freddie."

"Of course a woman might lie abed her whole term," said Dallington, rather uncomfortably.

"Yes, and what a terrible intrusion it must have seemed, when I asked why she cried out that way! A town can always convince you to abandon your reason, if you listen to enough of its gossip. I should have been more intelligent than to listen."

Dallington waved this away. "No, Musgrave was our chief suspect. It would have been irresponsible not to ask. At any rate, a knife with human blood upon it!"

"Yes. But might it not be her blood?"

"What, his wife's? You think her dead?"

"No, no. I mean, might it not be . . . but here you lose me," said Lenox. "I don't know what doctors do at all."

"They possess their own knives, certainly."

"Yes, you're right."

Dallington frowned. "We could ask Dr. Eastwood. Or write to McConnell. If there's any chance it was required for medical reasons one of them would know, in all likelihood."

"You're thinking more clearly than I am, John—that is what we shall do. Of course there is no proof that Captain Musgrave ever held the knife in his hand, much less used it."

Dallington nodded. "Your finding it in the slop bucket makes me think that somebody in the kitchen cut themselves and disposed of the knife there, fearing they had damaged it."

Lenox gave him a skeptical look. "Rather than rinsing it? I don't think the common sense of the average servant is so shallow as that. Perhaps if it was a young boy."

"How heavy was the blood?"

"There was a great deal of it, more than a small cut would have produced—though obviously not, of necessity, a fatal amount. No, let us leave the knife aside until the morrow, when we speak to Wells."

"As you please."

The next morning Lenox rode out across the countryside and again returned to the squire's excellent breakfast table, sharing eggs, bacon, toast, porridge and coffee with Lady Jane—and with the governess, whom even Lenox was force to admit had a new shine in her face. Perhaps the matchmaking had worked.

If Dallington was similarly affected he took care not to show it. "Are you ready to go to town?" he asked, resplendent in a gray morning suit, carnation in his buttonhole, as soon as he saw Lenox.

"Shall we walk? It's not much above a mile."

So they took the dogs and ambled toward Plumbley. When they reached the village green they dropped Bear and Rabbit in Fripp's shop. (Fripp, all his cricket-pitch glory shed, was deep in conversation with a woman who wanted to know which kind of apples made the best sauce, because her neighbor's Cox's Orange Pippins were too tart, and she liked it sweeter anyhow.) At the police station a sober Oates nodded them into the door.

"Gentlemen. Want a word with Wells, do you? He won't speak to me."

"Have you been trying often?" asked Dallington.

"Once in a way."

Wells had been kept so far in some comfort, was eating food brought from his home, had seen his wife and his son. He was to be transported to Bath the next day, because the evidence of his crimes originating there had become so incontrovertible that higher authorities than Frederick were demanding it.

As he sat in his cell, Wells must have heard the chimes of the church bells after Weston's funeral—nineteen of them, one for each year of the lad's life. Lenox wondered how he had felt.

His first impression when he saw Wells again was of how youthful the man looked. In his element, at the grain shop—green apron, black mustache, healthy, ruddy face—he had seemed somehow older. Here he looked a diminished soul. Lenox felt unbidden sympathy for him.

They had expected him not to respond to their questions, but in fact when Oates left them in the windowless room where they had interviewed Wells before, he spoke first.

"Who won the cricket?" he asked.

"The Oak."

"Did they? That'll wipe Millington's eye," said Wells with satisfaction.

Dallington raised his eyebrows. "I'm amazed you care, at such a juncture."

"Being in prison? I knew the risks."

"Why did you do it?" asked Lenox

Wells shrugged. "I didn't want to live out my life looking for farthings that had slipped down between the floorboards, like my father. It's no easy life, being a grain merchant. The big boys in London are after your customers, the marketplaces, people will go to Bath and Taunton. It was a losing proposition."

"We have a few questions."

"All right."

"Where is the knife that killed Weston?"

"With the man who killed him, I expect. Or tossed into a ditch nearby."

"It would not be in Captain Musgrave's house, I suppose?" said Lenox.

Wells narrowed his eyes, genuine bemusement on his face. "Why would it be there?"

"Musgrave was not your compatriot in all this?"

Wells laughed. "I know you heard about his getting angry with me for saying hello to Cat Scales—Catherine Musgrave, she must be now—because you asked. No, we wasn't compatriots, as you say."

"Randall and Fontaine worked for you," Dallington said. "Who else?"

Wells clammed up. "Nobody."

"How much coin could you produce in a month?" asked Lenox. It was a question to which the boys from London were eager to know the answer. They had run the machine but feared pressing it too hard, lest it break.

"Don't know. Made them as fast as I could."

Lenox decided he would leave the technical questions about the casting, the tools and dies, to other men. "Who sold you the machine?" he asked.

Wells laughed out loud. "A man with a hat," he said.

"Come, Wells, tell us and the judge may be lenient with you."

"It's not worth my skin, I told you already. I want Bessie and the boy to lead long lives, gentlemen."

The remaining few questions they asked took them down no new path. With a sigh they shook Wells's hand—who offered it quite generously—and left.

"We have our man, anyhow," Dallington said to Lenox after they had bidden Oates farewell.

It was a certainty—a peace of mind—that Lenox would wish he still had not long afterward.

CHAPTER FORTY-ONE

His realization came when he was asleep. He woke with a wrench, heart thudding, mind slow and fast at once. In the blind night he could not yet understand what. He stood up, poured himself a glass of water, and tried to collect his wits, waiting for his brain to catch up with his sense of panic.

Then he realized: Wells.

This was a relief, actually. It wasn't Sophia, wasn't Jane, wasn't Edmund in trouble, but as his senses returned he did see with three o'clock clarity (sometimes mistaken, sometimes revelatory) that it all felt wrong, about Wells. There was an error somewhere in the chain of logic.

He tried to calm himself. What were the details nagging at his thoughts? What had he overlooked, in his eagerness to solve the case, an old hack coming out of retirement? He cursed his pride.

The small room adjoining their bedroom, which he had been using as a study, was strewn with papers, books, pens, inkpots, flowers from the garden, tobacco. He went in and lit the lamp, shut the door so he wouldn't wake his wife. Two more sips of the water and his breathing had slowed to normal.

To begin with there was the knife. Perhaps the circumstances of its discovery had biased him toward thinking the knife was a meaningful clue—but how many concealed knives covered in human blood could a village like Plumbley possibly hold?

Still, it was not the knife that had roused him from sleep.

It was the black dog.

How had they accounted for that fourth vandalism? The first, upon Fripp's shop window, had been an accident; the second, when the thieves took Wells's clock, a message and a repossession; the third, a XXII upon the church door, had been a message to Wells from his partners in Bath, more certain and less dangerous than a private note, of when they would come for the money— and a reminder perhaps that they were not afraid to vandalize the village.

But the black dog that had appeared upon the church door five days before Lenox arrived: what accounted for that image? How stupid it was not to have asked Wells! Where had he even been when—

Here, Lenox suddenly perceived with a sinking heart, was his greatest misstep: *They had never checked Wells's alibi.* What had the man said to him, in the grain shop? Lenox had a gift for remembering alibis, and he ought to have remembered this one sooner: *My servants can attest to my presence at home yesterday evening. I was up rather late, past two in the morning, working on my books, and at least two of them stayed up with me, fetching drinks, managing the fire. They'll tell you I never left my study.*

What was the meaning of this? He had been quick to offer the statement, certainly. Too quick? It had the feel of a manufactured alibi, asking his servants to stay up late with him, and then mentioning that time, two in the morning, that put him just clear of possible responsibility for Weston's death.

There was nothing substantial to disprove Wells's guilt, and the man had admitted it himself, freely and openly. Why on earth would he have done that if his alibi were solid?

Still, that black dog . . . and with the knife, and Musgrave's abscondment, he wondered if there was a connection between Wells and the captain.

There must be some kind of explanation, he thought. He would speak with Dallington in the morning.

He felt heavy in his limbs and knew that, without much effort, he might fall back to sleep. It was necessary that he speak to Wells again—pose him these few questions, perhaps challenge him on his eagerness to provide an alibi—but it could wait until morning.

Lady Jane stirred when he returned to bed. "Are you quite well, Charles?"

"Hush now, go back to sleep."

"Is it your speech?"

"Yes," he said. "Just looking over it."

He knew it was what he ought to have been doing, less than a week from the most significant moment of his professional life, but there was no need to have lied. For the thousandth time since he entered Parliament he thought about the modest disappointment it had been to him—how he had loved politics so ardently from the outside, longed to be like his father and his brother, and how since achieving that aim, though he did his duty with great care, it had never excited his passion quite the way crime did. He couldn't recall waking up in the middle of the night over Parliament, and though it racked his nerves to worry about Wells there was a thrill to it as well, the thrill of his mind doing what it was best suited to do.

He woke several hours later without remembering that he had fallen asleep. The morning was again rainy, the sky steel-colored and sifted with cloud and mist, the outlandish green of the gardens more stark and differentiated than on a sunny day.

Lenox was an early riser, and most mornings in Everley he had used the time to ride out on Sadie. He would delay that pleasure now, until he had seen his cousin, Dallington, and Wells, in that order. He went to the butler in the front hall.

"Nash, is my cousin in his study?"

"No, sir, Mr. Ponsonby is upon the road to Bath with Constable Oates, accompanying Mr. Wells."

Lenox had forgotten. "Damn it all," he said. "They left early?"

"Yes, sir, by Mr. Ponsonby's carriage."

"I think he might have waited."

"Sir?"

"Oh, nothing. Could you ask Chalmers to set up Sadie for me?"

"Mr. Chalmers is driving the coach to Bath, sir, but his assistant will—"

"Yes, yes, that's fine." Then Lenox had a thought. Could he overtake them upon the road to Bath? "When did they leave?" he asked.

"Fifty minutes since."

It was no good—they would have covered too much of the distance. "Well, I'll take the horse, anyhow."

After Nash had left, Lenox realized something; his uncle would have had to stop and fetch both Oates and Wells. His carriage tended to move at a pretty stately pace, too. If Sadie took up a canter, perhaps . . .

Lenox ran to the breakfast room, tucked a piece of sausage into a piece of toast, gulped it down with a half-cup of coffee, and then went out to the stables. Nash, altogether in less haste, was just arriving.

"Never mind," said Lenox. "Tell my wife and Lord John that I'm riding after my uncle."

"Yes, sir."

By a stroke of good fortune Sadie was already warm and saddled, because Chalmers, that good man, had left word behind that she was to be prepared for Lenox from eight in the morning. He stroked her mane and offered her an apple, which she took from his palm with stupid and good-natured excitement, and then stepped up to the saddle.

"There is only one road to Bath from here, correct?" said Lenox.

The boy who had been left in charge of the stables—he couldn't have been above thirteen—nodded and pointed. "Yes, sir. And nice catch, sir, in the game."

Lenox laughed. "Out for a single run, however."

"It was hard luck, sir."

"Do you play?"

"Next year, I hope. I'm a wicket-keeper."

Lenox lifted his hat and made a note in his mind to have a catch with the boy upon his return—but now there was no time, if he wanted to chase down his quarry. He dug his heels into the horse's side and she dug her powerful back legs into the turf and bounded forward, almost immediately pushing herself into a hard run. Lenox had to clamp down his hat with his hand.

He had been riding over the fields since he arrived in Plumbley. He preferred that to riding along the road, but there was no question he was faster upon the dirt, even in wet weather. Sadie fled through the miles, after three or four still not even in any kind of sweat. He slowed her to a trot for a moment, thinking he ought to rest her, then decided he could trot all the way home if need be—he would catch up with Frederick, Oates, and Wells now if he could. He had seen a few old carts along the road, and one or two solitary riders, but it was relatively empty—the rain, perhaps.

As a result he saw the fresh rut of their tracks very clearly. There was a hard shoulder to the road that Sadie ran along. Good—another advantage in speed. Chalmers might be stopped and taking the mud off of the wheels right now.

Lenox rode hard for forty-five minutes before he started to doubt whether he would catch them at all. He was out of breath, Sadie too, and Lord knew how long ahead the carriage had gotten. Even at a brisk trot Freddie's horses kept a pretty lively pace.

Yet just as the first thought of turning back entered his mind he saw something a quarter mile down the straight road. It was a black hump in the middle of the path.

"That had better be a log," he muttered as he rode along toward it.

It was not; with a pulse of alarm throughout his whole body he saw that the figure was human, and in no very great state of health.

"Hoa!" he called down to Sadie when they were close and clicked his tongue; without any jerk in the saddle she pulled up. Down the road he shouted, "Hello? Hello?"

When there was no response he fairly leapt from the horse, trusting the beast to stay where she was—which she did—and ran to the body, falling to his knees beside it, praying that it was not Frederick. He turned the body onto its back.

It was Chalmers, dead. Upon his white shirt was a great bloom of bright red blood.

CHAPTER FORTY-TWO

O r was he dead? Crouched over Chalmers, Lenox thought he saw a flutter in the man's closed eyelids. Quickly he put two fingers to his throat and then waited, not breathing himself to make his hand more steady.

Yes, a pulse. It was barely there, but the groom was alive.

The question was what to do now. There had been a turnoff to the village of West Buckland less than a mile before, but down the road two miles was a larger village, Wellington. Would he have a better chance of finding a competent doctor there?

Chalmers's pulse was so inconstant, his breath so shallow, however, that Lenox decided he would go to the closer town and pray for the best. He stanched the wound—in the upper stomach, near the ribs—with a towel from Sadie's saddlebag, then took off his own riding jacket and wrapped it as tightly as he could around Chalmers's midsection. When this was done he pulled the man up and over the horse's haunch, very gingerly. Then he mounted the horse himself and nudged her into motion.

It was a delicate operation, riding to West Buckland; he wanted speed, but he didn't want to jostle Chalmers. Fortunately the village was close—in fifteen minutes he had reached it. His heart lifted when he saw that there was a doctor's red cross painted on a white sign over a door on the cobblestoned Main Street, just next to the pub.

"Doctor!" he called out to the empty street, still on his horse. "I need a doctor! A police constable, too!"

Nobody came out. He rode up just alongside the door and kicked it hard, trying to rouse somebody, but to his despair there was still no answer.

Just then a man appeared several doors down, pale, young, and with ink-black hair. "May I help?"

"Where is the doctor?"

The young man took in the situation. "A wound? The doctor is—well, perhaps I should look."

"Are you a doctor?"

He shook his head. "A veterinarian. But the doctor, by this hour—"

He had an honest face. "What, drink?"

"Bring him here," said the young man, and then called back into his office for his assistant. "What is his malady?"

"I found him upon the road, shot," said Lenox.

The young man nodded, calmly. Together the three of them took Chalmers past several waiting dogs and cats, one goat, and into the young veterinarian's office.

"I need to find the men who did this," Lenox said. "Do all you can for him—spare no expense. I am at Everley, but I shall return soon."

"You're leaving him here with—" Lenox handed the young surgeon a card. The lad looked at it and nodded. "Mr. Lenox."

"I or one of my friends shall return, you have my word of it."

In the street several boys were gawking at Sadie, touching the place on her withers that was slick with blood. "What happened, sir, please?" asked one of the boys.

"Where is the police station?" asked Lenox. The same boy pointed down the street. "You shall have a half-crown if you give this horse water and oats."

The boys burst into activity—"There, sir, it'll be a moment," "Oats *and* a carrot, I say"—and Lenox strode toward the police station.

The constable there was quick-witted, fortunately. He had heard of Wells's arrest, knew Lenox's name, and agreed to help. The only question was what they should do.

"There are so many paths they might have taken off the main road," said the constable, Jeffers.

"My uncle is in that carriage," said Lenox. "Alive, I hope. I mean to go after him. Fortunately the ground is wet."

"What can I do?"

"Telegram to Bath, go to Plumbley and tell—" But Lenox didn't know who to tell. Then he remembered. "Send word for a John Dallington at the big house, and tell a Mr. Fripp."

Jeffers nodded, somber. "Anything else?"

"The man to telegram in Bath is Archer. You may try any of them, though. They should be apprised of the situation immediately—and tell them to send men, if they can."

Lenox and Jeffers shook hands and the detective flew from the station, handed over his half-crown to the boys, and vaulted himself aboard Sadie, who with all the eagerness in the world turned her head again in the direction of the road.

He would never forgive himself if anything had happened to his uncle, he thought.

Out upon the road again he passed a carriage almost immediately, not the one he was looking for, and realized with dismay that he could no longer be sure which of the fresh carriage tracks in the mud belonged to Frederick's. Neither did he have a pistol, a constable, any means of convincing Wells to give up his cousin—for he was still convinced of Wells's intimate involvement in the business. Lenox worried that he might do more harm than good. Still he rode on.

What *did* Wells intend to do with Freddie? Lenox had yet to fully consider the circumstances because finding Chalmers in the road had driven him so definitely to action, not reflection. Presumably Wells had some plan to which the groom—but not Frederick, or indeed, Oates—was superfluous. Did he mean to hold them hostage? Had Chalmers simply been the one who fought back, and been shot for his troubles?

Then, though he was riding pell-mell, a realization came to Lenox in slow motion: If Wells had commandeered the carriage, he must have had an accomplice in his actions.

Why? For the simple reason that there was no chance Oates, Frederick, Chalmers, or Wells had been carrying a gun, and what Chalmers had suffered was a gunshot wound.

Perhaps Musgrave, or one of the coiners from Bath, had met Wells out here on the road. Perhaps the foreknowledge of that plan was what had made Wells seem so sanguine, so untroubled, in their interview the day before. Interested in the cricket, even. He had known he would be free again soon.

Think, Charles, he chided himself.

The rain began to come down harder. It cooled Sadie, but it slowed her, too. Lenox brought her to a trot for a moment to get his cloak from one of the saddlebags, and while he was in there fumbled out a cube of sugar. It had fallen into the mud but he knew she wouldn't mind—he wiped it against the saddle, blinking away the raindrops, and gave it to the horse, who was breathing heavily but seemed in no danger of outrunning herself.

The difficulty with the scenario was in its planning. How would

Wells have been in contact with Musgrave, or with any of his accomplices in Bath? Even if he had, why would they risk coming out to see him? Clearly when Musgrave had left Plumbley he wasn't worried about Wells shouldering the blame for Weston's death.

As he was mounting the horse again, Lenox felt a chill.

Who were the three men in the carriage, now? Wells. Frederick. And Oates.

It was impossible. Oates with his fleshy, impassive, unintelligent face, his grief over his cousin.

Yet wasn't he the most logical co-conspirator? There had been no evidence of another carriage stopping where Chalmers had fallen—only the one, Frederick's. And Wells couldn't have overpowered Oates, Chalmers, and Frederick together, even with a gun.

Lenox shook his head, yet a flood of inconsequential memories, small oddities of behavior, returned with great force to his mind. It was true that Oates had behaved strangely at moments. He hadn't wanted Lenox to look at Weston's correspondence, arguing overmuch for the boy's privacy. Had he been afraid of a note implicating him? Or the canvas of the town green: Oates had uncovered nobody to help them, while Fripp had produced Carmody within ten minutes.

And the note from Weston to Oates! "Swells" seemed such an obvious nickname for the grain merchant, and all the lads in the pub had known it at once. Wouldn't the constable have recognized it immediately? Wouldn't Weston have used only a nickname he was *sure* his cousin would understand?

Lenox's resistance to the idea was weakening. He hoped it wasn't Oates—but, he thought, who had been in the grain merchant's shop the first time Lenox visited? The constable.

Lenox remembered, too, Wells's somewhat unusual insistence that he stay in Oates's custody, the man from whom he should have most feared retribution. Beyond that there was Wells's alibi, and his true, convincing outrage when he was asked if he had killed Weston. What if Wells had only confessed because he knew he had a way out? That Oates would spring him?

It had already, after only a few hours, been a long day, and these small, agitating thoughts, arriving in Lenox's mind unbidden, seemed wrong, inaccurate. For half a mile of riding he dismissed the possibility from his mind.

Until, that is, he remembered a phrase from McConnell's letter: *The only fingerprints on the knife belonged to Constable Oates.*

How many dozens of times in his experienced had it been the murderer who found the body, who found the weapon? Hadn't Oates found the knife in the slop bucket at the last possible moment, that morning in the basement of Wells's house, at the last throw of the dice?

With a terrible sense of dread Lenox began to fear that the accomplice wasn't Musgrave at all. That it was Plumbley's police constable. That Weston's own cousin had murdered him.

CHAPTER FORTY-THREE

The rain was gone forty minutes later, the weak yellow of the sun glittering in the branches of the trees, blackened by their wetness, that lined the road. Lenox had lost all track of the carriage ruts, and nearly all hope, too. The thought of Oates working with Wells was too terrible to contemplate, but it solved so many niggling doubts. It explained Wells's behavior.

Now was the time to turn back. He had no way of knowing where Wells had taken Frederick—Wells and Oates, perhaps. His horse was getting genuinely tired. If Jeffers, the constable from West Buckland, had done as he said he would, by now they knew in Bath and Plumbley what had happened, and surely massive reinforcements would be patrolling this road soon.

Then there was Chalmers. Was he alive? If he was, could he tell them anything?

Yet something drove Lenox on. It was simple enough: his cousin, his mother's dearest friend within her family, was in the hands of a man, perhaps of two men, who had proved they didn't scruple at violence. If there was some chance of stumbling across them he had to try for it. He prayed for luck.

In the end, however, it wasn't luck but design that helped him.

As he was cantering along—a gallop now was too much for Sadie, who had white froth at her mouth—he saw, half-trapped in the mud of the road, a bright blue ribbon. He stopped the horse and got down, realizing with a fizz of joy as he did that it was Frederick's. It was the same ribbon, given to him by the garden society of Somerset, that he wore every day in his lapel.

Lenox knew Freddie; he would have dropped it from the window of the carriage on purpose. It was never the sort of thing to come loose on its own, either. How many times had Charles told his cousin of the importance of the trail of breadcrumbs in his cases, of small clues?

The question was why he had dropped it here, of all places.

Lenox looked around. The road had narrowed, vast tangles of maple branches intertwining to form a cathedral ceiling overhead. There was no evidence that he could see of a carriage stopping. Perhaps farther down the path.

He mounted the horse again and rode on, very slowly this time, his eyes scanning the space among the trees and along the ground. Nothing so far.

After a short distance, not above a tenth of a mile, he saw a shingle attached to a post. It read:

WILD BEAR COACHING STATION

PUBLIC HOUSE

HOT FOOD BEER BLACKSMITH STABLES

NEXT TURNING.

He could smell the smoke of the Wild Bear's woodfire. Was this where they had gone? Perhaps one of the horses had lost a shoe, perhaps one of the men needed food. Or perhaps it was a coincidence. Still, Lenox took the turning.

The inn was a squat, stone house with two modest gables in the upper story and a large stable attached to it, the sort of place where travelers stop for a bite and where local farmers congregate if it's closer than the village.

A boy appeared as he rode up. "Take your horse, sir?"

"Please. She's had a hard morning—water her and rub her down, if you would."

"Oh, yes, sir."

Lenox stepped down from the horse, gave the boy a coin, and passed him the hack's bridle. Might as well let her have ten minutes' rest, even if there was nothing else to keep her here. It might mean another hour's good riding down the road.

He waited until the boy had gone out of sight and then followed him with soft footsteps. He came to a door in the stable and pulled it slightly ajar.

With a thrill he saw, unmistakable in its trim and its construction, his cousin's carriage.

So they were here. Now he had to consider what he wanted to do.

He pulled his hat low over his eyes, so that it gave him some protection from recognition, and went around through the front door of the Wild Bear.

At this hour it ought to have been empty, but in fact it was rather full. A market day locally, perhaps. Or happy chance. Either way he accepted the luck with gratitude. The walls were dark from decades of smoke, and even now there was an eye-watering concentration of it floating constantly upward and collecting at the ceiling, from the badly ventilated hearth and from the pipes the men along the bar constantly refilled.

He moved toward the bar, catching the eye of the publican who stood behind it. "A half of stout, please," he said.

"Right away, sir."

When he had his drink he could sip it slowly, concealing his face, and scan the place. There were perhaps twenty people in the room all told, crowded around small tables and along benches at the back wall. He looked very carefully but saw that none of them was Oates, or Wells, or Frederick. He cursed under his breath.

Just as he was deciding that he ought to go straight to the coach and risk being shot, however, the door opened and there he was: Wells. Lenox saw him first, and quickly turned his back to the door. He wondered if he would stand out—dressed better than the men in here, no coat (that was still with Chalmers), and with dirt spattered up and down his breeches from the long morning of riding.

Wells approached the bar. "Pint of mild," he said, "and wrap up some sandwiches for us to take away. Six should do."

The barman nodded and pulled the pint of mild—contrary to its name the strongest of the ales that most public houses sold—before going into the kitchen through a pair of swinging doors behind him.

During the order Lenox had settled upon a plan. He took a deep breath, lifted his head, did a double-take, and then cried, from his end of the bar to the other, "Mr. Wells! Imagine seeing you here! What an unexpected pleasure!"

Wells had turned at his name, and when he saw Lenox his face blanched. He was caught off guard by the greeting, but other people were looking, so he played along. The two men shook hands. "Mr. Lenox. Excellent to see you again."

Almost immediately people stopped paying attention, the murmur of the pub increasing again, and Lenox could whisper to the coiner. "You and Oates in league, was it?"

Wells hesitated, but then nodded grimly. "Yes."

It was a sorrowful confirmation. Oates—he had seemed such a

good man, so incapable of surprising people. In the end greed had gotten to him, too. "Is my uncle safe?"

"Yes. We mean to leave this place, the three of us, or take out a fair few of you with us."

Lenox shook his head. "That is not necessary. Listen, I am quite alone. You have all the advantage. I only want my uncle. You may still go free. In fact, if my uncle's life is spared it is a matter of indifference to me whether you escape or not." This was false, but it was also true to a point. "It will be impossible to tell people that I didn't see you, but I will say, and it will be the case, that I have no idea where you might be going. London, Bath, the north, even overseas."

Wells shook his head. "You'd send up a cry. Then we couldn't get at—"

He cut himself off, but Lenox understood. They'd secured money somewhere, enough to fund their lives as fugitives, he and Oates, and they had to retrieve it before they escaped. "I can promise you, upon my word as a gentleman, that I will give you time to go. All that matters is my uncle's safety. You must understand that—I don't care if you're caught. Weston won't be any more or less dead. On the other hand if you were to harm Freddie or me, it would be national news—it would be the gallows. Would you rather be dead in a month or alive and away and rich? The choice is yours."

Wells smiled thinly. "That is precisely why we took your cousin. Thought he might buy us our life, if we did. But I need some guarantee."

"I have an idea," said Lenox. "Take me with you in the carriage. I don't mind. I'll leave my horse, and my uncle can stay here."

"He'll call the police."

Lenox thought for a moment, ignoring the faint relief in the back of his head at the rejection of that idea. "Then you must trust us. Take my horse, if you like, she's a runner. Leave the carriage behind and you'll go swifter. My uncle and I will have no means of catching you, of warning anybody. You'll be down the road, miles in whichever direction you like. I give you my word, my solemn word, that I'll tell them nothing other than that I exchanged my horse for my uncle."

Wells was a rational man. Oates had been drinking his sorrows away, was likely, at just this stage, capable of irrational action. The right man had come into the bar. Wells understood his situation: He wanted his money; he wanted to live.

"Very well," he said, at last. "Give me the money in your pockets, too, so you can't hire a carriage out of here."

Obediently Lenox handed over his billfold. "There are nearly twelve pounds in there."

Wells opened it greedily and verified the truth of this. "Nice to be a gentleman, ain't it. Come, we'll go to the carriage. You'll tell the boy we need your horse, and we'll take one off the carriage."

Lenox nodded. "Just remember, if you feel the urge to trick me, how much worse it should be for all of us—for you—if we don't make a clean exchange. Why should any of the four of us drop an ounce of blood?"

Wells laughed. "Don't worry on that count. I know where my bread is buttered. We'll make the exchange, I'll get Oates, and Freddie will stay in the carriage."

"No. I need to see my cousin before you go."

"Fine, then. He's taken a knock on the head, be warned."

Lenox mastered his anger at this, and nodded. Wells drained his drink, stood up, and led the way out of the Wild Bear.

In the stable there were two boys, the one who had taken Sadie and another, older one. He came forward. "Help you, sirs?"

Lenox said, "My horse—"

Wells interrupted sharply. "No. I need to speak with Oates first."

He went into the carriage, stayed a few minutes, and came out, apparently satisfied. "All well?" Lenox asked.

"Saddle up the horses. Food in the saddlebags." He pointed toward the better of the gray carriage mares and to Sadie. (Absurdly, Lenox felt a pang at losing the horse. He told himself to focus.) "When they're ready to go I'll whistle, and Oates will bring you your uncle."

The stable boy looked troubled. "Sir—"

"It's all right," said Lenox.

It was an agonizingly slow process—five minutes perhaps, but each passing as slowly as a Sunday hour. At last the horses were ready. Wells put two fingers in his teeth and gave a loud whistle.

Oates came out of the carriage, supporting Frederick. The squire of Everley looked sluggish but he was plainly alive. Lenox breathed a sigh of relief, and in doing so realized he had been holding that breath, after a fashion, since he found Chalmers.

Oates refused to look at him. Lenox couldn't help himself. "Oates!" he said.

The constable turned to him for an instant, and Lenox saw etched upon his face crazed, grief-stricken regret. "I'm sorry," he said.

"Quickly," said Wells.

The two men took their seats and without looking back kicked their horses away. Just like that, they were gone. Lenox—feeling it was a trade he would happily make again and again—ran to his uncle, muttering under his breath his thanks to God that the old man was still alive.

CHAPTER FORTY-FOUR

Likely they are in London," said John Dallington, speaking of the two fugitives. "I cannot imagine them stupid enough to place themselves within the confines of the city of Bath."

"And yet that is the most probable location of the money they stowed away," said Frederick, a bandage wrapped tightly around his head, face pale but eyes steady.

It was still wild with rain outside, the trees lashing into each other, but here, in the sitting room at Plumbley, the three men were warm, two of them sipping from well-deserved cups of hot wine.

Lenox shook his head. "I think Wells is too clever to have left his stockpile in Bath. He wanted a bolt-hole. I expect it's somewhere far from the Wild Bear, to be honest, perhaps several counties over. Otherwise he wouldn't have stopped to bother about the horse's shoe—he would have carried on though it permanently lamed the beast." For it had emerged that a hobble in one of the mares' gait was what had, fortuitously, caused Oates and Wells to stop. Frederick, though captive, had overheard this plan to lie by at the Wild Bear and dropped his ribbon from the carriage to warn

Lenox, or indeed any pursuers, that this was where they would stop. "If they have gone to Bath, however, they will be caught soon enough. Archer's telegram said that half the police force is crawling over the city, looking in every hostelry and back alley for two men answering to their description."

The men talked for a while longer, speculating about Wells and Oates and where they had gone. Both Lenox, who had seen it in his eyes, and Frederick, who had heard it from his mouth, also returned to Oates's regret at involving himself in the plot.

There was a knock at the door. It was Nash. "Dr. Eastwood, sir," he announced.

"Show him in," said Frederick.

It was Eastwood whom Frederick had insisted he see for the wound upon his head, inflicted by Wells a few miles outside of Plumbley with the butt of a revolver Oates had brought. It was also Wells who had shot Chalmers in cold blood; Oates hadn't known it was part of the plan.

On the other hand it was Oates himself who had killed Weston. Sobbing, in the carriage, he had told Frederick the terrible details, while his accomplice stared impassively on. There was no McCutcheon.

In his surgery Eastwood had pronounced Frederick wounded, but not dangerously. Now the squire sat quite comfortably with his wine; it was difficult to tell whether this ordeal of the past week had made him look older or younger. A bit of both, perhaps. Physically he was down to his last ounces of energy. At the same time he looked as if he had discovered within himself a new fortitude.

After wrapping Frederick's head Eastwood had borrowed a horse from the stables—the now badly depleted stables, which only had an old cart horse left, Sadie and one of the two gray mares being up-country—and ridden to West Buckland, to look after Chalmers. Now he was back. He accepted a scotch and soda.

"Well?" asked Lenox. "Any news?"

Eastwood, his handsome face graven with concern, said, "It is touch and go whether he shall survive. If he does it is because of your veterinarian, Mr. Lenox. That young man took excellent care of Chalmers. In return for the favor had an earful from the drunken doctor next door, Morris-McCarthy, about infringement upon his practice. I told them both a specialist in Harley Street could scarcely have improved on the job the veterinarian did, Jacklin was his name."

"What is your instinct?" said Freddie. "Will Chalmers survive?"

"I have not seen many gunshot cases, but I would say that his chances are fair. It all depends upon infection."

"Would it help to call doctors from London? Specialists, I mean, from Harley Street, as you say—I know that your education in general medicine is second to none," said Frederick.

"No. It is as straightforward a wound as I ever saw, no organs hit, thank Christ, three ribs broken from the impact, and the ball itself came straight out under Jacklin's knife. Now we can only wait."

"He has not spoken?" said Lenox.

"Not yet."

"Can he return to Everley for his recuperation?" asked Freddie.

"No. He shouldn't be moved."

Frederick acquiesced to this with a nod. Then he stood, though the doctor motioned him to sit. "Shake my hand—you have behaved damned handsomely today, Eastwood, patching me up and going to Buckland. In Plumbley we do not consider you much more than a passing visitor until you've been here a few decades, but I think I may say that you are as true a Plum as I ever knew."

Eastwood, like many men of reserved manners, took a compliment with unusual pleasure, flushing and declining and accepting all that Freddie had said. They shook hands. "And now I should go," he said.

"Nonsense," said Frederick. "My nephew will pour you another scotch and soda. You are as deeply involved in this horrible matter as any of us are. Charles, the doctor's drink?"

Eastwood declined. "I have patients waiting still," he said. "Please excuse me, gentlemen."

When he was gone Frederick looked after him. "I wish he had a wife to go home to, you know."

Supper had been cancelled—neither the squire nor Lenox feeling much like a social occasion—and so as they sat on, discussing Oates and Wells, Nash brought in plates of toasted cheese and cold chicken.

To his surprise Lenox found that he was famished, though he had eaten a quick bite when he first returned to Everley. It was the hardest exercise he had done in some time, riding as he had across half of Somerset. Thank goodness the Wild Bear had let them a coach to return to Everley in, and one with four horses, too, fast enough to cut the travel time in half.

Much of their conversation still revolved, unsurprisingly, around Oates. Apparently he had been half-drunk when Frederick had come to the police station, and as soon as he had handed the revolver from his cloak to Wells, he had taken his flask out and begun to drain it, all the while telling in great jags what he had done, and constantly asking Frederick for forgiveness. Wells had been happy to let Oates speak, even chiming in now and then with a detail.

"It was that which convinced me they didn't mean to let me live. A full confession to a magistrate—I believed they didn't care because I would be a corpse soon anyhow."

Dallington grimaced. "I can scarcely imagine a worse sensation."

Frederick's face was steely. "It shows a man what he wants from life, believing he will die."

"What did Oates tell you, then?"

"Just what I have told you—that it was he, not Wells, who treated with the men from Bath, and it was he, not Wells, who killed Weston. It broke his heart, I think. Anyhow he seemed barely a man."

"Nothing else of material interest?" asked Lenox.

"Oh—that he planted the knife at Musgrave's, too."

"Of course."

"That was where he dished himself," said Dallington. "He'd have been better off washing it and putting it back in his drawer."

"It might still have been matched to Weston's wounds, however," said Lenox.

"Throwing it into the woods, then."

"It was foolish, but one can imagine his reasoning. Musgrave was already suspected in Plumbley, and indeed made himself the prime suspect by fleeing the village altogether. The knife must have seemed like the final clue that would decide me—all of us—against Musgrave."

"I have a question. If Wells wanted Carmody to tell us about the horses, why did Oates pass him over?" asked Dallington.

Lenox shrugged, but Frederick knew. "They hadn't had time to speak yet. Wells mentioned that. Said he would have told Oates to bring Carmody to you later that day."

They talked for an hour more, perhaps two, smoothing over all the details of the case to their satisfaction, until it clicked together like a puzzle in all of their minds.

By now it was getting late. The wind whistled outside, the rain tapped the windows: It was a good night for a heavy sleep. "I suppose I had better retire," said Lenox at last. "Certainly you should, Uncle Freddie."

"Oh, I don't need as much sleep these days, and my head hardly smarts at all. John, will you sit up with me for another glass of hot wine? I wouldn't mind something else to eat, either."

They were the kindest and least reserved words the squire had spoken directly to the young lord, who smiled—he loved to be liked, and hated to have a bad reputation, though he always seemed to acquire one anyhow. Still, here was a chance; perhaps his ignominious arrival at Everley could be forgotten. "With great pleasure," he said. "It was the finest toasted cheese I've ever had."

"Mustard is the key," said Frederick as if revealing one of the secrets of the ages.

Lenox looked at him fondly and then rose. "I shall leave you to it. Good night, gentlemen."

Just as he reached the door, however, the butler appeared again.

"Nash?" said Freddie.

"It is a telegram, sir. For you and Mr. Lenox."

Frederick took it. He absorbed its contents quickly and crumpled it in his hand, eyes on the far wall. "It's from Archer," he said. "They've found Oates."

"But not Wells?" asked Dallington.

Frederick shook his head. "Oates was shot dead not far from the Wild Bear. They discovered his body a few hours ago. There's no sign of Wells at all."

CHAPTER FORTY-FIVE

The shock was over quickly; it couldn't have been plainer what had happened. Dallington said it. "He wanted all the money for himself."

"And Oates was in no condition for conspiracy, with his drinking and his chatter," added Frederick. "Down to Gehenna or up to the throne, he travels fastest who travels alone."

Lenox shook his head. "Poor soul. It is probably for the best, after all. He was ill-conditioned to live with a bad conscience."

Indeed, what had been the point of all this? It was hard to imagine a life more comfortable than Oates's; he lacked a wife but he had friends and family, a decent job of good work. Men like Wells, men of ambition, Lenox could understand their turning to crime. But Oates?

He went upstairs with a heavy heart, and knocked on the door to make sure he wasn't interrupting Jane. "It's Charles," he said.

He heard her lovely voice. "Imagine you knocking, Charles! Come in! I have just been to see Sophia, she is blooming—has no idea what kind of day her father had. You could not call her very interested in the affairs of others yet. I'm afraid in fact that she's rather a narcissist."

Lenox laughed and they met halfway across the room, where she leaned up to kiss him. "As we rode home I was thinking how sad it shall be when we can no longer spend as much time with her. Or when I cannot, in plain truth."

"What do you mean?"

"A mother always has a place in a nursery, but I don't believe I know a father who sees much of his children, at any rate not for longer than an hour in the evenings. That was as much as Ed and I saw of our father, though we loved him more than the world. Every day that she gets older I feel as if I am coming to the end of a wonderful voyage."

"She's only a few months old, Charles."

"You're right. There's time yet."

She heard him, and leaned her head into his chest. "We can be any kind of parents we like," she said, though both knew it was not precisely true.

"Yes. Perhaps I will make her have breakfast with me in the mornings, and convention be damned."

She laughed. "I call that a fine plan, but how are you feeling, my dear? Come, sit with me, I can put my feet under your legs—they're cold."

"I'm tired, but fair enough otherwise. Oates though—I have not told you of Oates."

He did, and she reacted with the same surprise, quickly trailed by comprehension, that the men had downstairs.

When Lenox had arrived home—covered in mud, with Chalmers's blood still upon him, and in Lady Jane's hand a telegram from the West Buckland constable that offered just enough information to scare her—his wife had been sitting by the pond outside the house, waiting to greet him in an uncontained flurry of grief and worry. She was a woman who seldom wanted for strength. When she had ascertained that he was alive she had ordered a bath for Lenox, had cleared the drawing room so that Eastwood could consult with Frederick, and had arranged for food and drink all around.

Once Lenox had rested for a while they sat together on this sofa for an hour or two, until at last she was satisfied that he was here—corporate, solid, unharmed—and then she had given him an embrace and sent him downstairs, to speak with Dallington and Frederick.

Now her worry was back, he could tell. "Are you quite unhappy?" he asked.

"I like it much better when you are sitting on the benches in the House, dozing off, without much more danger than crossing the street to bother you." She paused. "Francine Hudson lost Jonathan last year, you know."

"I remember."

"She is still in black, of course. And their child only two."

"I'm not a soldier in India, however, Jane. That is the flaw in your analogy, I have spotted it for you."

She smiled weakly. "Very humorous, I'm sure."

He took her in his arms. "I love you," he said.

"I love you, too," she said.

When he woke the next morning he was sore and sorrowful, but two pieces of good news greeted him when he went down to the dining room for breakfast.

Frederick was there—feeling very well, thank you, no the head is slightly sore but not too painful—and put down his gardening journal when Lenox entered. "Chalmers is well, according to your veterinarian. No fever. Eastwood is on his way over later today."

"That is excellent."

"And if you believe in good omens, here is one: Sadie has returned."

Lenox was in the midst of lifting a piece of toast to his mouth, but it stopped in midair. "Sadie? Your horse?"

Frederick smiled. "The very one."

"She must have been thirty miles away!"

"Apparently Wells loosed her. I'm surprised he didn't try to sell her to a farmer, but he must have figured it wasn't worth the risk of being caught."

"I'm amazed she made it back."

"As was I. It is a small miracle. It's a good thing she traveled under the cover of darkness, because certainly some unscrupulous traveler would have taken her up, if he had found her wandering loose upon the road during the day."

"Of course—a fine animal," said Lenox. He was unreasonably happy.

"The servants have rounded up every apple in Somerset and given it to her—she is an object of great wonder indeed. She shall lose her sweet tooth, I don't doubt."

"Any injuries?"

"A cut along one hock, incidental. Our own veterinarian is coming to look at her, but the boy, Chalmers's assistant, Peters, says she could run today."

"I won't chance it," said Lenox.

"No, better not."

"What about the papers?"

"Eh?"

"Wells—has he made the papers?"

"Ah, that. Yes, I'm afraid he has." Frederick pushed a copy of the Bath *Herald* across the table. "My name is out of it, thank

God, though Oates is mentioned. Too early to know whether Fleet Street has gotten hold of the story."

"I wonder where Wells is."

Frederick shook his head. "He might have let Oates live, even if he took the money for himself."

"Oates did not have much to live for."

"But that was not Wells's to determine."

"What will you do today, Uncle? Rest, I hope?"

"Rest! No, I mean to have busier days now. Miss Taylor has still yet to see half of the gardens, and there is a correspondent—a most vexing correspondent, Charles—who writes me on the subject of the peony; facts all wrong. I mean to put across a good letter to him in Wiltshire, set him firmly in his place on the subject of compound leaves."

Lenox planned to return to work upon his speech after breakfast. With a fluttering in his stomach he realized that it was now rather close, less than a week. A packed House of Commons.

These plans were upset by a succession of visitors. First there was Lucy, good-hearted niece of the redoubtable Emily Jasper, who had come to console Frederick for his ordeal. The squire, however, was on fire to write his letter to Wiltshire, so it was Lenox who entertained her, their easy rapport passing thirty minutes in what seemed like five, covering those eternal village subjects: the vicar; the vicar's wife; the town drunk; the old days. He extended her an invitation to London and was pleased when she said she would take him up on it. They had been friends in years past, and he always liked to pick up such strings again.

As she was leaving Dr. Eastwood came in. She curtsied to him, he bowed gravely, and then inquired, when she was gone, whether he might see Frederick.

"By all means, though he seems in the pink of health. Might his head injury have changed his personality?"

Eastwood laughed. "It is not likely. It was a soft blow, though I admit he has come up under it strong, very strong indeed."

Lenox lingered in the hallway reading *Cornhill* after Eastwood had gone to Frederick's study, waiting for the doctor to come out. As he was waiting the third and fourth visitors arrived. The bell rang and Lenox, being nearby, went to the door, but found that Nash had hurried, indeed rather pushed, beyond him, giving a soft exasperated sigh at Lenox's infringement upon his rightful terrain.

Nash stepped backward to admit the visitors. "Mr.—"

He needn't have said a word, though, for Lenox could have spotted the two gentlemen from a Somerset mile off. "Edmund! And Graham! What on earth are you two doing here!"

Edmund laughed, taking off his hat, handing over his cane and cloak to the butler. "The cavalry has arrived, Charles. We cannot have you getting knocked on the head and missing out on your speech and going into pistol fights with bit fakers. It won't do. And Graham has been pining to see the text you've drafted; he won't stop complaining."

One look at Graham's silent, smiling face showed that there was some truth in this. Lenox shook his hand, thrilled to see his old butler, now his political secretary—indeed one of the savviest political secretaries in the Commons, despite the handicap of his birth, as most such jobs went to recent graduates of the great public schools, sometimes even one of the two universities.

"It's true," he said, "I am desperate to see it, after the prime minister himself stopped me in the halls yesterday to ask about your progress."

CHAPTER FORTY-SIX

I t is the commonest observation in the world that a week can sometimes pass in an hour and an hour in a week, but it is true. Lenox's final days at Everley had been idyllic—long rides out on Sadie, afternoon tea in the great drawing room, walks in the garden with Sophie and Jane—and had passed in such a flash that now, sitting in a small anteroom outside the House of Commons, he felt practically dazed.

From the chamber there was a steady hum of human voices, each, because it belonged to a member of Parliament, more than usually accustomed to attention.

"Are they preparing for a great failure, do you think?" asked Lenox, and then laughed rather weakly.

Graham was the only other person in the dim room. Frabbs, their carrot-haired clerk, was at the door, prepared to reject entrance by anyone other than the prime minister himself. Or, if he were to stretch a point, the Queen. "I've no doubt they're speaking of their suppers and their women," said Graham.

"You are right of course."

They were on two blue leather sofas, with a mahogany table between them. There was a plate of biscuits and a bottle of claret there. Both were untouched as yet. Bottlesworth—that noble expert on comestibles who had advised Lenox to have two pints of porter and a passel of sandwiches before his speech—would have been distressed.

Lenox shuffled through the papers in his hand, looking at them and seeing nothing. He was all nerves; Lady Jane was in the visitors' gallery, McConnell too, and the press box, he had seen, was jammed. The prime minister had sent him a very civil communication, congratulating him on the tone of the speech and inviting him to dine together afterward.

"We shall see about that, if it goes badly," muttered Lenox.

"Sir?"

"Oh, nothing."

The door opened. Lenox assumed it was Frabbs and didn't turn, but then noticed with some consternation that a man in a snuff-colored suit of clothes had entered the room, and said, in a hoarse voice, "I have come to give my best wishes for your speech."

Lord preserve me from well-wishers, thought Charles, *and why has Frabbs*—but as he turned, artificial smile on his face to accept the compliment, he saw that it was his brother. Of course! Edmund had a cold in his head and shouldn't have been here at all, were it not for the occasion.

"Why, thank you, Ed." Charles's face was flushed with true pleasure as he spoke these words.

"I am prepared to hear a thumper."

"Lower your expectations, for the love of all that's good."

Edmund smiled. "Graham, I wish you joy of your achievement today, too."

"Thank you, sir."

"Will it be a third or a fourth, Charles?"

"Anyhow not a second."

In the brothers' experience there were four kinds of speeches delivered in the House of Commons, and this shorthand, long since developed, helped them communicate to each other—in the lobby of the House, for instance—whether it was necessary to go and sit upon the benches for a speech, or whether it could be tolerably missed.

Of the four types, two were good and two were bad. The first was a sympathetically bad speech, often full of painstaking research, mumbling, and indecisively argued points (for true intelligence welcomes dissent, unlike a good political speech); the second was an unsympathetically bad speech, full of bluster and steadily increasing passion without much bottom; the third was a powerful speech, with conviction and right on its side, also full of bluster and steadily increasing passion; but the fourth, the cynosure of parliamentary addresses, crowned all of these. It had circumspection, careful argument, passion, rhythm, suasion, wit, poignancy, ease, command, all stitched together seamlessly.

Lenox had aimed to make his speech a fourth. Time would tell.

Very little time, in fact. "A glass of wine, sir?" asked Graham.

"I think not, thank you."

"It would be wise to take something, Charles," said Edmund.

"I have spoken before the House, you know. Some thirty times."

Graham shook his head. "You cannot know how hungry you are, sir. You will rise and feel weak in the knees."

It was rare that Graham was insistent upon anything other than Lenox's schedule, and so the member took a half-cup of wine and a biscuit, albeit with great churlishness. Immediately he felt better and more solid. "A full House?" he asked his brother.

Edmund smiled. "Tolerably full."

"You ought to go in."

The older brother looked at his pocket-watch, their father's. "Yes, you're right. Two or three minutes is all that's in it. I say, good luck, Charles. Graham, mind that he doesn't bolt for the channel."

Graham and Lenox both laughed; then, as Edmund left to take his seat and Frabbs went out to check the composition of the house for them, they were alone.

For many, many years, since Lenox was an undergraduate at Balliol, they had lived almost changelessly together, the same house, the same daily pursuits, Graham often helping Lenox with his cases—the same rhythm of life. Then all had changed. Lenox had married, been elected to Parliament, had a child, cobbled his house together with Jane's into a rambling new hybrid. Most radically of all he had asked Graham, and not a lad fresh from Charterhouse or Downing, to act as his political secretary. It had been a change that demanded Graham endure the slights of those above him in station and work harder than he ever had before. Now, more thanks to his efforts than any other single man's, Lenox was opening Parliament. It was a friendship that Lenox reflected upon only very occasionally—perhaps because whenever he did he felt some strange emotion, which with greater deliberation he might have identified as true brotherly love. One might have used the word *loyal* about Graham, did it not imply one-sidedness: In their friendship the loyalty was mutual and equal in weight.

As they sat here that association filled the silence. At last, Lenox said, "You know, Graham—" He halted.

"Sir?"

"Oh, nothing. Only that I feel better for having had the wine and the biscuit."

"I'm glad to hear it, sir." He checked his own watch. "And now perhaps you should go into the chamber. Don't forget to bow to the Speaker and pay your respects to the opposition leader, before you shake the prime minister's hand."

The two men shook hands. Graham would watch from the sliver of the cracked secretaries' door, and be waiting there when it was all finished.

The benches of the chamber were jammed, and the doorways, through which members were still streaming, a positive fire hazard. Lenox paid his proper obeisances and then took a spot along the first bench. All of it was rather a blur. He had imagined there would be a great passage of time in which he might steel himself to the task, when in fact it happened in no time at all that he was called to speak. He stood up, legs watery, and addressed the chamber.

"Mr. Speaker, Prime Minister, good evening, and thank you," he said. "It is my humble honor to address the House of Commons at this opening, and my hope is that my words will incline you not toward partisan rancor but toward national pride; not toward meanness but toward generosity; not toward argument but toward reconciliation and progress. It ought only be such when we remember that we represent, together, the greatest nation the world has yet known.

"Indeed, we congregate here at the very center of the civilized world. I would ask you to set aside the next half of an hour to peer into the homes of those who still live as if in the last century, those who live solid, honest, British lives, but are afforded too little protection from the vicissitudes of fortune by their government. I would ask you to consider the poor."

It was a good speech, Lenox realized as he read on, but not a great one. It moved too much perhaps in the direction of fervor—the subject was too close to his heart. There was a passage about a family in Somerset who had to choose between medicine and food that was the God's honest truth, but might, he feared, have come across as nearly Dickensian.

But then why not? Dickens's greatest gifts had been humor and a conscience, two virtues that belonged in a political speech. As he spoke on about the Somerset family, about the shoeless children walking down frosted dirt paths, about the father who had one hot meal in a week, about the terror of the workhouse, Lenox felt his conviction rising.

He was aided by the men around him. On both sides, the right, the left, there were murmurs of assent. This was not the House of Lords, that ivoried domicile of the rich and remote. Among the men on the benches were brewers, stockbrokers, even publicans. They understood poverty. Most had seen it.

He remembered to take a sip of water after some time and realized his hand was trembling. It gave him confidence, strangely.

Just when the speech might have become the first kind, a mumbling recitation of facts, he saw his brother, and his voice strengthened. He offered a series of proposals and saw the nods around the chamber.

His conclusion was perhaps fanciful. He had been talking for well on thirty-five minutes, and his heart fell when he came to the last page. Was it a mistake to mention the coining, to have a little joke? In Everley it had seemed a clever idea, but here it seemed self-important. It had made the papers, yes, but . . .

He needn't have worried. "If only we could all turn coiners, the problems would be solved," he said, voice unsteady, and was instantly gratified to receive an enormous laugh. Even the Speaker, propriety personified, smiled.

He wouldn't remember finishing, only thanking the house and returning to his seat in silence. Ten or fifteen seconds passed before he realized that it was not silence at all, but wave after wave of applause.

CHAPTER FORTY-SEVEN

"He's gone," Lenox called back down the hallway at Hampden Lane.

His brother emerged from the Ugly Room, a drafty, dark parlor toward the rear of the house, in which Jane and Lenox never set foot because they stored in it all of their least favorite pieces of furniture, all of their most unfortunate works of art, objects they could not in all scrupulousness throw away—usually because they were the treasured bequest of some relative—but with which they had no desire to live daily life.

Edmund had been hiding from a particularly tedious liberal minister who would have wanted an hour's good conversation about India. He was only the latest in a long line of people who had come to congratulate Lenox on his speech.

"Was that tea coming in soon, Charles?"

"I forgot to ring for it. I'll do so now."

"It's rather cold."

"Well, you see the fire," said Charles, somewhat irritably. "Presumably you have not forgotten how to turn over a spade full of coal."

Edmund smiled. "Tired of your meetings?"

Lenox was at his desk, signing a stack of cards Graham had prepared to send to his constituents in Stirrington. "I am giving strong consideration to the idea of life as a hermit. On the one hand it would be irksome to grow a beard to my ankles; on the other I should never have to go to Lord Furze's for supper tonight, unless Lady Furze's taste has changed dramatically."

Edmund put more coal on the fire, and ordered the tea himself while his brother worked on. These tasks accomplished he settled into an armchair with an out-of-date copy of *Punch*.

After a while Lenox looked up from his work and out through the tall window. It had gotten colder, it was true. The fall had sharpened and deepened, the leaves upon the trees shading from the red and orange brilliance of their dying into the crackled brown of their deaths. The sunlight was paler now.

Though he had received the garlands of a victor after his speech there was some vague dissatisfaction in his heart. Perhaps it was that for all of this congratulation there seemed to be little real will to implement his ideas, and he knew, with an exhausted familiarity, that to pass anything through the House of Commons would mean months of persuasion and wrangling—that a single speech, though it had seemed so important, could not trim the sails of the ship of state.

He consoled himself—and his brother and Graham had consoled him—by remembering that he had placed the issue of poverty directly before his colleagues now. The papers had reported it so favorably, for the most part, that perhaps it would shame them into action. Even then there was the House of Lords to deal with, however; he had always found it fitting that just three people, shouting across each other, each a king upon his own remote plot of land, could make a quorum there. Maddening.

Presently the tea arrived. "Much better," said Edmund as they moved to Lenox's couches, nearer the fire. Between this and the tea the book-lined walls immediately seemed more welcoming, the thick blue carpet warmer.

A footman followed the tea tray in with the post. Amid the shuffle of letters Lenox found one postmarked from Everley, with the Ponsonby crest upon the seal. "A letter from Freddie," he said, slitting it open.

Lenox read in silence for a moment, while Edmund drank his grateful tea. "A *pro forma* thank-you, I imagine?" asked the older brother.

"No." Charles leaned across and handed the letter over. "See what you think of that."

Edmund read the letter.

September 23, 1874

Everley

Plumbley, Som.

Dear Charles,

First I must congratulate you on your speech, which we have just had details of this morning in the Bath papers. As you know Fripp and I are committed Tories, but both of us thought many of your points inarguable—as for those that break along party lines, neither of us doubts your good faith. Fripp did add that he hoped the next time you visited you worried less about farmers' shoes and more about covering your wicket, but I put him down straight away.

Everley is quiet since you left—Plumbley, too—and has reminded me why I feel, as you know, unequal to the ongoing task of her maintenance. In September I planted a line of spruce saplings along the west portico, against the better judgment of Rodgers—and now they have all but one of them died, which I view as final and irrefragable evidence that I have entered my senescence. It is a period I think better spent in a cottage in the village, a spacious and light-filled cottage, none of your dank rabbit holes, but a cottage nevertheless, and I therefore propose to come up to London on Monday next to see Wendell and discuss the transfer of ownership with him. There are three or six or even eight months of work left for me to do before I am satisfied that I have truly done my all by this house I have loved so much, and then it shall be his. I hope I may come to see you upon my arrival, however, as there are one or two subjects I should like to discuss before I see him.

Funny how quickly one grew accustomed to Jane, Sophia, and Miss Taylor! The house feels empty indeed. Return at any time the four of you please; and indeed if you do you shall have the best of Plumbley's hospitality, being rather more of a grandee than they realized when they had you in their grip.

Ever,
Frederick Ponsonby

"Well?" said Charles.

Edmund shrugged. "If he feels himself unequal to the work—"

"Does it not sadden you? To think of—well, of mother, I suppose? It is very like the end of an era."

"Eras go on ending," said Edmund gently. "It is the sign of a small—"

"A small mind to deplore change, yes," said Lenox crossly. "We had the same father, you know."

Edmund smiled at his brother, whose brooding eyes were turned toward the fire. "My primary thought on the matter—"

The world would have to wait for Sir Edmund Lenox's primary thought on the matter, however, because just then they heard the front door open. "Who could that be?" wondered Charles.

"Will it not be Jane?" Edmund asked.

Lenox said he thought not, that she was out visiting for the afternoon, that it was more probably Graham or someone unexpected, but within fifteen seconds the door of the study had made a liar of him. Lady Jane came in, surrounded by shopping bags, her bright smile and kind eyes alighting on each brother in turn.

"You wouldn't believe the weather—porpoises in Piccadilly—I saw Meredith Hance and thought her nose might fall off it was so red. That's terrible to say, Edmund I'm sorry. Oh, but Sophie! She must see her uncle! Miss Taylor! They are just in the hall."

"Was she quite warm?" said Charles.

"It is hard to remember whether she wore seventy-eight layers of wool or seventy-nine, but at any rate, yes, I imagine she was."

The governess, the red in her cheeks making her look rather prettier than usual, came in with Sophia, and then, the other three adults descending upon the child at once, made her safely to the sofa and sat sipping a very welcome cup of tea.

"I have clean forgotten," said Jane, when at last they looked up from Sophia. "Edmund, we saw Molly."

"Did you? In the park?"

"Yes. She invited us to supper tonight."

"I hope you'll come."

"Certainly we shall. I do not think either of us is bespoken, Charles?"

"Lord Furze," said Lenox shortly, and with a petulant sigh returned to the tottering stacks of paperwork upon his desk.

CHAPTER FORTY-EIGHT

By great fortune Dallington had almost immediately, upon returning to London, received another case. His health was fully intact again—that remarkable resilience of the young—and while he sent Lenox small notes, apprising him of new facts as they arose, the two men did not see each other after their return from Everley.

When he was announced as a visitor that Saturday morning, Lenox assumed it was because the young lord wished to consult with him about the case. It was a theft of some important blueprints from a clockmaker and watchmaker in Clerkenwell. Because there was no evidence of forced entry Scotland Yard refused to make an investigation, but Inspector Jenkins, returned from his foray into the gin-soaked parts of Belgium, had passed the matter onto Dallington.

"Clerkenwell?" he asked when Dallington came in.

The young man was holding a clutch of flowers. "For Lady Jane," he said, though Lenox wondered, rather to his own surprise, whether they had been in fact intended for Miss Taylor. "And about Clerken-well—no, that is finished. It was Aguetti."

"The watchmaker next door?"

"Yes. Not a matter of professional interest, either, for he is far and away the better craftsman. No, Thomson was carrying on with his wife, and Aguetti wished to harm his business."

"How is it being handled?"

"By the Yard, you mean? I have not passed it to them. Aguetti made restitution of the papers and apologized, Thomson apologized too, and they are in the Coach and Horses, drinking pint after pint of ale. Mrs. Aguetti is in a fine pique, being ignored as she is—both men have sworn off of her."

Lenox smiled. "Just a social call, then?"

"No—but where is my brain! It is this!" From his back pocket Dallington produced a telegram. "It is from Archer—have you not received it?"

"No."

"Then I daresay yours will be coming soon, if it has not already."

Lenox rang the bell and asked if there had been any telegrams; in fact there had been one while he and Lady Jane were at a champagne breakfast for the First Lord of the Navy, whose daughter had been married, but it had been forgotten, perhaps mislaid, the footman was most terribly sorry, it would never happen again—at any rate here it was.

"Shall I read it or will you tell me?"

"It's Musgrave. He was run to ground. Among other things they found him with six sea chests of false coin."

Lenox, who had stood to receive the telegram, stopped where he was, looking agape at Dallington. "Where?" he said.

"Read the telegram, if you like."

Archer did offer a location—Musgrave had been hidden away at a rented estate in Surrey—but little more, promising only that he would write again should further information make itself available.

Dallington had taken a seat upon his sofa and was snipping the end of a short cigar. "Odd, no?"

Lenox still stood. "I'm a fool."

"Come now."

"Really I am. It is the clearest conspiracy I ever saw. Musgrave had the machine, but Bath had obviously become too hot to hold him, and he wanted to apportion the risk to somebody else. Wells could take that on, and had both space in his shop and the opportunity for distribution, as well as being above suspicion. Having poor Oates on their side squared away any chance of local detection."

"You stopped Wells and Oates."

"Not before Weston died." Lenox slumped down into his chair. "From the start I should have asked myself how Wells had made criminal contacts, a country grain merchant. Clearly it was Musgrave who came to him. For that matter, I should also have asked myself why Musgrave ever moved to Plumbley."

"For his wife, was it not?"

"I imagine his wife would have been perfectly content to live in Bath. I also think Musgrave needed to leave; that perhaps his wife introduced him to Wells. I wonder whether she was complicit. Anyhow their argument on the town green will not have been about her, but about the money."

"But the vandals?"

Lenox shook his head. "No doubt Musgrave had partners still in Bath. And the black dog upon the church door—perhaps it was a signal that they needed to see him, to consult with him. Or a threat?" At this Lenox smiled, despite his anger with himself.

"What is it?" asked Dallington.

"Only that for all their seeming hysteria, the people of Plumbley are proved quite correct in the end. Musgrave was an evil presence, and that black dog of his, Cincinnatus, corresponded to the black dog painted upon the church door."

"A stopped clock is right twice a day."

Lenox read the telegram again. "We must hope that Musgrave peaches on his friends in Bath."

"Funny that Wells should have been so afraid to name Musgrave even after he had left."

"No, I saw the shading of a terrible temper in the captain. Perhaps Wells did too, that day when they argued on the Plumbley green. When McConnell suggested that Mrs. Musgrave was with child I dismissed her husband from my mind as a suspect, but I ought to have done better. It is well that I'm out of the business, John."

"I cannot agree." Dallington lit his cigar, now tidily cut. "Do you think the wife was involved?"

"Time will tell."

This they would never know, in fact, for Plumbley took her in, her and her new daughter as well, and cloaked her in its silent care. Cousins, friends, enemies, all of them together provided her with a small set of rooms, with food, with friendship, and above all with silence. She had undergone a dreadful pregnancy, indeed seemed half a ghost and would never speak of Musgrave's treatment of her, or indeed of his affiliation with Wells. The village's propensity for judgment stilled itself and withered away in this case, replaced with generosity. She was, after all, a broken woman. Some time later, when Lenox very gently broached the subject to Fripp, the fruit-and-vegetable seller said, "It is all in the past—and better to let it lie there." In this sentence he summed up Plumbley's attitude toward Cat Scales, as had been Cat Musgrave.

All of that was in the months to come. As Dallington and Lenox sat in the study at Hampden Lane, chewing over the case anew, Musgrave was being taken to a prison in Bath.

In the next week many different people attempted to make him speak, but he would not; in the end they could only charge him with possession of fraudulent monies, a great deal of it, to be sure, but never enough to put him in jail for a very long term. His solicitors said there was no proof whatsoever that Musgrave knew the money was fake at all.

At the trial, in which both Dallington and Lenox testified, he received a sentence of two years. Yet it might be just as well to round off the tale here, and say that, despite the assiduous scrutiny of police in both Bath and London, upon his release Musgrave did nothing illegal, until one day, three or four months after his release, he took a train bound for Manchester, a very small valise in hand. He never came out at any of the stations along the voyage, and, as a final trick, didn't alight at Manchester either—in fact seemed to vanish straight into thin air. The police were confident he would appear in London, but in this they were wrong. Nobody caught sight of him again.

As for Wells, there was only ever one incident that proved him still alive.

His wife and his son had gone down in the world upon his departure, sold off their carriage, sold off their weekday china. Still, by dint of hard work in the shop they did manage to keep their large house, and to retain one of their horses. It helped that Mrs. Wells was a very pretty woman—blond, plump, and flirtatious, and the men of Taunton and Bath liked to deal with her. Slowly the shop, still called Wells and Son, grew to be successful.

At last, when she had saved enough capital, she and her sisters began a small sideline in selling scents. This was a talent they had cultivated since girlhood, and though at first only a small, dim shelf in the shop was devoted to their perfumes, after they received the patronage of Emily Jasper and several of her friends in

Bath, this part of the business began to grow—until at last there was no more grain merchant at all upon the town green, and Mrs. Wells's small, crystal bottles of lavender and primrose adorned the bureaus even of Mayfair.

Only she was no longer called Mrs. Wells—her name now, after a small ceremony presided over by the groom's master, was Mrs. Chalmers.

In a village as small as Plumbley no wedding is ever wholly surprising. This one came near it, however. Mrs. Wells had gone to visit the groom when he was recuperating and their friendship had, in the course of several slow years, grown into love. Her marriage having been dissolved by a court, on grounds of desertion, she was free to wed the man her husband had nearly killed.

Around the time of the wedding, and not long after the conversion of the shop to its new business, was when Wells popped his head out. A postcard arrived at the house one day that said, without any additional comment, FOR SHAME, MY FATHER'S SHOP.

It was tracked to a sailor in Kilkenny, who said he had been asked to post it by a man in Paris—but there the tracks ran cold. Lenox, for his part, never looked back on the case with much fondness or satisfaction, because the two men who bore perhaps the most responsibility for its crimes were somewhere out upon the face of the earth, settled and, if not contented, at any rate still free. While Weston and Oates were both cold in the churchyard of St. Stephen's.

If it bothered him overmuch, however, he consoled himself with two thoughts: first, that Chalmers was alive and well, still at the stables of Everley, and freshly married to, of all people born to womanhood, irony of ironies, Mrs. Wells; and second, that his Uncle Freddie might yet live to a ripe old age.

CHAPTER FORTY-NINE

I s your uncle quite well?" Dallington asked Lenox, still smoking his small cigar on that autumn day in Hampden Lane.

"Yes—in fact, he shall be here Monday, if you would like to dine with us."

"Oh, happily. Perhaps he will have more news from Archer."

After another fifteen minutes Dallington took his leave, eyeing the flowers as he went.

Almost immediately there was a knock at the door—another Parliamentary visitor for Lenox, who greeted him with a very convincing false cheer that, even as he acted it out, sent a chill down his spine.

At last I have truly become a politician, he realized. Yet he wanted desperately to change the laws of his country, and if this was the way to do it, so it should go, he thought. He took the man into his study, gave him a glass of sherry, and straight away began to cajole and bargain him around to supporting the new poor laws he had proposed.

That Saturday and Sunday passed as the days before them had, in great avalanches of parliamentary chatter. Graham for his part slept not more than three or four hours a night, while Lenox was constantly between his desk at home and his offices in Whitehall, rarely eating more than a piece of cheese between two breads.

"People speak ill of the Earl of Sandwich but I am grateful to him," he said to his brother when they passed each other in Bellamy's one day.

Therefore he had nearly forgotten that Frederick was arriving on that Monday. Fortunately it was a bank holiday, and the Commons wouldn't sit until the next evening. There were still meetings to attend, but by five o'clock he was home.

Jane was in her small rose-colored drawing room, writing at her desk, as Sophia slept in the bassinet next to her; the last lines of yellow light crossed the floor at a diagonal. When they had been simply friends it had been this room Lenox found the most comforting and homey of all the ones he knew, and still it offered him some evanescent pleasure—a woman's touch in the small framed mezzotints, in the particular draw of the lace curtains, in the ornate cedar coffee table.

"What news?" asked Lenox. He kept his voice soft.

She sat down by him, having kissed him on the cheek. "Sad news, I'm afraid."

"Oh?"

"It's Toto. I've just had a letter from her, down at her father's."

Lenox's heart fell. "Have they been arguing?"

"She has Georgianna with her, too. It must be terrible for Thomas—he so dotes on them both."

"But what quarrel can she possibly have with him?"

"Her letter is unclear on that point—only says that she cannot tolerate London at the moment, cannot tolerate the country either, and feels heartily sick of it all."

"I hope there is nothing of a permanent rift."

Jane raised her eyebrows. "It is difficult to say. I wonder whether I should go down to see her."

"Are you not planning the ball?"

"I would miss it, of course, for Toto."

"Shall I speak to Thomas?"

"No, don't. Or let him speak to you, if he likes."

Lenox shook his head. "I cannot imagine he will."

"As long as he has not taken advantage of the solitude to—anyhow, you know as well as I do."

"He didn't have his laboratory, his experiments, his marine studies, back in those drinking days. Not to so great an extent. Work is a great distraction."

She leaned her head against his shoulder. "Shall I call tea for you?"

"Thank you, no. We dine early tonight, do we not?"

"At seven, if Freddie really does come."

Lenox gestured toward the desk. "You were returning Toto's letter?"

"Oh, no, that is already sent. I was only—but can I tell you tomorrow?"

"Of course," he said.

She smiled up at him. "I think you will like the surprise."

They sat in companionable silence for some moments then, watching the listless light lose its color and then begin to disappear altogether. Through the window he could see smoke rising from the chimneys in Grosvenor Square. How nice it was to be inside and warm, on such a day; how fortunate. "Has Sophia had a productive day?"

"Miss Taylor read to her this morning, and she dined on a very great—a prodigious piece of meringue."

Lenox frowned. "Can that be healthy?"

"Children need eggs and milk, as far as I can gather."

"So much sugar, though?"

Jane laughed, pulling a strand of glossy dark hair behind her ear. "She is not so roly-poly as some children."

"No, she is perfect, of course. I suppose I should not wake her?"

"You may as well, or she won't sleep tonight. I shall ask Miss Taylor to change her into something fetching, too, for Freddie—her little yellow dress, perhaps."

The squire of Everley arrived punctually at a quarter to six that evening. As he always did in London he looked more harried than easy. He offered up some parcels to the footman, and took off his coat. "Cabman shouted at me," he said.

"Did he?" asked Lady Jane. "How rude!"

"I did fall asleep in his cab, I suppose, and we were blocking a line of traffic, from what I saw as I was . . . as I was hustled out. Still."

"Was your journey down happy?" asked Lady Jane, guiding him toward the drawing room and setting him in an armchair.

"Endurable, thank you."

"And Plumbley? Plumbley is well?"

Here they launched into a conversation about Musgrave—the town was taking it with shocking smugness, and also relief that the ordeal was finished.

There were other guests to arrive soon: Edmund and his wife; Dallington; and one or two of Frederick's acquaintances from schooldays. Jane thought that before they did and the tone of the evening grew more formal Sophia might be brought down.

She was, by Miss Taylor, who wore a fetching blue dress. "That reminds me," said Frederick. "Charles, if one of your men could fetch my parcels? I brought you, Miss Taylor, some cuttings of the flowers we spoke about in Somerset."

"How kind of you!" she said.

There was a knock at the door as he was presenting her with this parcel—it was Dallington, who came in, saw her, and rather seemed to blush. He was able to put a good countenance on his embarrassment. Lenox wondered whether there was anything at all to Jane's speculations. Perhaps, he thought.

It was a long dinner, with a great deal of laughter and storytelling. When it was finally over, and the men were putting on their cloaks in the hallway, Frederick started to don his as well. They had offered him a room here, on Hampden Lane, when he planned his visit, but he was an old bachelor and admitted freely that his club would best tolerate his idiosyncrasies.

"Did you not want to speak to me?" Lenox asked him. "Your letter—"

Frederick smiled at him. "Not just now. Perhaps in the morning you would have breakfast with me, at the Carlton? I will know my mind better then—best not to speak on serious subjects after a day of travel, a rich dinner, and a few glasses of wine."

"I should be very glad to breakfast with you. Eight, shall we say?"

"Capital." Frederick smiled, and Lenox recognized some ghost of his mother's smile therein, a fine lineament. "Charles," he said, the din of the other guests' conversation still covering their voices, "you will not be too down in the mouth, when I pass Everley on?"

"Not in the slightest," said Lenox stoutly, at last, in this very moment, having determined himself not to be.

"I'm glad to hear it. Until the morning, then."

"Until the morning."

CHAPTER FIFTY

Lenox had grown accustomed to rising with the daylight this past week, with so much to do, and having taken the previous evening off he was at his desk at six the next morning, reading the minutes of meetings he had skipped, answering his correspondence, and poring over lists of the members of the House who attended sessions infrequently, in the hopes of finding a name or two that might be rehabilitated and brought into the fold. Every so often he rubbed his eyes or took a sip of coffee. Otherwise there was no break in the work.

At half-seven he went upstairs to change from his comfortable morning coat, with its tattered hems at the wrist and the heel, into a smarter suit of clothes, appropriate for dining at Frederick's club. He felt tired in his bones as he mounted the stairs, but brightened when he saw Jane was upstairs, dressed for a morning round of calls.

"Have you seen Miss Taylor?" she said.

"I have not."

"She wished to speak to us."

"It will have to wait, unless it is about Sophia's health, in which case—"

"No, no, it is nothing of the kind. I shall tell her it must be later, though she was rather pressing in her request."

Upon saying this, Jane looked at him meaningfully: Dallington. Lenox frowned. "I hope she won't want to leave us. Just when we are all so used to each other's ways."

"In all likelihood it's some trifle. She's a methodical young woman."

"Let us hope so. In the meanwhile help me with this watch-chain, would you dear? I must be on my way to see my cousin."

The Carlton Club was a sleek and stuffy place—mahogany, red velvet, quiet voices. Quite foreign territory for Lenox, since it was occupied primarily by conservative politicians. In the dining room he waited for Frederick at a table, covered with a white cloth, laid out with silver and a slender crystal vase that held a rose. As he studied the flower two men from the opposite benches passed him with a cordial salutation. "Coming to our side, is it, Lenox?"

He laughed. "At any rate to your club."

Frederick, when he came down, looked fresh, not as dulled and battered as he had the night before. In fact Lenox would have told him he looked younger, if it didn't sound fanciful.

He skipped the last step up to see Lenox. "Charles! There you are! Here, I shall sit, don't stand—but look." He put the folded newspaper that had been tucked under his arm onto the table. "I find in the *Times* that you are made very great! You might have told me last night, anyhow."

Lenox frowned. "What have they reported?"

"Is it not true that you are to be a Junior Lord of the Treasury?"

"Ah, so they've got hold of that, have they? Yes, Hilary asked me on Wednesday. I must give him my decision tomorrow. It will be yes, I think. It must be yes."

"A thousand pounds a year, Charles! And then, the Treasury—you will be able to find Wells."

Lenox laughed. "No, no, it's nothing like that. There are plenty of men better equipped to handle the treasury than I am. It's more in the line of a . . . you might call me a whip. It will be a great deal of work, I fear."

"You look almost wistful, but it is a high achievement, Charles! Your father would have been proud. Your mother, too."

"I thank you. As to it's being a high achievement—they sent round a few sheets of paper with all the trivial details of the post, and there they hastened to remind me that even in this exalted new position, I must enter a room after the eldest sons of viscounts. They included a list, who else was it? The youngest sons of earls—"

"The eldest of baronets, the youngest of viscounts—"

"And the commissioner of Bankruptcy may positively lord his situation over me! While I am a very inferior creature, not even in the same field of play as the Master of Horse."

Both were smiling now. "Still, I propose a toast. Hail that man and ask for champagne."

Lenox did it. His smile came from pleasure in Frederick's company, not from the promotion—of course it was happy news, but like all happy news it carried with it an implication of forsaken choices. Nevertheless Lenox accepted his cousin's congratulations with good grace.

The waiter came back with the champagne. "Shall I open it?"

Lenox was about to nod, but Frederick said, "After we've eaten, Sam, thank you. If we might have eggs, fried bread, a few sausages, and a good deal of coffee—Charles, is there anything else you would like?"

"Thank you, no."

A silence crept into the moment after the waiter had gone, and then began to expand until it became rather embarrassed. Both men were conscious that they had now to address whatever it was that the elder of the two had wished to speak about, and Lenox, for his part, disliked to push the issue. After fifteen or twenty seconds they both undertook to speak at the same time.

"No, you must begin," said Lenox.

"I do have one or two things I should like to discuss with you."

He steeled himself. There would be legal matters over Everley's ownership, advice to ask about the old-planted forests—might they be protected from cutting for some term of years—and perhaps even a confidential word or two about Wendell, that Lenox should bear him some special kindness.

There was still a pang in his heart as he contemplated these questions, but it was muffled now. He had made up his mind to let go of Everley.

As it happened, however, his expectations of the conversation were incorrect. What Frederick actually had to say astonished him.

"At my age there is no refined way of saying this, Charles." He coughed and looked down at the table, adjusted his fork and knife. "I am to be married."

At this very crucial moment, when Lenox was agog with interest at what his cousin said, a white-haired gentleman came to their table. "Mr. Lenox," he said. "I agreed whole-heartedly with your speech."

Both of the men rose. "Baron Rothschild. I know of all you did in the famine in Ireland, so your support is not unexpected—but I am very glad indeed to hear of it."

"Much good may it do you—I think I shall very probably be turned out of my seat at the next election." He laughed, croakily.

This was Lionel Rothschild, scion of the great banking family. He had had one of the most interesting careers in the history of English politics; many years before he had won a seat in the Commons, but, because he was Jewish and therefore would not make the Anglican oath of office, had been barred from taking it. In protest he had left the seat vacant for a decade. To his eternal credit, Lord John Russell—off-and-on-again prime minister, and one of Lenox's closest allies in politics—had forced a law through the Houses permitting Jews to sit in Parliament. Nevertheless Victoria, the Queen, had, despite the entreaties of many powerful men, positively refused to elevate Rothschild to the House of Lords—to her eternal discredit, some might say.

"Do you know my cousin, Frederick Ponsonby?"

Frederick shook hands and said, "I don't know that we have met, but I once saw one of your horses at Epsom, in 'sixty-eight. A beautiful creature."

The old man smiled; he had been very handsome once, but now stood rather rickety. "We shall win Epsom one of these times, too. Good day, gentlemen."

They bowed, and when Rothschild had paced off some ten slow feet away from them sat down again. "My goodness," said Lenox in a low voice, "you do keep your cards hidden, Freddie. You have my sincere congratulations. Who is the woman?"

"There is another piece of news to go along with this."

"Oh?"

"I was quite sincere when I said I was coming to London in order to see Wendell, to speak with him about the transfer of Everley's ownership. But I think that my new plans—well, I knew that I would throw the dice one final time, and it happens by pure luck that they have turned up in my favor. I shall keep Everley for myself a while longer, to put it plainly. With a partner it may be easier, I hope."

Lenox felt his heart rise with joy. "Then I shall love the woman even more. But who is she?"

"I suppose I must seem mysterious, but it is only because I must ask your indulgence."

"Mine? Why?"

"The young lady in question is your governess, you see. Miss Taylor."

CHAPTER FIFTY-ONE

Lenox was speechless.

"Well, Charles?"

"You have my congratulations! I scarcely know what else to say, I'm so surprised." Amid all of the various puzzlements the news presented, one stood out. "You only saw her in passing yesterday, though, I believe? Has this been settled for some time?"

Frederick shook his head. "With the parcel of cuttings I left for her yesterday evening was a letter, and this morning I had her acceptance by messenger. I had scarcely dreamed she would say yes—had fully planned on proceeding with my plans to hand Everley over to Wendell—but now this wonderful thing has happened, you see, it changes everything. You are not dissatisfied with my conduct, Charles? She is a wonderful woman."

"Dissatisfied, never, so long as Miss Taylor is happy. Merely knocked for a loop, cousin."

"The gap in our ages is very great."

"Lord Wrexham married a seventeen-year-old when he was in

the back half of his eighties. I don't think you and Miss Taylor will excite much comment."

"Except in Plumbley."

Lenox laughed. "It's true, they'll be surprised in Plumbley."

Frederick put a hand on the champagne bottle that stood in its silver bucket by the table. "Perhaps we might have our toast now?"

As the idea lost its newness over the course of their breakfast, as he grew accustomed to its counters, it came to seem less outlandish to Lenox. He pictured them as they had been at Everley, amiably walking through the gardens, she with a sobriety beyond her years, after the annealing tragedies of her youth, he with a long provincial gentleness that looked, perhaps, something like youth.

Then her birth was good, if not excellent, and her character was sterling.

He recalled the glint in Freddie's eye after his long day upon the road to Bath with Wells and Oates. What had he said that night? *It shows a man what he wants from life, believing he will die.* The past weeks had certainly changed him. It was a happy change, too; after their second glass of champagne together, the squire's face was shining with an unwonted joy, with a vitality that had been missing a month before.

What would Jane think? he wondered.

Dallington might be disappointed. Still, he would have dozens of chances to marry, if he wished, while Freddie must have given up on the idea, what, ten or twenty years before. It was providence that had brought Miss Taylor to his home.

"Have you spoken about when you are to be married?" Lenox asked, spearing a sausage on his fork

"No. I am inclined to wait until the spring. At any rate I am staying in London a few days longer than I had anticipated, that I might see her." A troubled look passed over his face. "Perhaps a wedding would be undignified, though."

"Never in life. It needn't be a large wedding, or a town wedding, of course."

"The difficulty of being married in Everley is that I'm the magistrate."

"Rodgers can do it," said Lenox, smiling.

Frederick laughed. "It is not unlikely that I can persuade the vicar to do the job."

After they were finished they went to the club's library and sat among its lines of morocco-bound books, smoking and talking in low voices. Frederick was an unexcitable soul, but there was a placid euphoria in his words and gestures.

After they had parted, the squire off to see his heir, Lenox stopped by the Commons briefly to have a word with Graham, then returned to Hampden Lane. There he found his wife pacing the front hallway.

Lady Jane had a combination of warmth and reserve that Lenox loved; she was rarely discomposed, and absorbed news quietly and methodically, but never coldly. He was surprised, therefore, to observe her agitation.

"Jane," he said.

"You had better come into the drawing room. Miss Taylor would like a word with us together."

"Is everything quite well with Sophia?"

"Yes. Did your uncle tell you—no, come in, speak with her for yourself."

He put a hand on her wrist to stop her pacing. "Freddie told me. You are not upset, surely?"

"I am upset for John Dallington, yes, and I think it entirely inappropriate that two people of their respective ages should break convention and make themselves a spectacle."

"Come, this is not like you," he said in a quiet voice. "It means Freddie will keep Everley."

"As if I cared a fig for that."

Suddenly Lenox perceived that Jane's plans for Dallington and Miss Taylor had borne a far greater weight of aspiration than he had previously understood. The Duchess of Marchmain was one of her closest friends, her concerns quite intimately Jane's concerns. "Is she quite upset, Dallington's mother?"

"You were always as blind as a mole, Charles. Everyone in London is speaking about her son's behavior at Gordon's. She hasn't slept in weeks, she hasn't—"

There was more to it than that. They were losing their governess, she was a new mother, easily rattled, she had put Lenox's speech before her own needs for many weeks now. And her friends were, perhaps, all unhappy. "Did the post this morning bring anything else from Toto?"

She looked him in the eye, her lip trembling. "No, unfortunately, it did not."

"Come and sit with me for a moment in the study, my dear. You shall have a glass of sherry."

"At eleven in the morning?"

"At eleven in the morning."

It was low of him, but he felt a kind of pleasure in bringing his own calm to bear on her consternation for once. So often it had been the reverse. He led her into his study, sat her by the fire—low and glowing orange now, soon rekindled—and stayed with her there until she had regained her composure. In time, he knew, she would find great happiness in Freddie's betrothal.

After ten minutes, she said, "Miss Taylor is still in the drawing room, Charles. She'll have heard you come home."

When he entered the drawing room Lenox smiled kindly at the governess. She was more self-possessed than Lady Jane, but he didn't know what words had passed between them, and there was a certain color in her cheeks that might have indicated high emotion. Then again it was a cool day.

"I'm so sorry it has taken me this long to come and see you, Miss Taylor," he said.

She rose. "I received this letter from your cousin yesterday, Mr. Lenox—"

"I don't need to read it, only to offer my congratulations."

"I would feel happier if you read it, since I live under your auspices, currently."

To oblige her he took the note. It was written very formally and rather beautifully, too. *Since I first walked with you in the west gardens a fortnight ago,* Frederick began, *I have entertained the liveliest affection for you—indeed I might call it love, if I did not fear it would be a trespass against your goodwill. I write now to ask whether you might reciprocate my emotions.* It went on to describe his situation in detail, what she might expect as an allowance, the society of Plumbley, his general aversion to London (though he agreed that he might take a house in town for "a week or two in the season, should we be wed, preferably the shorter duration"), and ended by describing all that he found congenial in her character, and restating his admiration of her.

"I think it is a very fine letter," said Lenox, "and again, can only offer you my congratulations. We shall be sorry to lose your services, of course, but it will be a delight for Sophia to know you as an aunt."

"Do you think him a good man?" asked the governess, waving away his politeness.

"I know of none better." Lenox hesitated for a moment. "For some time I thought John Dallington might have been courting you, however."

She smiled. "John? He's only half a boy, you know. About Freddie—you do not think I would be making a mistake? I believe I love him," she said, and for the first time he heard the tone of petition in her voice.

It was because of this tone that he saw what he had not before. What she sought was not his congratulations, but something else, something she could not find elsewhere: a father's advice.

With a sense of tenderness, mingled with pity, he gestured for her to sit down. "Let us take it point by point," he said, and semi-conciously his voice lowered a half-step. "First let us discuss his social position, then, and after that we can move on to his finances, and then we ought to review his—"

"Oh, yes, thank you," she said, sitting back, and her face was flooded with relief.

CHAPTER FIFTY-TWO

That was a very cold winter in London. In the House of Commons one could see one's breath, and for Lenox, in his new position, the hours and days and weeks were taken up with work, with long, exhausting meetings, too often unproductive, and—just as often—with coaxing recalcitrant liberal members to vote as the leaders of the party wished. These conferences were almost always made under a social pretext, and he grew wholly tired of the sight of his club on Pall Mall, which had once been a refuge to him.

Still, each morning he permitted himself a half hour with Sophia. She was growing rapidly, it seemed to both him and Jane, and she could sit unsupported now, even recognized voices from other rooms; her taste in toys, meanwhile, had become positively sophisticated, though she had a regrettable fondness for the loud rattle, painted a lethal shade of mauve, that her uncle Edmund had given her.

Miss Taylor was still living there, because in all truth she had nowhere else to which she might remove herself, unless it be lodgings, and all concerned, especially Frederick, considered this too dreary a prospect. It helped to have her in the house: From afar, Jane was planning the wedding at Everley.

It was not her only project.

Late one evening, while Lenox struggled to keep his eyes open over a report on sheep farming in Northumberland, she came to his study. "Hello, dear," he said, standing. "I thought you had gone to sleep."

"Not by a long shot," she said. She was holding something behind her back. "Are you busy with your reading, Charles?"

"I would pay ten pounds to the person who gave me an excuse to stop," he said, smiling and stifling a yawn, stretching his arms out.

"Do you remember when I was so secretive at Everley? You stopped asking—which I take kindly, you know." She smiled at him softly. "Pressure never does, with this kind of thing."

"Of course," he said—but in truth he had forgotten all about it, once they were out of Somerset and he had less occasion to notice her habits.

Shyly she handed him a book. "Here it is."

He furrowed his brow and took a loose sheaf of papers from her, perhaps twenty pages of them. "*The Adventure of the Lucy*," he said. There was a picture of a small gray mouse below the title, wearing a morning jacket and looking out to sea through a telescope from the taffrail of a ship. "Is it a story?" he asked, smiling with the dawning realization that it was.

"It's nothing much," she said and stood up, then began to fix the cushions on his sofa. "I thought I might show you—one or two other people—for Sophia, you understand, after my great tour of the children's books left me desirous of something different."

"Who did the drawings, Jane?"

"Oh, Molly."

That was Edmund's wife, who was talented with watercolors. She made compact drawings, full of detail, often rather wistful; he should have recognized them straight away. "Come sit by me as I read it," he said. "Please."

She laughed skeptically—would have snorted, had her upbringing been different—and said, "I couldn't. But read it if you like."

So he did, awake now, with a glass of whisky in hand.

Once there was a mouse named Bancroft, and you will be surprised to learn that though he was only a mouse, and at that rather a small mouse, with a kind intelligent little face, he commanded one of the finest ships to sail the seven seas. She was called the Lucy, and in all respects she was like any other ship of England—ask your father, who has probably been on one and bumped his head on the low ceiling, and he will tell you all about it—with one notable exception: There were to be no shipboard cats. It would be much more difficult to find the lost Lady Sophia, after all, if the mice of the Lucy were at all hours listening for the footsteps of an enemy.

After only these few words Lenox was charmed, and as he read on his enchantment increased. The book told the tale of this troop of mice, and in many of its particulars—its gentler particulars—it mirrored the voyage he had made, not quite a year before, to Egypt. There were differences, needless to say. The mice successfully captured a pirate ship (full of cats) and landed on an island with a solitary human being living upon it, tired of London and committed to living there until he had grown a beard all the way to his feet. Their true mission—the recapture of a mouse girl named Sophia, who had been put on the wrong ship in Portsmouth—they fulfilled on the second to last page. On the last page they all had Christmas together, in Portsmouth again.

The book was funny, slightly magical, more contemplative and less madcap than many children's books—certainly less moralizing, too. He felt proud of her. There was no question that it was a book that could find a public. Its pages went by before you realized you were reading at all.

Yet for some reason that he could not quite explain, reading the book and looking at its drawings filled him with a bittersweet sorrow, almost too heavy to bear. It felt as if it belonged to the past, perhaps that was it—the book had a lightness of tone and spirit that their lives had once had, too, but now, in this cold winter, had lost.

So often as one looked back on life one saw a multiplicity of choices, reduced, not quite at random, to one. There were so many houses he might have taken in London; so many women he might have fallen into marriage with; so many cases he might have taken. Rarely was there a clear path, with two choices.

Here was one, however, that he had made. Reading about the *Lucy* reminded him that what he loved—travel, adventure, detection—he had now traded for a different kind of work.

After he had finished reading he sat and stared into the fire for some time, sipping his drink. He didn't know how long had passed when he heard a soft knock on the door; then, of course, he leaped to his feet and congratulated his wife on her triumph.

Throughout the first week of December both Lady Jane and the governess were closeted in the upstairs drawing room, planning for the wedding. Occasionally another person would stop in—Toto, who was back in London and rather pale, but couldn't resist talk of a wedding—and all three of them would discuss invitations, dresses, food. (The one responsibility Frederick had retained for himself was the flowers.) It was all to happen in April.

"I always say that an April wedding is loveliest, you know," Lenox could hear Toto saying one bright morning, "though Elizabeth Wallace was married on the first of the month, in Oxford, and as far as I can gather she would have done better to marry a mule, her husband—"

"Toto!" said Jane.

"It's true, though."

Miss Taylor was always the person who retrieved the conversation. "The point is that I cannot wear white. I've been too old for that since I was twenty-two."

"What tosh," said Toto. "You'll look lovely—you have just the complexion for an ivory white." Lenox, still eavesdropping, smiled to himself. "The only question is whether you ought to be married sooner."

"Sooner?"

"Why wait, I say?"

"Toto," said Jane, but she ought to have known her cousin was irrepressible.

"I think a Christmas wedding would be the finest thing I ever saw."

"Toto, you scarcely know Miss Taylor."

"How rude you are, Jane, really I think you are—here we are, three friends—aren't I coming to Everley to see you wed, dear heart?"

The governess laughed happily. "I should like it very much if you would."

"See? There. Now the great virtue of a Christmas wedding . . ."

So, after only ten hours or so of discussion, Miss Taylor was pushed toward a writing desk to ask Frederick whether they might be married sooner than he had anticipated. He wrote back by the next post: No haste was too great for him, and he knew just the holly tree he could cut from, the true *Ilex aquifolium* by Everley's lake.

CHAPTER FIFTY-THREE

In the very early hours of Christmas that year, it snowed in Plumbley.

"What a pity," said Lady Jane when they woke to see the world white and angelic, the trees fringed with powder, Everley's long lanes unbroken by footprints.

"What can you mean?" asked Lenox.

"Snow is so messy. I warned Toto."

"You're not much of a romantic, my dear."

They dressed and ate breakfast alone, Frederick having taken his breakfast in his room, while his soon-to-be wife was staying with Toto, her chief adviser now, in the dower house, McConnell, only partially back in her good graces, nearby at Everley. At nine o'clock Lenox and Jane stepped into one of the carriages that waited along the avenue. The horses that pulled them into town were strangers, hired for the day, but Lenox had gone to see Sadie in her stable the day before. He had tried to sneak her a carrot but she turned her nose up at it, having become very spoiled, now, and snorting until she received an apple each morning.

The village had rarely looked better. The town green was a smooth white. Steps away, on the porch of St. Stephen's, there was a great mass of black coats and top hats, people speaking to each other between the merrily green-garlanded pillars of the church.

Everyone had turned out, it seemed. There was Fripp, who placed a proprietary hand on Lenox's elbow and walked him around; Millington, the blacksmith and cricket captain; fat Mr. Kempe, red from the cold; and dozens besides, all full of "Happy Christmas" and sure that the snow was a sign of good luck.

Then, too, there was someone Lenox had particularly hoped to see, Dr. Eastwood, with his newly betrothed: Lucy, the niece of Emily Jasper and Lenox's old Plumbley friend.

The news was fresh, and so was Lucy, who looked giddy with happiness. She had the feminine beauty—there is none like it in the world, not even in the loveliest eighteen year old—that comes to a woman who has thought her time was gone and past, who has resigned herself to a life alone, and then finds herself truly in love. It was a kind of radiance beyond radiance. She ducked her head and blushed when Lenox congratulated her, her lined eyes full of joy, and held tighter to Eastwood's arm. For his part the doctor seemed so pleased as to be a new man.

"The great virtue of getting married today is that they shall have to see very little of me." He looked at Lucy. "We shall get married on a Monday, too, perhaps."

Lenox looked at him quizzically. "Why is that?"

"You remember, Charles," said Lady Jane, "Marry on Monday for health, Tuesday for wealth, Wednesday the best day of all, Thursday for crosses, Friday for losses, and Saturday for no luck at all."

"What day did we get married, dear?"

"Can you have forgotten? It was a Saturday."

"Then I think it a very stupid rhyme."

"Perhaps it should be Saturday for the most luck of all," said Lucy.

"I like that better."

Besides the villagers, Lenox shook hands with a great many distant cousins, glad to exchange a word with them: Plans were made for suppers and luncheons in London, news of the old house in Devon was passed from mouth to mouth, and cousin Wendell, beatific and plump, said he had driven past Everley that morning when he arrived and it looked "capital, simply capital."

Lenox felt a fondness for the man now. "When it is yours, will you keep the trees as Frederick has them?" he asked.

"Wouldn't think of changing 'em—always liked a tree, myself, I think them a very companionable sort of person."

Soon, by some mysterious common consent, they made their way into the church and filled the pews. Lenox and Lady Jane sat in the third row; already there was Dallington, who was staying at the King's Arms. He had seemed slightly wan when the subject of Frederick and the governess arose in the past months, but he had always set his mouth firmly and said that he was, "Delighted for them—no, and I shall send them a cracking great hogshead of champagne for their wedding day."

Rushing in at the last minute, having caught an early train apparently, was Edmund, accompanied by his wife, Molly, a cheery fuschia ribbon tying her hair up, and, to Lenox's surprise and joy, their son, Teddy. He looked taller at fifteen than he had even six months earlier. He didn't wear his midshipman's uniform, but his bearing seemed, nevertheless, naval.

Lenox stood up, and in a church whisper, said, "My dear Teddy, you came! How long are you ashore?"

"Only two weeks. But have you heard I'm studying for lieutenant? And there's so much to report from the *Lucy*. Carrow told me especially to say hello, and Cresswell said—"

The opening chords of the organ hushed him, and they crowded into a row together. Frederick, looking unflustered and with a sprig of something wintry in his buttonhole, appeared at the altar—and then the bride came in.

It was uncommon indeed for a bride past the age of twenty to wear white—indeed that color was only consecrated as the ideal twenty-four years earlier, when Victoria had worn it to marry Albert—and no doubt when she married Eastwood, Lucy would opt for gray or blue. Yet with the light of a recent snow still falling gently through the windows, the world clear and soft, it looked beautiful, looked eternal. Lenox felt a fatherly sensation as he watched the governess walk down the aisle and then thought of Sophia—and realized, with gratitude, that the world was always offering him lessons, if he chose to take them. One day the little infant beside him would walk down an aisle like this. Time! How it played you forward, how it filled the world with people to love, how cruel and wonderful at once it could seem. When Miss Taylor stopped at the altar he thought, for a very brief moment, that tears might come into his eyes. Soon enough he mastered himself and the ceremony began.

An hour later they were back at Everley, part of a great multitude of people who were congregated in the hall to celebrate with Mr. and Mrs. Ponsonby.

"Charlie!" called Fripp, holding a glass of champagne.

"Wish you much joy, Mr. Fripp," said Lenox, smiling.

"There hasn't been a turn-out like this that I can recall since the old squire's funeral."

"A cheery observation."

Fripp laughed. "Try an orange, there on the sideboard, if you like. I brought them up this morning, as a present, you know."

You could say for the village that it annihilated some distinctions of class that the metropolis enforced; there was to be a supper later only for the cousins and the likes of Emily Jasper, but this wedding breakfast saw every stripe of person come together. Lady

Jane was speaking to some of the women from the cricket pavilion; Toto was fretting with a farmer's wife about the state of the bride's train; Dallington and Wendell were reminiscing with the veterinarian from West Buckland about Wells and his coining operation.

Perhaps it wasn't the village, though; perhaps it was Frederick.

Finding himself alone for a moment, Lenox watched the bride and groom. He was pleased, so very pleased, that they would stay in Everley. He didn't quite understand why. It was something to do with his mother, in truth: He had believed, before he lost anyone, that after a person died there was a process of comprehension for those left behind, a waning sense of loss. In fact all that happened was that days went on passing, whether you wished them to or not—even for the suffering the sun would rise, casting its inhuman chemistries over the earth, even for the suffering there was food, water, and what color to paint the second bedroom. The formality of a funeral was a deceit; everything that followed it was strayness, pangs, forgetting, remembering, unguided, and unnegotiable.

Then there was Parliament. Every generation no doubt considers themselves especially burdened, their souls harried and pent— certainly each finds of itself that it falls very late in history, as no doubt the Vikings did, to exist so many hundreds of years beyond the legends, or the medieval priests who knew that it had been a thousand years since the birth of Christ. Lenox was not immune from this feeling; and Everley, perhaps, while Freddie was there, represented an inoculation against it.

At about two that afternoon most of the people left, and there was a brief lull in the schedule before supper. "Shall we take Sophia for a walk?" asked Lenox.

"Isn't it too cold?"

"It's brightened up now, and we can bundle her up."

To their surprise the child's old caretaker, now Mrs. Ponsonby, overheard them and asked if she might come, too. "Everyone imagines me much busier than I am," she said. "Mostly it has been waiting." Then Freddie decided that he might as well come, too—there were some very fine waxberries if they walked the loop around the pond.

So they bundled the young girl, with her alert eyes, her pink cheeks, in a mountain of warm clothes, set her in her pram—sturdy enough to conquer the snow, certainly—and set out to walk the path along the pond, happily chattering about the morning, in anticipation of the goose that was being cooked for the evening.

In the library Edmund and Teddy were both reading, the father a parliamentary report, the son a manual on the azimuth compass.

When he noticed his brother outside, Edmund stood up and walked to the cold glass window, close enough that he could press his nose against it. How happy they looked!

As Edmund watched, half a smile on his face, Freddie stopped his guests' procession under a broad-branched evergreen and began to lecture them; when he tapped the trunk knowledgably with his cane, however, a great bank of snow shifted in the tree and crashed over them.

Edmund laughed out loud. "Teddy, go and fetch a cloak to the front door for your aunt and your cousin, if you would. I think they'll have need of it." Indeed, the whole party had by now already begun to turn back, smiling, laughing, and, in Jane's case, rather exasperated: making together for the warmth of home.

Turn the page for a sneak peek at
Charles Finch's new novel

AN OLD BETRAYAL

Available Fall 2013

CHAPTER ONE

The long green benches of the House of Commons were half-deserted as the evening session began, scattered with perhaps a few dozen men. It was only six o'clock. As the hours moved toward midnight these rows would fill, and the voices speaking would grow louder to be heard, but for now many of the Members of Parliament were still attending to the chops, the pints of porter, and the ceaseless gossip of the House's private dining room.

In the front bench to the left side of the chamber sat a man with a short beard and kind, intelligent eyes, rather thinner than most gentlemen who were just beyond, as he was, the age of forty. He wore a quiet gray evening suit, and though by now many along the benches had begun to lounge backwards and even, in some instances, close their eyes, his face and posture evinced no rebellion against the more or less limitless boredom that the House was capable of inflicting upon its observers. His name was Charles Lenox: once upon a time he had been a practicing detective, and while he still kept a careful eye upon the criminal world, for some years he had been the Member of Parliament for Stirrington, and politics now comprised the chief work of his life.

"Lenox?" whispered a voice behind him.

He turned and saw that it was the Prime Minister. In his early days in Parliament such an informal address from such a figure would have awed Lenox, but now, having moved by his own industry from the backbenches to the front, he was accustomed to Disraeli's presence—if perhaps not his company. Rising to an inconspicuous stoop, he said, "Good evening, Prime Minister."

Disraeli motioned him down and sat beside him, then went on, still in a low voice, "I cannot imagine why you have brought yourself here so early in the evening. Not to hear Swick?"

Across the aisle, several rows up, a gentleman was speaking. He was Augustus Swick, a notorious crank. His speech had begun, several minutes before, with the comforting assertion that in his view England had never been in a worse position. Now he had moved on to more personal issues. As he spoke his enormous white moustache shook at its fringes.

"It is 1875, gentlemen, and still I cannot walk across St. James's Street to the Carlton Club without being harassed by every variety of vehicle, your omnibus, your reckless hansom cab, your landau, your rapid, far too rapid, clarence—"

"Pierpont!" called out a lazy voice from a backbench.

"I am delighted to hear that name, sir!" cried Swick, reddening, his brow set so grimly that this profession of delight seemed less than sincere. "Yes, Pierpont! I had hoped his name might arise, because I must enquire of this chamber, are we all to go to private expense, as Colonel Pierpont did, to install islands in the middle of every road we wish to cross? Do every man's means extend so far? Can private citizens be expected to bear such a burden? I ask you, gentlemen, where will it end? Will it take a horse trampling me to death in Jermyn Street before the attention of this chamber is drawn to the problem of London's traffic?"

"May as well try it and find out," called out the same voice, to mild laughter.

Swick, outraged, drew himself up further and Disraeli, with a wink, took the opportunity to move to the front bench across the aisle—for he was a Conservative, though he liked to stop in among his foes for a friendly word when the chamber was empty. He was sharp, this fellow. He had turned out Lenox's own party's leader, William Gladstone, the year before, but since then he had very carefully won around both sides of the House by tempering his imperial ambitions for England with an unexpected social conscience. Just that evening they were going to discuss the Artisans' and Labourers' Dwellings Improvement Act—a bill that sounded as if it might have come from Gladstone himself.

And in fact this was why Lenox had come to the chamber early. He had a word to get in.

By the time Swick had finished speaking, ten or fifteen more men had filed into the Commons and the serious business of the evening was near its commencement. The Speaker recognized the only man to stand after Swick—Edward Twinkleton, a midlands glue baron. He began to address Disraeli's act.

The housing of the poor was a serious issue, perhaps the one to which Lenox had, in recent months, devoted more time than any other. Only that morning he had driven to the slums of Hungerford to see the problem firsthand.

Despite its origin in his own conservative benches, Twinkleton stood firmly against the bill, and was now making a long-winded argument about the idle poor. When he had concluded Lenox stood up and, after recognition from the Speaker, began his response.

"The chief issue is not, as my honorable friend presumes, one of the comfort of our poorer citizens, but of their health. May I ask whether he is familiar with the usual, and vile, practice of the builders in these neighborhoods? Commissioned by Her Majesty's government to construct new edifices, they take the very fine gravel we, the taxpayers, have purchased—for the construction of the foundation—and they sell it on the black market. Then they replace it with something called 'dry core,' gentlemen, a mixture of trash, dead animals, and vegetables. It is only March, but in the summer, I am informed, the smell is beyond belief. Can we rightly call this England, if Parliament gives its endorsement, this evening, to such practices?"

Lenox sat down and thought he saw Disraeli incline his head slightly across the aisle in thanks—though perhaps not.

Twinkleton rose. "I commend my honorable friend's insight into the issue, and yet it cannot be lost on him that these people have always lived in the city, always in suchlike conditions, and that there seem to be more of them than ever! No amount of dry core reduces their number!"

Lenox stood to respond. "The honorable gentleman from Edgbaston neglects to consider, perhaps, the historical context of our time. During the period of the honorable gentleman's childhood—"

"As I did not receive a card from my honorable friend upon the occasion of my birthday, I do not see how he can be so certain of my age."

This drew a big laugh, but Lenox bore onward. "During the period of the honorable gentleman's childhood," he said, "or thereabouts, one in five Britons lived in a city. Now it is edging toward four in five. Even to a very dim intellect that must be acknowledged a change."

There was laughter on the one side, and a diffident round of hissing and catcalling on the other, all very usual, at this slight, and as Lenox sat down upon the green baize bench, smiling faintly, Twinkleton rose up, his face also traced with amusement, clearly raring for battle. But the Speaker, chary perhaps of any further devolution of courtesy in the chamber, chose to call for rebuttal instead on Montague, a Member from Liverpool. Twinkleton would have his chance again in a moment. In the meanwhile, Montague, who had all the charisma and verve of a dying houseplant, returned the tone of the House's discourse to its proper tedium.

When Montague had been speaking for ten minutes or so, Lenox saw that a red-haired boy was approaching him, having darted down one of the aisles. This was Frabbs, his clerk, a bright and attentive lad. He handed Lenox a note. "Just came to the office, sir," he said.

"Thank you," said Lenox.

He tore the envelope and read the short note inside. Interesting. "Any reply, sir?" asked Frabbs.

"No, but find Graham and ask him whether the vote on this bill will come in this evening, or if he thinks there will be another day of debate. You can signal me from the door, I shall keep an eye on it."

"Yes, sir."

Graham was Lenox's political secretary, his most important ally; it was a position in most instances occupied by some ambitious son of the upper classes, fresh from Charterhouse or Eton, but Graham was, unusually—perhaps even uniquely—a former servant. For many years he had been Lenox's valet. A compact, sandy-haired, and shrewd fellow, he had taken to the position without faltering, and now had more to do with the running of Parliament than fully half of the body's own Members.

As Montague bored onward, down into the depths of his prepared remarks, Lenox's eyes kept flitting to the side door where

Frabbs would appear. Catching himself at it once too often, he smiled: it was the old internal debate, the mild pleasures of Parliament, the sense of duty he felt to be there, laid against the thrill of being out on the hunt. Detective work.

Lenox's father had been a great man in the Commons, and now his older brother Sir Edmund Lenox stood among the two or three chiefs of the party. For his part, Charles had always taken a great interest in politics too—had sometimes wished that the seat in the family's bestowal, which of course Edmund took, might have been his—and had been thrilled when he won his own. It felt like an ascent, for in truth many of his class looked upon Lenox's previous career as a folly, even an embarrassment.

But how he missed the old life! Twice in the past two years he had emerged briefly from retirement, on both occasions in singular circumstances, and now he often thought of those cases, their particular details, with a longing to be back in the middle of them. No morning passed in which he did not pore over the crime columns of the newspapers, coffee growing cold in its cup.

He thought of all this because of the note Frabbs had passed him: it was from his former protégé in detection Lord John Dallington, asking for help on a case. Having read it ten minutes before, Lenox itched with irritation at his position already, eager to be gone from the Commons.

It was true that he had promised Disraeli, and several other men, that he would be an assiduous participant in these debates. But he had already exchanged words with Twinkleton once, and for an hour or two's absence he would hardly be missed. Particularly if the vote was to be delayed beyond that evening.

Ah! There was Frabbs's head, popping around the doorjamb—and yes, there was the thumb in the air. With a murmuring goodbye to the men on his bench, and a promise that he would return just after the break, Lenox stood and made for the exit, happier than he had been since he left the house that morning. A strange circumstance, Dallington's note had promised. Lenox smiled. Who knew what might await him out there in the great fervid rousing muddle of London?

CHAPTER TWO

A stroll up and across Green Park took Lenox to Half Moon Street, where Dallington lived. The address was a fashionable one, popular especially among the young and idle rich, lying as it did close by both their clubs and Hyde Park, where they might ride their horses in the morning. Dallington lived toward the Curzon Street end, almost precisely halfway between Parliament and Lenox's own house in Hampden Lane, which was situated in the leafy, more sedate precincts of Grosvenor Square.

John Dallington, the youngest son of a very kindly duke and duchess, must have been twenty-seven or -eight by now—but he was fixed in many London minds as a disreputable cad of twenty, who had been sent down from Cambridge in sordid circumstances, then spent the next years making the acquaintance of every gin hall and debauched aristocrat in Mayfair.

This image might have been just once, but by now it was unfair. Lenox knew as much firsthand. Several years before, Dallington had, to the older man's very great astonishment, expressed an interest in detective work, and though the lad was still prone, in times of boredom, to relapse, to visit with friends from that less seemly era of his life, by and large he had settled into adulthood. His apprenticeship to Lenox had been profitable to both men. Indeed, through his own intelligence and industry he had now succeeded Lenox as the premier private detective in the city—or at the very least trailing just behind one or two other men who followed the same calling.

Dallington inhabited a chalk-colored building of four floors, taking the large second story to himself. At the front door now was the neighborhood's postman, in his familiar uniform, the scarlet tunic and high black hat. Dallington's landlady—a redoubtable and highly proper personage in her twenty-fifth month of mourning for her husband, only a little black crepe around her shoulders— answered the door and took the post, then saw Lenox further down the steps.

"Mr. Lenox?" she said, as the postman touched his hat and retreated.

"How do you do, Mrs. Lucas?" Lenox asked, rising to the top of the steps.

"Are you here to see Lord John, sir?"

"If I might."

"Perhaps you can convince him to take his toast and water."

"Has he been ill?" Toast and water was the food considered most suitable for convalescents, at least for those who belonged to the generation of Lenox, of Mrs. Lucas, of Twinkleton—boiling water poured over burnt toast, and mashed into something like gruel. Personally Lenox had never found it palatable.

This made sense of the note, at any rate, which had contained a postscript apologizing that the young Lord couldn't come to him.

"You shall see for yourself," she said, turning and leading him into the dim hallway.

"Not contagious, is he?"

"Only his mood, sir."

"I see."

She lifted a candle from the table in the front hall and led him up the stairs. A boy was sweeping them, but made way.

"Mr. Lenox, here to see you," called the landlady when they reached Dallington's door, tapping it chidingly with her nails.

"Push him in!" called out the young Lord. "Unless he doesn't like to get consumption."

"Ignore him," she whispered. "Good evening, Mr. Lenox."

"Good evening, Mrs. Lucas."

By contrast to the shadowy stairwell, Dallington's rooms were a riot of light, candles and lamps everywhere. Such was his preference. Because of that the air was always tolerably warm there, especially now, in the spring. The sitting room one entered from the hall was pleasant, comfortable, with dog-eared books in piles upon the mantle and one of the sofas, watercolors of Scotland upon the wall, and a cottage piano in the corner.

"How do you do, Dallington?" said Lenox, smiling.

The young man lay upon a divan, surrounded by discarded newspapers and letters stuffed back into their envelopes. He wore—the privilege of the ill—comfortable clothes, a soft jacket of blue merino and gray woolen trousers, with scarlet slippers on his feet. "Oh, not all that badly."

"I'm glad to hear it. Now—"

"Though if I die I would like you to have my collection of neckties."

"They're too colorful for me. But it might be that an especially garish meat-pie seller would agree to take possession of the more subdued ones."

Dallington laughed. "In truth it's only a head cold, but I must keep Lucas on her toes, or she's liable to come it pretty high. Toast and water, indeed."

His appearance made a lie of this deprecation, however. Despite his years of drink he was usually healthy-looking, face unlined, hair sleek and black. At the moment, by contrast, his skin was pallid, his eyes red, his person disheveled, and on top of that he had a nearly continuous cough, though he managed mostly to stifle it into a handkerchief. It seemed no wonder that he didn't feel equal to venturing out upon a case.

"I can't stay long," Lenox said.

"Of course, and thank you for coming—I thought perhaps you might not be able to get away from the Commons at all. It's only that I'm due out to meet a client at eight in the morning, and finally decided two hours ago that I don't think I can go."

"You couldn't reschedule?"

"That's the damnable bit, I—" Here Dallington broke into a fit of coughing, before finally going on in a hoarse voice. "I have no way of reaching the person who sent the note. An enigmatic missive, too. You can pick it out from the birdcage, if you like, the red envelope."

This brass birdcage, absent of avian life, was where Dallington kept his professional correspondence. It hung near the window. Lenox went to it and found the letter Dallington meant, tucked between two bars. It was undated.

Mr. Dallington,

The police cannot possibly help me; perhaps you might. If you are amenable to meeting, I will be at Gilbert's Restaurant in Charing Cross station from eight o'clock Wednesday morning, for a space of thirty-five minutes. If you cannot contrive to meet me then I will write to you again soon, God

324 | Charles Finch

324 | Charles Finch

willing. You will know me because I am dining alone, and by my light-colored hair and the striped black umbrella I always carry.

Please please come.

"Well, what do you make of that?" Dallington asked. "It is unsigned, of course, which tells us that he desires anonymity."

"Yes."

"Moreover he cannot know me very well, to address me as Mr. Dallington. I don't stand upon much titled formality, but I generally receive it anyhow."

"What else?"

Dallington shrugged. "I cannot see much further into it."

"There are one or two telling details," said Lenox. "Here, for instance, where he says he'll wait for thirty-five minutes."

"Why is that odd?"

"Such a specific length of time? Given that he proposes meeting at a train station, it suggests, to me, that he will catch a train shortly after 8:35. Do you have a Bradshaw?"

"On the shelf there," said Dallington.

Lenox pulled the railway guide down and browsed through it, frowning, until he found the listings for Charing Cross. "There is an 8:38 for Canterbury. The following train doesn't leave until 8:49. I think we may presume that your correspondent is traveling to Kent."

"Bravo," said Dallington. "Is there anything else?"

"Yes," said Lenox. He paused, trying to define his reaction in his own mind before he told it to Dallington; for the letter had unsettled him.

"Well?"

"It is something in the tone, in every line of the letter. I don't know that I can identify it precisely." He gestured toward the page. "Its despairing scorn for the police, for instance. His carefully generic description of himself."

"He is being cautious, you mean?"

Lenox shook his head. "More than that. This phrase, "God willing," and then this rather desperate final line. All of it together makes me believe that the man who wrote this letter is living in a state of mortal fear."

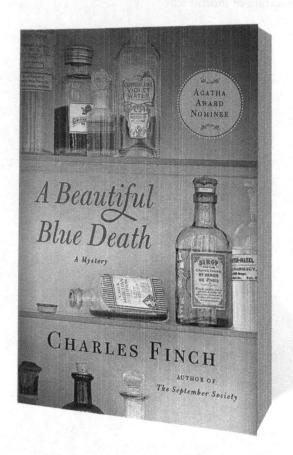